What W

What Will Survive of Us

HOWARD JACOBSON

JONATHAN CAPE
LONDON

1 3 5 7 9 10 8 6 4 2

Jonathan Cape, an imprint of Vintage, is part of the Penguin Random House group
of companies whose addresses can be found at global.penguinrandomhouse.com

Penguin
Random House
UK

First published by Jonathan Cape in 2024

penguin.co.uk/vintage

Typeset in 12/14.75 pt Bembo Book MT Pro by Jouve (UK), Milton Keynes
Printed and bound in Great Britain by Clays Ltd, Elcograf S.p.A.

The authorised representative in the EEA is Penguin Random House Ireland,
Morrison Chambers, 32 Nassau Street, Dublin D02 YH68

A CIP catalogue record for this book is available from the British Library

HB ISBN 9781787334823
TPB ISBN 9781787334830

Penguin Random House is committed to a sustainable future
for our business, our readers and our planet. This book is made
from Forest Stewardship Council® certified paper.

MIX
Paper | Supporting
responsible forestry
FSC® C018179

To Jenny

For you, always you

Our almost-instinct almost true:
What will survive of us is love.

Philip Larkin, 'An Arundel Tomb'

PART I

MISS PICKY

DAY ONE

Kerpow!

Funny – unless it's ominous – she had put that very word down on a Scrabble board only a day or two before. Jubilant, the k scoring triple. Her opponent – the man she had known for over twenty years, slept with for five, no longer slept with for however many more that left, and now played Scrabble with instead – contested the spelling. Kapow, yes. Kerpow, no. They fought over it. Have it your way, she said in the end. Which meant she had to remove a garment.

What? They were still up to those tricks? No, no, truly they weren't. Idly, because they'd found themselves at home together for the first time in months and opened an expensive bottle of wine, they dared each other, laughing, in honour of the good old days.

She'd raised herself from the chair, not looking at him. Was this how they used to do it? *Christ! – playing strip Scrabble at forty-seven.* Was she really that old or did she exaggerate her age to aggravate her shame?

And now, *kerpow!*

How she kept her balance she didn't know.

It could only have been that she'd had just enough warning, a shapeless presentiment, as she stood ringing the bell, in that atom of time that prepares the mind for irrecoverable shock.

He had opened the door to her. The Wunderkind – all right, the Once-Wunderkind – himself. That she hadn't expected. As a rule, for appointments with men who win prizes, she would be met by an assistant, secretary, housekeeper, wife. She had even heard tell of a liveried butler. Write a successful musical and there was no limit to what you had to have. But men who wrote musicals were of no interest to her. It was words or nothing. Otherwise, these exploratory meetings were much of a muchness. 'Good morning. You must be So-and-So. I'll tell His Wordship OBE, FRSL you're here.' A short wait, time for her to check how she looked in the hall mirror if there was one, clear her throat and decide whether to tuck her blue A4 notebook under her arm to show she was in control or hold it loosely to show she had a devil-may-care spirit. Then up silent carpeted stairs – *hush, thoughts germinating* – through palisades of family portraits, carefully disarranged playscripts, programmes and original lithographs of Sarah Bernhardt as Cleopatra – and into the engine room of genius where she would find X at his desk, head down, so absorbed he didn't hear her announced. So why not today? Why, today, had the man she had come to see acted as amanuensis to himself? Later, wanting to make it all miraculously synchronous, he would tell her it was because he too must have had an inkling of what was about to befall him.

She shook her head. *Inkling* indeed. He understood very little, if he could use a tepid term like that, to describe the tremor that had rocked her body.

It was neither welcome nor expected. She was too busy to be looking for adventure. There were dozens of those blue A4 notebooks on her shelves, bursting with research notes, scripts and schedules, records of programmes she'd made, outlines of programmes she still hoped to make. If there was to be a man again after Hal he would have to come to her. She wouldn't squander her life waiting for him to put in an appearance or wondering if he'd be worth it when he did. She'd know.

And when the Wunderkind opened his door to her she knew to a certainty.

Knew what?

Just knew.

Kerpow!

A single blast of him was all it took.

He stood on the doorstep, just about smiling, and appraised her incrementally. He couldn't help himself. What men did. He didn't need telling that a woman was more than a piece of fruit that came apart in segments. Miss Gore, head of English, had taken the class through the sins of masculinist evaluation practised by every poet since Catullus. 'Two hundred years to adore each breast, for heaven's sake!'

'But "thirty thousand to the rest", Miss,' he'd put in, mistakenly assuming that she didn't think two hundred years anything like enough.

'The rest!'

What had he said wrong? He coloured.

'Is that all a woman is to you, Quaid, two breasts and *the rest?*'

'No, Miss.'

'So do you have an alternative computation?'

'Not offhand, Miss.'

The class guffawed. He would remember forever the heat of his embarrassment – a fiery furnace of confusion and shame, fuelled by a woman's snort of derision.

All right, all right. He would try to avoid such mistakes in the future. But have a heart, teacher. Centuries of errancy couldn't be remedied all at once and in his single person, no matter how ready he was to forswear the cultural history of being a man. Just give me a little more time, Miss Gore. I don't know how much more. But measuring years as the poet measured, say thirty thousand.

Today he'd call her out as a bully. Don't tell me what I'm allowed to look at and like!

Oh, and by the way – two hundred years of adoration is a hyperbolic fucking joke.

Edina Gore. Bright red lips, big eyes swimming behind fish-bowl spectacles, arms crossed on her chest, now like a nun's, now like a wrestler's. All this time later he can recall the distaste he felt for those arms which seemed to be extruded from her breasts like sausage-meat. Though now he knows he shouldn't. Distaste was worse than the wrong sort of desire. Like a woman's arms too much and you were sunk. Like them too little and you were sunk a second time. What was he supposed to do – keep his eyes off a woman's body altogether?

Yes.

And do what?

Look at something else.

It was unfair. He respected women. Revered them, in the abstract, to the point of madness. Woman! My God! Would he ever attain to one? Would he ever have one to call his own – no, no, no, no, no, not his own as in his *property*, but his as in to have and to hold.

My own to love and cherish, Miss Gore.

Here was the ironic thing – in picking on him, Miss Gore had picked on probably the least sexually experienced boy in the class. He'd read a lot of poems, that was all. He could talk a good love lyric. But of real breasts (and don't even talk about the *rest*) he would leave school knowing nothing. But for the surly com-plaisance of a prostitute he would have gone to university knowing nothing too.

Now that he is older, Miss Gore would be within her rights to think of him as a lost cause after all, entirely unimproved the moment he comes face to face with an unknown woman, pick-ing her off part by part. Today's woman being no exception. There the hair, blowing in the wind like Mary's of Peter, Paul And; there the mouth, stern and narrowed so as to give nothing away, but he knows what to look for and sees the blood pulsing under the pale lips; there the breasts (move on, move on); and there the legs, muscular, like a dancer's or a gymnast's. She catches his eyes flick down to her legs and wonders why she'd chosen to wear a skirt instead of her usual trousers. Mistake or not?

A purely professional question.

His eyes ascended again, noting that her nails were painted as blazingly red as Edina Gore's lips, and that she left her hand in his a little longer than was customary, as though to be sure he felt the firmness of her grasp and, just possibly, the weight of a gold ring she wore, he couldn't quite tell on which finger. And then, despite her apparent assurance, there was the startled look with which she greeted him, as though she'd known him all her life and not expected him, of all people, to open the door to her, unless he was so unlike anyone she'd ever met before she feared they wouldn't speak each other's language. This was difficult to describe or explain.

Vanity took him some of the way. Why wouldn't a woman have been startled by his appearance? He was tall. His nostrils flared like a flamenco dancer's. He had louche, lazy eyes and hair that a journalist had described as enraged. He had a broken nose from the only fight he'd ever fought and his cheek was interestingly scarred as a consequence of a firework he lit for his stepdaughter's birthday going off prematurely. 'Mummy, quick, Stepdaddy's face is on fire' – a phrase enshrined in family history. All in all, as another journalist had written, he resembled a pirate with a degree in fine art.

Plus – he was full of plusses – he was an arts-page celebrity. Or at least *had been* an arts-page celebrity, no longer on the front page but in the paper somewhere if you took the trouble to look for him. Scraps of high if misremembered accomplishment still clung to him like flies on flypaper. People remembered a play of his they'd been to years ago. Not its title or what it was about exactly, but the interviews he gave, the buzz, the queues, the cost of the programme. Others, who had no idea what a starred first was, somehow knew Oxford had awarded him one at the age of only twenty.

No longer being front-page worked for him in the perverse way of celebrity. It made him more attractive. Allowed him to be irascible and rebellious, unkempt, contemptuous of those still scrabbling to be known. He was to fame what torn jeans were to fashion.

This is not to blow his trumpet for him. It is simply to explain why a woman, unimproved by the warnings of a Mr Gore to keep her eyes to herself, might have breathed a little harder when he opened his door. Or looked twice at him in the street.

But there was something more he couldn't account for and that had to do with her, not him. Something to do with her capacity to register. He loved the eyes of women on him. In their reflection he saw a version of who he was that beat the version he had started to carry around in his head. But in this woman's eyes he saw a man he feared he might never be able to live up to.

Startled by her startlement, he was unable to think of anything to say. He should have welcome-kissed her on the doorstep. Not unlike the hero of his early show-off play, *Don Juan in Oxford*, who believed he could tell everything he was ever going to feel about a woman from a single kiss, Quaid believed a single kiss would reveal everything a woman would ever feel about *him*.

DAY TWO

She hasn't slept. She often doesn't when her head is full of a new programme. She will get up in the middle of the night, pad softly to her study so as to cause no disturbance, and start making notes. But this time she lies for hours in bed before deciding it is distasteful, not to say disloyal – marginally disloyal – to have such thoughts in such a place with a man she respects – *respects*, notice – beside her. So she goes down to the kitchen to make tea, tea being the most calming substance she knows, and relives the encounter.

It isn't only that she can see him. She can smell him. In the past she has left men whose smell she can't abide. When things go wrong between a man and a woman, she believes, the first sign of it is the smell. You needn't especially have loved the smell at first. You might simply not have noticed it. But then you do and that's that. An affair going off stinks to high heaven. What's new to her is noticing and liking the smell of a man at the outset.

At the outset! This is why she hasn't slept. She has let futurity in. At the very least she has opened the window to it.

On the strength of what? A smell she cannot describe. An aureole of zesty hair. A dry, sarcastic mouth. Maybe kind, maybe not, half-closed eyes. A rugby-player's shoulders. And a fore-knowledge of his wordsmithery – not to be confused with any *inkling* – that was so heated with anticipation that she marvelled at the way he spoke before he had a chance to say three words. She laughs at herself. He says 'Come in,' and her heart stops beating. How will she be when he makes his first speech explaining why, though he is flattered by her offer, and notwithstanding the radio talks he's given, he is not a media personality, and certainly not a television presenter, it being a matter of artistic faith to him to have no presence beyond his work, to make no utterances that are not the utterances of art, for it is only art that speaks the words he wishes to be known by, in short to respect the sibylline silence of creation, which he is confident that she, as an intelligent and well-read woman, will surely have listened to with awe herself in those moments when what's visionary and half-glimpsed asserts its ancient primacy over the gross actuality of a liquid-crystal display . . . ?

How will she be? Well, she now knows the answer to that. Somewhat insulted. 'Gross actuality' is not a fair description of what she does. No matter. She will deal with that. She will make space for the sibylline silences of a man unable to stop talking. Thereafter, ask her how she is and she will close her eyes. Unslept, is how she is.

The house is all hers after nine o'clock. Over breakfast she takes out his card. It was a mystery why he'd ever given it to her. Writers don't have cards, he told her. She knew that. She'd never yet met a writer who had a card. It went against – well, whatever it went against. It's actually my wife's, he'd added with a queer little laugh.

'Selena Pallister, Painter'

She'd kept her maiden name but shared a phone. *My wife's.* Was that a warning or a come-on? She wants to ring him to apologise for being peremptory about his suggestion to include Dickens in the mix. She has never much liked Dickens and wonders whether that explained her reluctance. Maybe they can work out a way of doing it after all. In fact there was no conceivable way without changing the entire premise of her series. Dickens had not travelled to escape a country he loathed and that had rejected him. But she can't think of any other convincing reason for making the call, and it's a call she has to make. It is as though she had scaled a remote peak and forgotten to plant a flag to show she'd been there. If she is to stake any sort of claim to the territory, no matter how gestural, she must plant that flag. She lets another hour go before ringing him. His wife's voice – peremptory and even ill-tempered – is on the answering machine. We are not available, it says.

We.

She drives a fast car not because speed excites her but because she can afford a fast car and has no children to ferry to school, so she might as well. More than that, she has always claimed for herself the freedom and esteem men enjoy, and a fast car that people gawp at in the street is one way of accessing those advantages. *Comme des garçons.* Otherwise, she affects an indifference to what she drives and pretends she doesn't remember the make. 'I think it's Italian.' She might want the freedom of being a man, but she also wants freedom from the objects that captivate men's minds.

Driving to work, tired and preoccupied, she passes an accident. It looks serious. More than one police car, more than one ambulance. Normally the sirens would make her heart race and she would come off the main road as soon as she could. At the very least slow down. Today the flashing lights don't touch her. She is somewhere else. Has steel entered her soul?

She has a meeting with the series commissioner.

'So he's interested?'

'He says he wants to think about it, but I'm confident he'll agree.'

'Which one is he veering towards? Ibsen in Sorrento is too obvious, I assume. Lawrence in Taos, I'll bet.'

'As it happens, no. And you're right about Ibsen. "Done that to death," he said. Joyce in Trieste looks the most likely. Or just maybe Byron in Missolonghi. I fancy he might think of himself as Byronic. Whereas Joyce was weedy and half-blind.'

'And D. H. Lawrence tubercular.'

'Well more than that. He says Lawrence's genius alarms him. He says he has only to read two words of Lawrence to want to be him. Whereas he knows that if Lawrence were to have read two words of his he'd have hated them both. For which reason – not to paraphrase – he loathes the fucker.'

'That could make a good programme.'

'That's what I told him but he said he wouldn't give the fucker the satisfaction.'

'He does know Lawrence is dead?'

'Yes, but not dead enough.'

'Ah well. Too much affinity, I suppose. Sex-obsessed, angry Northerners.'

'I suspect he'd reject that way of categorising him. The writer he says he does feel closest to is Dickens. Bad husband, great writer. Often the way. Said he'd quite fancy doing Dickens in America. Our subject's exile, I reminded him, and Dickens in America is not a story of exile. "All art is exile," he said.'

'I suppose he has a point.'

'He does, and I've a feeling he's made it many times before, but we're not the *Culture Show*. And anyway, I prefer Lawrence to Dickens even if he doesn't. I have a soft spot for those angry Northerners you speak of.' (As for the sex-obsessed, she had nothing to say.)

'And you're confident that whoever he goes for you'll be able to work with him?'

'Oh, yes. Why shouldn't I be?'

'He has a reputation for being difficult.'

'Writers are difficult. That's why they're writers.'

'That sounds like a point *you*'ve made before.'

'I've worked with enough of them.'

And she had. Difficult writers were her speciality. Pigs, prigs, pricks, pedants – they were all thrown her way.

'I still think it might be worth steering him on to Lawrence. It'll make a better programme if he doesn't get on with Lawrence, especially if you do.'

She doesn't answer. She is thinking about Lawrence's notorious public brawls with his wife. The last time she made a programme with a Northern genius he brought his wife along on the shoot, demanded she be part of the action, and bickered with her endlessly. Before the filming was through, the bickering had become the story.

The Northern genius never forgave her for exposing his marriage on television.

'No, you did that,' she told him. 'My job as a director is to let the tale unfold.'

A Lawrentian sort of thing to say.

She is wearing a black suit with a faint stripe and not-too-high black patent shoes. More daggers than rapiers. On the way out, her head down, her narrow face harbouring shadows, she passes a senior producer who once propositioned her at a Corporation party. He has been awkward with her since, though she has never held a proposition against any man. He takes her in at a glance and suppresses a shudder. He's amazed he ever had the courage to try it on. She looks like an assassin, he thinks.

DAY THREE

Thanks to that phenomenal memory of his, Quaid is able to give after-dinner talks without notes. 'On this, at least, Plato, Jesus Christ and John Lennon agreed,' he tells audiences, 'all you need is love.' He doesn't go on to say what he thinks, which is that love isn't just all you need but all there is. The rest is death. You don't bring up the subject of death at a cancer-charity dinner in the Dorchester.

The rest. He can never hear that phrase without remembering his attempt to defend the poet Andrew Marvell against Edina Gore's derision. 'But thirty thousand to the *rest*, Miss.' Much of his subsequent thinking is directed at her.

'"To His Coy Mistress" isn't a poem about desire,' he wrote to her from Oxford. 'It is a poem about death. *But at my back I always hear / Time's wingèd chariot hurrying near.* Not sometimes, Miss Gore – *always*. The time the poet imagines lavishing on the woman's breasts is time he knows he doesn't have.'

When he doesn't hear back he assumes the wingèd chariot must have whisked her away.

Despite believing that his work should do the talking for him, the Once-Wunderkind discusses it frequently at conferences and seminars. He has a good voice and likes the sound of it when he's in the mood to hear himself. You can break every writerly rule for charity . . . and an appreciative audience.

Though he believes it becomes him as playwright to be seen in jeans and a dirty black t-shirt, for such an event as this he wears a velvet suit (also stylishly in need of a dry-clean) and

Byronic necktie that make him look like a French symbolist poet just come in from a long night walking the streets of Paris. He knows that audiences of women of an age to be charitable want a speaker to take them where they've never been. He sheds a decade when he speaks. He is witty and risqué. The husbands don't much like him. This is a matter of satisfaction to him.

Yes, he's come a long way from the nervous schoolboy who knew nothing of women other than what he'd read about them in *The Oxford Book of English Verse*. Ask why he has to keep telling himself that and he will answer that the nervous schoolboy never leaves the grown man altogether. He is every man's secret.

On the front row next to the honorary life president of the charity is his wife. A waspish observer might remark that she too looks as though she's come in from a long night walking the streets of Paris. She sits round-shouldered, showing a weary cleavage and looking cold, in a sequinned dress which, like her expression, she has worn for evenings at the Dorchester listening to her husband being brilliant far too often. A number of her sequins have gone missing. Not impossibly she has pulled them off.

Her mouth is twisted into a hellish smile.

The honorary life president leans into her and whispers in her ear. 'Is your husband always as wickedly funny as this?' she wants to know.

'Always,' his wife says. 'He is a riot from morning to night.'

'You are lucky in that case,' the honorary life president says. 'Mine hasn't told a joke or cracked a smile in twenty years.'

'And mine's done nothing else,' his wife says.

Selena. They originally met at a reading he was giving on the stage of the National Theatre. She was there to sketch him for a magazine but couldn't concentrate on his appearance. If only she'd known how to draw sentences. They spiralled out of him without pause or punctuation, as though from an invisible and inexhaustible source. They ensorcelled her, enveloping her in the smoky perfume of their fluency, evocative of the Northern city he came from – flat, built-up and tarmacked – and yet at the same time airily fanciful, as though promising a life of abstraction everlasting. 'Just tell me things,' she said when he took her to his bed. 'Teach me about English literature. Start with the drama. Who wrote the first ever play? I don't ask who wrote the best. I know the answer to that.'

How he loved appreciation.

How he *needed* appreciation.

Who am I, he would ask himself when his confidence would suddenly – unaccountably – drop to dangerously low levels. I am not what I seem to be. I am a lodger in my own mind. I don't belong there. I am burned-out. I am fraudulent. I confuse sentimentality with feeling. I call this self-criticism but it is self-indulgence, or would be if I had a self. I am never not banal. I am yesterday's man. I regurgitate clapped-out thoughts.

Not true. When he wrote, words appeared that weren't other people's. They weren't his either, but that didn't matter. As a book or play took shape, so did he.

The only time this happened outside of writing was when he was in the arms of a woman. He went to her bed as shapeless and as unformed as clay and she blew into his nostrils whereupon, miracle of miracles – MAN. A woman not only made him a person, she woke him up. Made him almost of his time.

Before they both realised they were embracing cadavers.

The morbid fuck.

Charmed by how charmed she was by him, he talked to this new wonderful, willing, willowy woman with a sibilant, silvery name – Selena – as no man ever had before, bestowing centuries of praise on everything about her that had no specific name: her aura, her presence, her indefinable desirability. Though his admiration of her made her blush with its extravagance, she would find it hard, in later years, to remember a single thing he'd actually said. He was no more succinct as a lover than he was as a writer. Explicitness horrified him. It was as though language had the power to release a terrible unseemliness which he was tasked with keeping forever out of sight.

Tasked by whom?

You might as well ask who commanded him to write.

'What did you actually say to make me feel so sexy?' Selena would ask years later, still trying to work out why she'd ever fallen for him.

Quaid pulled his Oxford distaste face. '*Sexy*? You know I hate that word. Next you'll be asking why I *fancied* you.'

'Why did you fancy me?'

'I didn't. I felt the force of you.'

'Like being run over on a motorway?'

'More like being blown over in a gale.'

His vocabulary wasn't just chaste, it was circumventive. The one adjective she can remember from that first night that spoke with any sensual directness to her was 'open'.

'I blush to this day remembering you say it,' she would tell him.

'Precisely,' was his reply. 'When it comes to desire, the less said the—'

'—sexier?'

He laughed. He no longer loved her but was reminded why he had.

'But tell me,' she went on, 'I've never understood. Why is *sexy* wrong but *open* right? What's implicit about *open*?'

'I don't say sexy is wrong, I say it's popular, common and borrowed. It doesn't describe what anyone sees for themselves. *Open* – well sometimes there is only one word that describes what you *do* see.'

17

'And what part of me was so open that you could find no other word?'

'All of you.'

They are no longer getting on. 'Closed' is the word for them now. She is jealous of the woman she was.

On his way to relieve himself, he sees his visitor of a couple of days before in front of him. He increases his pace to catch up with her and taps her on the shoulder. 'Well here's a surprise,' he says. In the event, it's too much of a one. It isn't her. When she turns, she shows him soft, blue, pellucid eyes. The eyes he was expecting to see were a stormy Atlantic grey. The foreheads are different too. This woman has a far lower hairline, a brow less troubled, less commodious, less gracefully arched. Heavens! *A commodious brow*. Had he noticed that much about her?

Tonight, surprised by this moment of disappointment, he sleeps badly. He doesn't like to have made a social blunder, however small. Will the stranger think he was making a pass? He is too quick to feel a fool. And then too quick to be annoyed with himself for caring. But mistaking one person for another is surely not sufficient to explain this. Something else is wrong.

I'm lonely, he thinks. In the past, whenever he felt lonely he would go looking for someone to share his loneliness with. Not in a rapacious spirit. More little boy lost. He hasn't progressed much, but at least now he has work to fall back on. A play a day keeps the doctor away. And he no longer experiences loneliness as a non-specific ache. These days he has to have a woman in mind before he realises how lonely he is without her.

He keeps *The Oxford Book of English Verse* by his bed. It was once his boast that he knew half of it by heart. Especially the two great ages of love poetry – the early seventeenth century when love was valued as an accomplishment, an expression of character and intellect; and the late nineteenth when it was feared as an illness. He can recite more of the seventeenth century than the nineteenth, but enjoys declaiming 'The Lady of Shalott' when he's feeling feverish. Lancelot Quaid, riding down to Camelot with his armour ringing. 'I see you more as the Lady,' Selena says, with an acid laugh. 'Waiting for the curse to come upon you – as I did.'

To calm his agitation he goes looking for a poem – any poem – whose familiarity will relax him. The book opens where it was opened last, and opened a thousand times before, at Thomas Wyatt's 'They Flee From Me', a poem said to describe the poet's dangerous liaison with Anne Boleyn in the days before – for her safety and no doubt for his too – she ran from him like a startled deer. It is a poem whose sad recollection of happier, hotter times, when Anne Boleyn *all sweetly did him kiss*, makes Quaid shiver with the cold of loneliness.

All sweetly, all sweetly – God in his mercy!

A man of Quaid's sentimental, romantic bent, needs to be *all sweetly kissed* every day of the week.

He drifts off to sleep at last with Anne Boleyn's arms about his neck.

DAY FOUR

'He needs to get out more,' Lily thinks, swotting up on everything of his she can lay her hands on.

She is rereading *Ibsen in Sorrento*, Quaid's first success outside Oxford. She calls it rereading but in fact she hasn't read it before, only seen it. Twice. Once with her mother who went to see everything at the Almeida but in the interval told her daughter she wanted to go home; once with a passing fancy who couldn't tell if it was meant to be funny. 'Bit gloomy for me,' he'd whispered, wondering if and when he dared touch Lily's knee. 'A play about Ibsen couldn't really be anything else,' Lily whispered in return. She didn't much care whether her companion touched her knee or not.

'But no one made him write about Ibsen,' he replied.

Lily vowed never to go to the theatre with anyone again.

In the interval she conceded that Ibsen was a strange choice. Strindberg would have been more interesting.

'Certainly hotter,' the young man said, bringing her an ice cream.

If I give him my knee, maybe he'll shut up, Lily thinks.

Reading it, she isn't sure gloomy is the right word. But certainly claustrophobic. 'My subject is the inside of people's heads,' Quaid wrote when the play first came out. 'I don't care much what happens anywhere else.'

What kind of lover will he be in that case, Lily muses. This is to jump the gun, but what will it feel like having him rooting around inside my brain?

Making allowances for the age of the playwright when he wrote it, Lily decides the play's not bad in a knockabout, absurdist way: the sombre Norwegian dramatist, for whom love is tainted, incestuous and unsatisfying, succumbing little by little to the charms of scurrilous Neapolitans who don't care what love is so long as they can sing about it. She likes the scene when he is taught the words of 'Torna a Surriento' – that soppiest of all soppy exilic songs – by Enrico Caruso who, if one wanted to be pedantic about it, was yet to be born when Ibsen lived there.

'And Cleopatra couldn't have played billiards with her eunuch because billiards had not yet been invented,' she has found a recording of him snapping at an interviewer. 'Take the matter up with the Bard.'

Shakespeare is his get-out-of-jail-free card. He takes it everywhere with him.

Lily has played the recording twice. He has a good speaking voice, she thinks. It has bitumen and sandstone in it. He is a man you graze your shins against. The wisdom is that he is too sarcastic for television. He has too superior an air. Not that that worries her. She has fixed many a superior air in her time. It's all but written into her contract to do so.

She can see why he doesn't want to do Ibsen in Sorrento for her series. Done is done. But imagining his singing voice being as good as his speaking voice she visualises a scene in which he performs a trio with the ghosts of Ibsen and Caruso. It's part of the play's spectral surrealism that it shows Ibsen finishing *Ghosts* in the Imperial Hotel Tramontano. As a rule she doesn't favour tricksy directing but getting Quaid to come out of himself is a challenge she might relish.

Apart from anything else, it would be nice to be in Sorrento.

Eating pasta in the sun.

Laughing.

Talking.

In the Hotel Tramontano.

With the Very Devil.

DAY FIVE

He is working on a new play. He doesn't yet know its subject. Famously troubled men, if his previous plays are anything to go by. Man out of time and place. Man marooned. Man Gored. Any resemblance to himself being purely incidental.

Only the act of writing will decide what the new play's about. This is the best time, waiting for the 'about' to reveal itself. Notwithstanding his reputation for being spiky and unyielding, he submits ecstatically to the capricious wiles of language. The words will look after him.

It's their way of saying thank you. He looks after words, they look after him.

His wife is still half-asleep at 9.30 when he brings her coffee. She drank too much the night before and calls for water. In their early days they drank freely together, laughing as they uncorked yet another bottle. 'How are you?' he would ask when they opened their eyes late into a new day. 'Pissed-blind,' she'd say and he'd gather her into his arms, as though a pissed-blind lover with long flanks was the most precious commodity in the world.

'You?' she'd ask.

'The same.'

Then she would roll out of his arms and gather him into hers. Now, pissed-blind is no longer endearing to either of them.

Selena was thirty when they met. Already divorced and with two daughters, less substantial than her, both as light and long-legged as dragonflies. He shook their hands when he met them. Hello girls. Which exhausted his interest in children. She – the mother – was a book illustrator in the style of a roughed-up Cicely Mary Barker with ambitions to be a portrait artist she wasn't yet sure in the style of whom. He had a proposal for her. No, not that. In idle hours, when he couldn't see how to get from Act I to Act II, he penned world-weary fables in which he affected a disillusionment beyond his years. He had even put a small, loose-leafed book of them together, tentatively entitled *The Ostrich That Had Seen Enough*. It would do, he thought, as a gift. Would Selena like to illustrate it? He can't recall now what became of her attempts. Not cynical enough, he thinks. She couldn't draw a nihilistic ostrich.

It was he who made her think that their careers were following a similar trajectory, though he, at twenty-six, was the Wunderkind, with two successful plays and countless critical pieces he called Amusements to his name. Why he went on soaring and she never quite took off is hard to explain. Talent for talent, he assured her, they were fairly matched. Success, however, is wanton. And responds well to ambition, of which he had more than her. But wasn't he ambitious enough for two – great writer and great painter, the all-creative, all-charismatic, all-conquering colour-supplement pair, gifted, caustic, and nearly twelve feet tall between them? Only trouble was, he forgot to ask her if this was a partnership she wanted. Looking over his shoulder, one day, to be sure she was keeping up with him, he saw she was not there. 'Rush, rush, rush,' she breathlessly shouted after him. 'Pushing and shoving and smarming, to get where?'

She had a point. They were artists, not entrepreneurs of art. The rush was not something he could explain. Was it that his meteoric start demanded nothing less than a meteoric future? Vultures waited for him to fail. He wondered if he was one of those vultures himself. Had he already exceeded his desserts? Did he hope that if he moved fast enough no one would see in him what he, on bad days, saw – namely, not very much at all?

But none of this was relevant; if she didn't want to keep up, that was her business.

'How about,' she pleaded with him one day, 'you just go at your own speed and allow me to go at mine?'

He fell to his knees and apologised. Her frustrations were all his fault. He had uprooted her from her natural habitat of quiet concentration. He had thrown her in the path of rowdy failure.

'Get up, Quaid,' she said. 'I don't need any of this.'

'What do you need?'

'For you to leave me the fuck alone.'

A fond pleasure in beholding Selena hasn't gone entirely. It returns unexpectedly and in degrees. This morning, aroused by the sight of an uncovered breast, still as blue-veined and milky as a dairymaid's, desire – or is it the memory of desire? – stirs in him. With one arm still extended, waiting for water, she has gone back to sleep. There is a libidinousness in accidentality. Stealthily, like a biblical villain, like one of those lascivious Elders or Noah's sons, he leans across the bed and with trembling fingers uncovers her breasts a little more – a man secretly spying on his own wife's nakedness.

A dozen questions nag at his conscience. Is desire transferable? In stealing a look at Selena is he actually stealing a promissory look at another woman altogether? And if there is another woman – he is only saying *if* – is it a betrayal of that other woman to be looking in this way at breasts that are not hers? Can one look betray the whole sex?

He covers her up – the eternal, eye-ravished wife – and leaves the room on quiet feet, a fugitive from his own marriage bed.

DAY SIX

The Scrabble board sits abandoned on the dining-room table, an unfinished orgy, the tiles scattered, the little white muslin bag upended. They don't eat at home a lot, or together.

The dispiritedness with which she'd removed her jacket and then her silk camisole had not gone unnoticed by her opponent, Hal, the man she'd lived with for many years, sometimes irritably but for the most fondly as the heat went out of them. He'd unbuttoned his own shirt and unbuckled his own belt with no more zest. They didn't even have the heart to go on with the game. Maybe they'd invite another couple round. Maybe they wouldn't. The one time they'd tried had been an agony. Laughter had saved them – just. But they had bags of cruel time ahead of them. Bags almost as full as the bag of Scrabble tiles. How much more laughter, over the coming years, could they call on?

It had, of course, been his suggestion. As had the photographs. And her taking her top off at the beach. All perfectly harmless in intention, she knew, but they harmed her. You can be modest without being prudish, she thought. Or at least she could. You can not want to play along for the perfectly good reason that you simply don't.

'You look really good,' he told her, as though how she looked – meaning how she looked to him, and to whoever else gawped at her on the beach – was the problem. She knew how she looked and liked how she looked. She looked after herself, *for* herself. Self-respect, her mother called it. She saw it more as self-honour. What people called 'a bit of fun' was only fun if you found it so. Otherwise, it was trespass.

She cared for Hal. That she could no longer express her feelings for him with greater fervour saddened her. For him, she thought, the kindest thing would be a mistress, if he didn't already have one. She was not going to suggest that. She knew there was nothing like permission to take the zip out of an infidelity. She wouldn't have wanted him telling her she was free to find a lover. They were each the reason the other had to look elsewhere, each equally to blame and each equally blameless and, except when they carelessly allowed staleness to stare them in the face, as on the beach or when playing Scrabble, the ancient rituals for saving marriages or sort-of marriages worked well enough for them. To her mind, spicing up the home front was a sort of blasphemy. You honour feelings that were once important by letting them wear themselves out naturally. When time is up, time is up. You don't say 'Darling, we need to talk.' You don't use the word 'space'. You remember your manners, stay out late and tell lies.

That, too, was a species of love.

It helps that they are both successful in spheres so antithetical there is no likelihood of their circumferences ever touching. She does words, he does things. He has the bigger company, manufacturing executive games and gadgets of his own invention. Right this minute – the year is 1995 – he has an idea for an electric scooter for adults. Her production company is niche, making low-budget television programmes, in which people speak a lot, for the smaller channels. That she earns a reasonable amount of money is down to Asian countries, and occasionally America enjoying, or at the very least buying, the programmes she makes. Though she doesn't always work for the BBC, everything about her programmes suggests the BBC, to Asians and Americans at least.

Each respects how well the other has done. But because it would upset them to sit and remember the schemes they hatched as half-dating sixth-formers, when her greatest ambition was to be a librarian, and his to invent machines that would appeal to men in a hurry like him – because fruition is as melancholy as frustration when it no longer unites in happiness those who planned and dreamed – they steer clear of the subject. Words of formal congratulation do the job of kisses and champagne. The proof of their having loved each other once is that they have the practical decency not to refer to it.

She has lunch with her friend Lucasta whose husband has left her for an older woman. 'He says he is desperate to have some excitement in his life,' the friend says.

'An *older* woman? It would seem, in that case, that he is desperate to have some quiet.'

'Older doesn't mean quieter, as you know full well.'

'Old doesn't mean quieter, I agree. Old*er* is something else. She can't be more vivacious than you.'

'That's not for me to say. But she is quite the livewire, I'll give her that.'

'Oh God, Lucasta, you've met her!'

'We work together.'

'Worse and worse. So tell me what makes her so lively that a man would leave you for her. Does she chair-dance?'

'I can see what he sees in her, is all I'm saying.'

'Then why don't *you* run off with her?'

'If I were to run off with any woman—'

They both laugh at the outlandishness of that suggestion.

They call for the bill. 'We'll just have to see,' the friend says.

'What do you mean "We'll just have to see"?'

'How long it lasts. This isn't the end of the story.' A few tears flow but she recovers quickly. 'He'll come back.'

'You know that?'

'I know that. He's done it before.'

'Ah!'

'Ah what?'

'Just ah. And you'll take him?'

'Wouldn't you?'

'I doubt I would.'

'I've never thought of you as the jealous type, Lily.'

'Everyone is the jealous type. But it wouldn't be jealousy in this case. I'd find it hard to forgive him the discourtesy.'

'I don't even know what that means.'

'He shouldn't involve you in his search for whatever it is he wants.'

'We're friends. He has to talk to me.'

'Friends! You're married.'

More tears. 'Things aren't so black and white.'

'All right, you're married friends. But we are supposed to spare our friends.'

'What if I'm to blame?'

'For what?'

'For not giving him . . . whatever.'

'You're not. He's just as much to blame for wanting it so badly. A human want is not a human right. And he's more to blame for making you feel responsible.'

'So what's he to do? Take up yoga? Run a marathon?'

'Tell him to take himself in hand.'

'Don't be disgusting.'

'Nothing disgusting about it. Americans do it all the time. Americans actually think that's what sex is. And it's worked fine for the rest of the world for millennia. What's disgusting is making you question yourself. He didn't have to tell you you don't excite him.'

'We have been together a long time.'

'We've all been together a long time.'

'We've been together longer than most. We met when we

were fourteen. That's more than thirty years ago. He says he wants to know what he's been missing.'

'With an older woman he knows what he's been missing. I presume he had a mother.'

'I think I am a little more understanding than you.'

'So will you now take an older lover while you're waiting for him to decide when he's had enough of his?'

'In my place, would you?'

She lets her eyes glide around the restaurant, without settling on anyone or anything in particular. At the next table two City men pause from laughing over nothing to slurping oysters. It would seem they are in a race to see who can slurp the most.

'Only if one presented himself.'

'And if one doesn't?'

'I'd stay in and read a book.'

Miss Picky – that was her girlfriends' nickname for her. Well, Miss Picky, not everyone could afford the luxury of waiting.

DAY SEVEN

He can't fully explain why he's been thinking about her as much as he has. She doesn't fit his usual category of chimera woman. She doesn't flit, faerie-like, through his imagination. He likes women who are unfinished in some way so that he can complete them, but this woman gives off a forbidding self-sufficiency – slender, elegant, carefully styled (nothing left to chance), in the prime of her early middle age, with stormy eyes and that *commodious* brow, conscious of her power to persuade. 'No, please don't involve your agent at this stage,' she had asked him. Implored him? No. Too confident to implore. But not frightened to play the supplicant. He liked the way she said 'please' with challenging eyes, as though she meant to baffle him. Who was asking what from whom? Otherwise, attentive, sleek, like those thrushes in a Ted Hughes poem he'd read at school. Yes, she reminded him of a bird. Terrifying? That was to go too far too soon. But she eyed him, as a bird might. What did she see, he'd been wondering. Danger or prey?

He cares too much what women see.

If women stopped seeing him, he wonders, would he exist?

Scrub that. It's a false piece of wondering. It's as though he's rehearsing shedding the man in him to see how he would feel without it.

But scrub that, too.

He is always being asked why he writes. One day, he says to be invisible. Another, he says to allay shame. His best answer is: to be someone else. Above all, he tells groups of would-be writers,

I urge you to reject the cliché that we write in order to find ourselves. If we did we'd be horrified and never write a word again. Good writers write like summer snakes, to slough their skins.

Secretly, he suspects he writes to get his own back on Miss Gore who planted a seed of doubt slap bang in the garden of his tentative maleness in the hope that only doubt would grow there. He writes to fool her into thinking she was wrong.

Looking at the words on his latest unevolving manuscript he isn't sure he's succeeded. Leaving it to the genius of words worked fine when he was super-young. You have to be relaxed and flexible to do that. You have to be confident that words will find their way through you. You need there to be no hairs on your chin. Forty-whatever-he-is is not exactly decrepit. One interviewer recently called him 'boyish'. But the passages through which art flows are not as unclogged as they were. His concentration, too, is fogging over. Something's scratching at his brain with the promise of a diversion. It's like the end of term. Vacation. A boy on holiday doesn't have to be a man. He's feeling provisional, the sure sign of which is that he's toying with writing the sort of fables he composed at school. *How the elephant forgot. How the hyena lost its sense of humour. How the man lost his balls.*

In the garden of his productive maleness the tree of doubt has grown so many leaves it blots out the sun.

Sun or no sun, he is tired of the view.

WEEK TWO

I want him, I want him not, I want him . . .

Isn't she a bit old to be sitting cross-legged on the grass in Regent's Park plucking petals off a daisy?

What's the flower you pluck to see if you're too old to be plucking it?

As a schoolgirl she played this game with cherry stones. *Shiny cherries, round and sweet. Count your cherry stones, who will you meet?* But it was a bit late for that. She'd already met him.

One thing she is just the right age for is a week in a wellness centre in the south of France listening to whale music.

'There's a lot of stiffness in your shoulders,' the masseur tells her.

'You don't say!'

'*Comment?*'

'That's what I'm here for you to fix,' she shouldn't have to explain.

But she knows there's no fixing what's really wrong. Short of—

Once, parents with enough money to act promptly on their fears would send wayward daughters abroad under the supervision of a chaperone, or escort them out of harm's way themselves. *Once* might suggest a far-distant era of sexual anxiety, but it was more recently that Lily's mother had led her teenage daughter away – 'in chains' was how Lily described it in her diary at the time – from scandal and heartbreak. They had crossed the Channel by ferry then travelled through France by train, her mother never letting go of her wrists, she in tears for the whole journey, until the light of Juan-les-Pins and the smiles of waiters roused her spirits, whereupon her mother had to decide whether it wouldn't be better, all things considered, to take her back home.

Lily had brought it on herself. 'How does one know when one's in love with someone?' she'd made the mistake of asking her mother.

'*One?*'

'A woman. How does a woman know?'

'You're not a woman.'

'I will be next year.'

'Then ask me then.'

Lily skipped away, pretending to be a little girl. But her mother knew the signs. For her own part, she'd decided with such finality *not* to be – not to be in love with her husband any longer, late in the piece though that was – that her family had wondered whether a change of air wouldn't do her good too. She hadn't left him for another man. Strictly speaking she hadn't left him at all. Just pushed him away, not so far that he couldn't occasionally see his daughter if he so wished – and, more importantly, if *she* so wished – but far enough so that he would never see his wife again.

Countless are the ways a husband might contrive to betray his wife. And countless were the ways – she had tried to count them, so she knew – a woman might forgive or tolerate her husband. But this husband had failed the most fundamental test of decency and not kept himself physically clean. He had returned from a business trip – some business trip! – not with his head full of another woman but with his body full of lice. She didn't mean it in the slightest bit fancifully when she vowed to disinfect the house of all trace of him. 'I knew you to be a louse in your own person,' were her final words to him, 'what I cannot tolerate is your being the bearer of other people's.'

He knew not to try his famously handsome smile, so bowed his head and left, scratching himself for shame. There's something about contracting a low-grade infection that will make even the most irresponsible of men wish they'd stayed away from home a little longer.

Thereafter, Lily's mother occasionally allowed herself to be taken by an admirer to a romantic restaurant. Less frequently she would let one of them into her bed. It was hard to rid her imagination of disgust or her body of the horror of contact. And she had a growing daughter to instruct by example.

She sent her to an obscure all-girls public school in a leafy suburb of Northamptonshire. Nothing was risk-free: the girl might form an infatuation for a teacher there or put her arms around another girl when the lights went out, but on balance these were small, hygienic transgressions. Soon, rumour reached her that her daughter had been caught trying to climb out of the dorm window in the dead of night to keep an assignation with the gardener. The girl denied anything had happened. Three separate doctors confirmed her story. She bore no sign, other than a small brown tooth mark on her neck, such as a hamster might have left, of advanced lovemaking.

'Then you've been lucky,' her mother had said.

'No, I have not,' she answered. 'I've been careful. Despite what you think' – forgive her, she was of that age when girls find it necessary to shock their mothers – 'I'm not that desperate to be penetrated.'

She was speaking the truth. She wanted to be held, kissed gently and precisely – she hated being smothered in wet, approximate kisses – and talked to about serious things. Even the bite she could have done without.

But bitten she had been, and the next thing she was in Juan-les-Pins, where, managing to slip her mother, she found a nightclub, danced until the early hours – dancing being her first passion – and was bitten again.

★

34

It isn't for a repeat of the experience that, nearly thirty years later, she has taken herself away. The adage that one nail drives out another might have been true for her teenage self, but the last thing she is looking for now is the distraction of *another lover* before she knows what status to accord the current contender.

Contender! Did she just say *contender*? For what? Her heart? Her hand? Her bed?

Foolish girl, she thinks. Foolish woman.

So what has she taken herself away for?

A few quiet days, that's all. Some sunshine. A lounger to read a book on. A soothing massage.

In the event she is enticed out to a bar by a pretty Italian boy who changes the towels at the spa. He must be no more than half her age, knows his way around the cocktail menu and dances well. She wonders, after the first couple of dances, whether he knows somewhere a bit more seedy.

'Seedy?'

'Low. Disreputable. A dive.'

'Dive' he knows.

But he's surprised. She doesn't look a dive sort of woman.

'Careful,' her mother used to say to her, after the house had been cleaned – and not just of her father – 'you're walking it all back in.'

They were in a state of constant war about her carelessness in the matter of walking it all back in. 'Walk all *what* back in, Ma?'

Her mother didn't think she had to go into details. All that was out there that she didn't want to see walked in. The dirty world.

The girl took after her in the end. 'Careful,' she shouts to the man with whom she shares a house. 'You're walking it all back in.'

When it doesn't make him furious, he laughs about it. She would like to laugh about it herself, but can't. She hates dirt, dust, dross – everything that should stay out there coming into

35

her space. But when she is out there herself it's different. It's what makes her a good documentary-maker, her fascination with life she knows nothing about and wouldn't want in her house. So long as she's already out there, the dirtier the world she encounters, the better.

The boy from the spa makes the wholly understandable error of confusing her request to be taken somewhere disreputable with a desire to be disreputable herself. In the malodorous dark of an immigrant jazz cellar he presses himself upon her. It's all very flattering. Why not?

But then again, why?

She hasn't changed much from the girl who assured her mother that penetration was not top of her to-do list. She doesn't hate it – unless it's hour-long, jack-hammer penetration which makes her sore and causes her ears to pop – just doesn't go overboard for it. There are many things men want to do to her, or want her to do to them, that she doesn't especially dislike but can take or leave alone. Once she can't see their faces there isn't a lot remaining that she does want to see.

'We could either dance or leave,' she says, squeezing the boy's shoulder companionably. Her great skill is to refuse without giving offence.

He doesn't much like being here himself. He too has a mother who has warned him against walking it all back in.

They leave.

She spends a day on the beach making a list. It was something her mother had taught her to do. Make a list of what you're going to wear the day before you go somewhere special. Make a list of the necessary contents of your suitcase before you pack it. Make a list of the qualities of someone you're thinking of going out with – for and against. Lily doesn't say her mother's list didn't help much with her own choice of husband.

Lily writes down what the new man in her imagination has going for him and what he hasn't.

PRO	CON
Hair	Married
Voice	
Shoulders	
Pheromones	
Vocabulary	
Syntax	

She returns to Muswell Hill rested and browner than when she left, but when her old university friend Amaryllis asks her if anything exciting happened while she was away she is being entirely honest when she scratches her head and says, no, nothing that springs to mind.

'I don't believe you,' Amaryllis says. 'You've got fireworks going off in your eyes. Who did you meet? What's he like?'

'Amaryllis, do you really think a woman my age can find a man interesting? I have more important things to think about.'

'*A woman your age*? Lily, you're the same age as me and I'm still waiting to grow up. Look at you! Your legs are like a schoolgirl's. I bet you can still fit into your old hockey skirt. And as for there being more important things to think about, we both know there are none.'

Lily suspected Amaryllis of having being in love with Hal since they were all students together. Was she waiting for Lily to move aside? How could Lily tell her that wasn't necessary. Just take whatever delights your fancy, Amaryllis. I'm busy.

WEEK THREE

I love her, I love her not . . .

He *must* be in love with her. The sure sign is that he has started to think about death every hour of the day, not just in the morning.

Selena knows something is up. It is her working assumption that there is always something up, but she recognises the split second of silence on the answerphone as the guilty hesitancy of a person wondering whether to leave a message and then deciding it is not safe to do so. So something is doubly up.

'Your mistress has been trying to get you,' she says.

He isn't sure which to search first – his memory or his conscience. As it happens, both are clear. Mistress? No. Much as he likes the grown-up sound of it, he's never had a *mistress qua mistress*. This doesn't mean it hasn't crossed his mind. At the height of his fame he would let his gaze brush any woman who happened to be looking his way – it didn't matter where or at what time of the day – as though to make her feel they were opportunities they'd both missed. 'In another life it could have been us,' his eyes would say. 'Ah well.' The sadness of it.

Whether any of the passing women grasped his meaning, he couldn't have said. Unlikely. Not everyone lives on such a precipice of if-onlys. But he's stopped doing it anyway. A couple of poorly received plays and he no longer feels he is a modern Midas with stores of priceless happiness to distribute.

'Mistress! Don't be ridiculous,' he says.

'And you don't treat me like a fool.'

'Just because someone doesn't leave a message, doesn't mean she's in an intimate relationship with me.'

'So you admit it was a she who was trying to reach you?'

'*A she*! For God's sake, Selena. No, I admit no such thing. It might just as easily have been *a he* trying to reach you.'

'My men don't sneak around, waiting until the coast is clear. They have the balls to leave a message.'

My men. Her first instinct when hurt was to hurt back, twice as hard. Let him dare take a lover and she would take ten. Let him dare take two, she'd take a hundred.

So who'd started this unending quid pro quo of discontent? He supposed he had. Years ago she'd found a letter of reproach. 'You should try learning some manners,' it had said. But an anti-love letter to her husband was still not something a wife wanted to read. She accused him of deliberately leaving it where she could find it. 'You intended me to read it,' she said.

'Why would I do that?'

'To cause me pain.'

'And why would I want to do that?'

'To destabilise me. To make me jealous. To prove to me you're attractive to other women. Because you're a cunt.'

'I have nothing to gain from making you jealous.'

'Then why didn't you destroy it?'

He saw the trap. To have destroyed it meant he had a secret. Not to have destroyed it denoted carelessness, and carelessness in a marriage is contempt.

'I can't win this one,' he said.

'No, you can't,' she said. 'You're a cunt either way.'

And either way he'd cut the silken cord that had once bound them.

Sooner or later isn't that what always happens? One party or another takes out a knife and slashes.

'So who is she?'

39

'There is no she.'

'Don't tell me I'm mad. I know what I heard.'

'And what did you hear?'

'The incriminating silence.'

He shakes his head. 'Listening to silences incriminates the listener.'

It's a line from one of his plays. His wife recognises it. 'Quoting oneself incriminates the quoter,' she says.

They may have reached that point in a marriage when they are both mad.

Back at his desk, he wonders if the director with the brow as broad as a full moon could have been ringing and not leaving messages. But why? Everything is above board. What can't she say?

I wouldn't be human if I were not intrigued, he tells himself.

But he wouldn't be human if he were not also irritated. If it is her, she's causing him trouble in his marriage.

He has the decency to laugh at himself. *His marriage* indeed.

But he jumps whenever the phone rings.

WEEK FOUR

He rings her.

'I've been rereading Lawrence's *Mornings in Mexico* and I am warming rather to a month in Taos,' he says before she can even say hello.

She too has been reading *Mornings in Mexico*, on the off-chance. Fiesta time in a pueblo the shape and colour of a giant chocolate cake – how would that be? *Mindless, without effort, under the hot sun, unceasing, yet never perspiring nor even breathing heavily, they dance on and on.* He has only to say the word Taos for her to hear feet stomping on the hot clay. A month there! A whole mindless month. Dancing.

'Is that a decision?' she asks.

'Would you like it to be?'

'Just a minute,' she says, coughing.

'Is that toast I hear you eating?'

'Yes. Soldiers.'

'You're breakfasting with soldiers?'

She laughs. But behind the jest she hears a trap. Is he ringing at breakfast time in order to learn more about her domestic situation? Husband? Children?

Does he want her to say, come live with me and I'll make you soldiers?

Breakfast, she thinks, is the most intimate of meals. No wine, no candlelight, no music – so how come the intimacy?

It's obvious. Breakfast is bed-warmed. She, for example, is still wearing pyjamas. Though not the pyjamas she'd wear if she were not alone. And he?

She imagines he has good legs. Long, sinewy, if a little hairy. Silence falls between them. Is he undressing her?

'I was wondering,' he says, with clumsy suddenness, 'if you'd been trying to get hold of me . . .'

What's this? *I was wondering.*

'No.'

'If you'd rung me . . .'

'No. Ah. Hang on. Yes. I did call, but your answerphone was on.'

'You left no message?'

'No. I wasn't aware I was obliged to.'

He doesn't know what to say now. But she can say it for him: *If, in the future, you must call, please leave a message, otherwise . . .*

She leaves him to find his own way out of this. Otherwise what?

But she can fill in the blanks for herself. *Otherwise my wife . . .*

And that he can't say because to introduce the wife is to concede the mistress . . .

There she now sits, anyway, Mrs Playwright, on a silver breakfast platter between them, like a Sunday joint, her eyes dead, her mouth open with an apple in it.

Enough. I am supposed to be a feminist. I am not in the business of stealing husbands from their wives. This has to stop before it begins.

'I won't call again,' she says.

'No, all I'm saying—'

'Don't worry your pretty little head about it,' is what she thinks. What she says is, 'Rest assured – I won't call. Let me know if you do settle on Lawrence.' Whereupon she puts the phone down.

'Because if you do,' she says to herself, 'I'll sort you out another director.'

★

The next day she amends her list. In the CON column she writes:

>Pusillanimous
>Conceited
>Arsehole

So that's it. Whatever it is, or it isn't, it's stopped.

But the scent of war has entered their negotiations. Whoever pulls out now will have admitted defeat. And defeat in love – even incipient love – is unbearable.

WEEK FIVE

Someone from his agent's rang to ask for her address.

The very thing she'd tried to avoid from the start, third-party intervention. Things slipping from her control.

Two days later a postcard from him arrived:

We are rather conscious, verbal beings, you and I, don't you think, to be venturing together into Lawrence country? We could make ourselves look very foolish.

Q

Q? The affected bastard. His Christian name was Sam.

The card itself was from a gallery in Romania and showed Ionesco looking playfully bored in a Chaplinesque hat.

Cute bastard. Not Ionesco, Q.

She put a message on his answerphone, loud and clear. 'No need to say it again, Sam. Got you loud and clear.' And, louder and clearer still, L.

L for Love? No, L for Lily.

And then. 'No need to call back.'

She set her mouth, returned her blue book to the shelf and rang her commissioning editor to say progress on the Lawrence film had stalled.

'Good timing,' he said. 'We're a director down, can you do Byron?'

SHE STOPS COUNTING

In Venice, doing Byron, she sleeps with the sound-recordist.

She is pleased with herself. Let her rephrase that: she is not *dis*pleased with herself. Sleeping with a sound-recordist is a witty thing to do. No one sleeps with a sound-recordist. If you are going to sleep with anyone on a shoot you sleep with the cameraman.

Even the sound-recordist agrees. 'This isn't a pity-fuck is it?' he wakes up in the middle of the Venetian night to ask.

She is already awake. She is always awake on shoots or when she's sleeping with someone there is no good reason to sleep with. 'Of course not,' she says, 'I don't do those.'

His asking only goes to show why sound-recordists are largely shunned. They harbour the dark and bitter thoughts of the lowly. Not for them the heroic early morning stride to greet the rising sun-god; they must hang back, ever a stride or two behind the big cheeses – the cameraman, the director and even the fly-by-night talent – to fiddle with the knobs on a back-breaking reel-to-reel recorder in order to moderate the howling of the wind or the screaming of the cicadas. And who cares about the sound they record, even if they manage to record it well, anyway? In a visual world, they are yesterday's men.

As it happens, she is one of those who trusts sound more than she trusts pictures. She has worked with this sound-recordist before and likes him. Only *likes*, but that will get her through. He tells her he has wanted her since the first film they made together fifteen years ago when she told him his cicadas were spot on.

The film is shaping up to be beautiful. Byron had been careful to exile himself only in gorgeous locations. But her heart isn't in it. Self-delighting, Byronic man is not to her taste right now.

The presenter is a fastidiously handsome Anglo-Italian art dealer who swallows spaghetti a spaghetto at a time and has ambitions to be presenting a food programme. Her heart isn't in him either.

Yesterday they filmed in the Calle della Piscina where Byron lodged for a while, acting as 'cavalier servente' to his landlord's young wife, a woman 'in her appearance altogether like an antelope'.

Grudgingly, she granted him the poetic felicity of antelope.

What graceful creature would Byon have likened her to?

From the lagoon came the tenor braggadocio of the gondoliers which the sound-recordist, tearing his hair, could do little to muffle.

She was relieved to remember that in two days she'd be in Geneva where Byron kept a list of his lovers – 'countesses, cobblers' wives, some noble, some middling, some low: all whores' – and where there'd be a different crew.

And where, also, to her complete surprise, she finds a gift from the playwright waiting for her at her hotel.

How did he know she was here? She shrugs. Who cares? It's a copy of the first American edition of Lawrence's *Mornings in Mexico*. It is signed *Love, Sam*. Shame. *Love, David Herbert*, would have made the book precious.

But *Love, Sam* had its own interest. Sam, not Q. Love, not sincere regards.

So the filming's on again, is it? The nerve of the man! Did he think she had nothing better to do than wait on his vacillations?

It was all she could do not to sleep with the replacement sound-recordist.

PART 2
TAOS AND BEYOND

CHERRY STONES

Virtue, Lawrence wrote, watching the Pueblo Indians dancing, lies in the heroic response to the *creative wonder*.

She marks the page with her napkin, takes a sip of tea and pulls a face. She is in the breakfast room of the hotel in Albuquerque where she's been for the last week, making phone calls, and where the crew will rendezvous. Quaid should have been here the night before but his plane was delayed. She consults her watch and then opens the Lawrence again. *In woman it is the putting forth of all herself in a delicate, marvellous sensitiveness . . .* She marks the passage with another napkin. The volume now contains more napkins than pages.

He sees her before she sees him. She is wearing a red, cable-knit, off-the-shoulder sweater. A garment he loves, though he didn't know he loved it till he sees her wearing it. He would like to go straight over and tell her she has beautiful Grecian shoulders, but it's a little early in the piece for that. And, anyway, she probably knows.

It's a *kerpow* moment for her once again. She hasn't seen him since their first encounter or spoken to him on the phone more than a handful of times after he hung up his objectionable No Trespassing notice, but he still makes her throat tighten. She's forgotten nothing about him, except the degree to which everything she remembered doesn't quite measure up, doesn't quite do justice to his queer galvanic quality, as though a bolt of fire had raced through him, charring his skin and making the hairs on his head bristle like singed serpents. She imagines that men

49

who'd been to war returned looking like this, allowing that he also looked as though he'd never so much as crossed a road at rush hour.

What can explain it? Her mother is an old woman and doesn't hear well but she has a theory. 'The bolt of fire has run through you, my dear,' she'd say were she here. 'I felt the same about your father, the lice-bearer. Some men just know how to get a woman to invent them. I'd be very careful if I were you and wash regularly.'

He, on the other hand, has allowed his first impression of her to dull. He is an out-of-sight, out-of-mind kind of man and doesn't only forget but actually goes off people when he doesn't see them. In the weeks since she called on him with her modest proposal he has blurred her, made her less of a distraction to his thoughts, flattened her shape, dimmed the challenging Atlantic grey of her eyes, lengthened her skirts, suppressed all memory of that look of hectic alarm that could break out at any moment and make him worry he'd done or said something amiss, and then make him want to be the person who could clear it.

Is his forgetfulness a function of his inability to be faithful in his head to more than one woman at a time? He doesn't know. But ask him to describe his wife this minute and he won't be able to.

He has read that there is an inexplicable electrical murmur in the vicinity of Taos, said by some to be caused by extraterrestrial visitations and by others to be what's left of the psychic vibrations bequeathed by the distinguished mind-benders – Carl Jung was one – who flocked here in the 1920s looking for enlightenment. But Albuquerque is more than a hundred miles from Taos. So could the ringing in his ears be the sound of deck-chairs being rearranged again on the sinking deck of his decency?

'Good to see you, Lily,' he says, taking her elbows and kissing her, but scrupulously, in the way you do when meeting a remote relative off a plane.

She leans, she fears, just a little too far forward to receive his kiss. 'Good to see you, Sam.'

They stand for half a minute letting their words of conventional greeting dissolve, pleased with what they see. It is a wonderful thing to like the look of someone with whom you are about to spend time. They are still smiling when they sit. She orders him boiled egg and soldiers.

The waitress doesn't understand why that makes the air between them hiss.

The crew, too, have been held up, which means they have time on their hands. They agree to go shopping in town. He is excited by the prospect. He hasn't shopped with a woman in years.

She needs new sunglasses. 'You?' she asks.

He shakes his head.

She sits back in her chair to take a look at him. 'What are you intending to wear for the shoot?'

They should have had this conversation before but his moodiness has made her wary.

'This,' he says. He is wearing a heavy brown leather backwoodsman jacket over jeans. 'I'm told it gets cold in New Mexico.'

'In winter.'

'Ah – so what are we in?'

'Summer.'

'What would you say I need then? Shorts?'

'Not for pieces to camera. Unless you have amazing legs.'

'I have amazing legs.'

'What else do you have?'

'Amazing arms.'

'To wear.'

'Other than this and a few t-shirts, a velvet smoking jacket.'

'Then let's get you something.'

So they go looking for an outfit appropriate to doing pieces to camera in a pueblo and find an oatmeal linen travel-writer's suit from a shop which, to their amusement, is called Lawrence's Wearhouse. But he also wants shorts, for the hell of buying them with her, and tries on a baggy pair in khaki.

'What say you to these?' he asks. 'Do you think they make me look like D. H. Lawrence?'

It is, he thinks, a seminal moment. If this were his wife shopping for shorts with another man he'd – well, right at this moment he wouldn't give a damn.

'No,' she says. 'In the only photographs I've seen of Lawrence in Taos he is wearing a black undertaker's suit.'

But the shop assistant likes them. 'Your husband looks good in those,' she says as he changes back into his winter wardrobe. Lily flushes and hopes he hasn't heard. 'He isn't my husband,' she says, rather definitely, as though it matters what an assistant in a gents' outfitters in Albuquerque thinks.

Could he have heard? Will he be angry if he has?

They no sooner leave the shop than she has to dash back in. He assumes she's left something on the counter but he's wrong. 'For you,' she says, handing him a paper carrier. It contains a plaited leather belt with a snake buckle. Made by local Indians. 'To go with your new suit.'

As they navigate the unfamiliar city he is protective of her, laying a steadying hand on her back as they cross the road. By the time they return to the hotel their fingers are touching.

He is first down for dinner. He wants to see her arrive.

He thought of turning up in his new shorts but decides against putting a joke before whatever the word is for what they're doing. Better, tonight at least, to be a symbolist poet, without the floppy bow. He wishes he hadn't given up cigarettes. He would like to see her through plumes of smoke. In the event, his eyes steam up of their own accord when she arrives in a wrap-around floral dress of such fine material he could whistle it off her. He stands to kiss her, using his height, but again they kiss chastely.

'I'm sorry,' he says.

'What for?'

'I seem to be over-kissing you.'

'Two in one day is hardly excessive. Especially on my birthday.'

'It's your birthday! You look too young to have a birthday.' And this time he kisses her on the lips.

'I've been wondering,' he says.

'What?'

'What you taste like.'

'And?'

'Now I know.'

'No, you don't. Now you only know what my lipstick tastes like.'

They have the regulation pre-affair ground-rules conversation while pretending to be talking about something else. She was brought up virtually without a father. In a manner of speaking, so was he. Mine wasn't in a manner of speaking, she says. Sorry, he says. They both had overprotective mothers. She read psychology at university. He read English. University was the best time of both their lives. Her first job was as an editor on a men's magazine. No, not that sort of magazine. She means a blokes' magazine. Cars. She got into television accidentally, through someone she edited on the magazine who wanted her to edit him forever. He looks hard at her. Did they . . . ? No, no they didn't. He directed his first play as a student and was given an internship at the National. He was writing full-time by the age of twenty-five. She has never had or wanted children and is now too old to change her mind. You can't be that old? I can. And if she weren't too old? Still no. He the same. Does that make them selfish? No. Quite the contrary. They don't seek their perpetuation in mirror images of themselves. They don't mind dying out. Though maybe I will when the time comes, he laughs. She doesn't think she will, so long as the life she's led gets close to what she's wanted of it. Which is? Activity. Interest. Company. Talk. Love? Yes, but love as defined by activity, interest, company, talk. You? Yes, to all those. Such concurrence! He has, though, by the by, two stepdaughters, one sired on his wife by a tree-hugging hippie before he met her, another by a concrete poet, ditto. Where are they now? The fathers? No, the daughters. He shrugs. At university . . . he thinks. Her? If she is not the mothering type is she the marrying type? No. But living with someone, he imagines. Yes. In what she supposes could be called a fairly stable relationship. Only fairly? Well probably *un*fairly – to him. Because? Oh, time. Not that they – this after a decent pause – are open-relationship people. They don't discuss what would be too upsetting to discuss. She has never been in love. He neither, which is a lie. But he doesn't want to devalue this moment by alluding to others like it. Not that . . . They are both straight. She is not experimental. He is, within the confines of straight, but says he isn't.

Does she invite him to her room or does he invite himself?

Neither is entirely certain. But she asks him to give her thirty minutes. To show he understands women he gives her a full hour. Time enough to call his wife, but he doesn't.

She opens the door to him wearing a white silk kimono which parts and comes together again with a sound like breathing, filling his famed nostrils with her perfume.

This will be the smell of the second half of my life, he thinks.

He is astonished by himself. Has he decided?

His olfactory organ has.

She is surprised by how lightly he holds her and how bristly he isn't. She imagined him spikey like his character, his arms and chest covered in coarse black hair, but under his shirt he is fair and feathery.

He relaxes quickly under her touch. She owned a bendy doll when she was a little girl, Captain Twisty, whose arms she could knot behind his back. She feels she could easily do the same with Quaid's.

Funny, she now thinks she wants to call him Quaid.

He is hamstrung by his education. He slides his hands under the silk of her kimono but can't tell her she has beautiful breasts. 'No, you don't,' Miss Gore warns him. 'Mmm!' he says instead. The sound takes him back more than forty years to the first breasts he ever saw and thought Mmm about. He lowers his head and suckles.

Strange creatures, men.

'Mmm,' she says.

Once a man has suckled a woman's breast can he ever again be a man in her eyes?

Or in his own?

As though to reassert some sort of authority, if only of appraisal, he takes a half-step back to look at her. She turns her head away in shyness.

Voluptuous is not a word he likes to use. It is not a writer's word, unless what you write is soft porn. But how else is he to

describe – to himself – the unexpected fullness of her, the plenitude, the easeful fleshliness which is somehow – miraculously –
compatible with her being slender and even slight?

But why does he need to find a word at all? Why, if she is
marvellous, can't he just marvel?

Because he is a writer and a writer is not fully alive to himself
until he has found the language that tells him he is.

She isn't sure who initiates the kiss. The kiss proper. Neither of
them has good teeth so they are both careful to keep their
mouths a secret in conversation. And not to laugh with abandon. Behind his lips she imagines a harsh and fiery tongue.
There's a joke. Behind hers he imagines a small, warm cavity like
a chinchilla's nest. In the event they are both wide of the mark.
His mouth is soft and yielding. Hers is scented and capacious.

'Hot tongue,' she says, pulling away to catch her breath.

'Cool mouth,' he answers. 'I feel I have been swimming in a
temple pool in Andalucia.'

Who'd have thought so austere a speaker would be so flowery
a lover? 'Not drowning, I hope.'

Drowning? Not any more. 'Floating,' he says.

They laugh nervously, unamused. Their eyes daren't meet. He
thinks hers could blow up in his face, like his stepdaughters'
firework.

She opens the minibar, asking him what he wants, her robe
flying open.

'Everything I have ever desired is here,' he says.

'In the minibar?'

They laugh again, but now their eyes do meet. What has he
just said? *Everything* he has ever desired!

'Don't,' she says.

He is afraid he has gone too far too soon. Yes, it's months since he first set eyes on her, but this is Day One of the Creation of the World and you don't show your heart on Day One unless you want it to be broken before you even make it to Day Two. But it's *her* heart she's protecting. She says 'don't' because she knows the risk to herself of thinking 'do'.

But now he's started he can't stop. Is this what his linguistic reserve has all along been about? Has he been holding back a tide which, once allowed the slightest ingress, will come flooding in?

'Greedy boy,' a woman twice his age had called him once. Abashed, he'd turned away, put his hands in his pockets and left with nothing. Such are the errors of youth. Let Lily call him a greedy boy and he will devour her in her own sanctum in a single bite. Desire can make a hungry man religious. Lawrence's acolytes called him a Priest of Love. Quaid is too much the ironist to see himself like that but he doesn't find it absurd to think of Lily as a Priestess of Love and he her votary. Her perfume is myrrh and spices, cedar and sandalwood, swung in a silver thurible. Her fluttering robe invites prostration. 'I wonder,' he asks, peering once more into the minibar, 'if they have sacramental wine in here.'

She kisses him again. She thinks of saying *all the sacramental wine you will ever need is on these lips*, but she guesses – correctly – that her action requires no explication. Without any fuss, they have entered the hushed Vale of What Doesn't Need To Be Said. He drinks so deep of her she fears she will faint.

DREAD

'Whoever falls in love lets dread into his soul.'

Quaid, suddenly awake, hears a line from one of his early plays. Nearly all his plays are early plays. He is an early man. And that goes for love.

Slow down, he tells himself.

Unknown to him, Lily too is awake. She has not yet fallen asleep and it will be a while before she does. She lies there in the silence, reading his thoughts. How often, she wonders, does he fear he has allowed dread into his soul?

Does that mean she has allowed dread into hers? No. She is more practical in her fears. Not dread. Suspicion.

They find each other's hands in the dark.

DEAR HEART, HOW LIKE YOU THIS?

They will remember their first night together as so transcendent that they expected light to do the decent thing and retreat from sight. She had warned him that he would have to creep silently from her room in the early hours so as not to be seen by any of the crew, but even as he was getting his things together the camera-man rang from London. Their plane was still on the ground. Normally, such a delay to a tight shooting schedule would have rendered Lily apoplectic. This morning, 'Ah well,' was all she said.

She ordered breakfast in her room. For two.

'Say it again,' Quaid said.

'Say what?'

'*For two.*'

Was he going to turn out more romantically needy than her, she wondered. She had travelled the world and breakfasted happily alone in a thousand hotels. *For two* didn't hold the magic for her it did for him. But she said it and he clutched his heart.

Dread in his soul, milk and water in his heart.

They talked all day, even lunching in bed, waiting for more night.

'But I don't care if it never comes,' he said. 'I have all the time in the world.'

'The shoot is only three weeks,' she reminded him. 'And we're in the process of losing a day of it.'

'There is a life after a shoot,' he said, waving away conse-quences with the hand that wasn't irritating her by drawing absent-minded circles on her thigh.

'Mr Reckless,' she said.

'Why the sarcasm?'

'Last night you warned me against turning up on your doorstep.'

'I did no such thing.'

'You told me about a woman who followed you back from a signing and camped outside your house. Why?'

'Why did she camp outside my house?'

'Why did you tell me about her? Are you afraid I might do something similar?'

'Of course not. I just – well, I don't know.'

'I do. You *just* wanted to remind me you are a married man with responsibilities. As you did when you told me that ringing and not leaving a message made your wife suspicious. I have not forgotten you have a wife.'

'Then maybe I have.'

'Don't say that. If you had forgotten you have a wife you wouldn't start whenever there's a knock at the bedroom door. Are you worried she might have followed you from Notting Hill?'

They managed to summon a dark laugh when, that very minute, there was indeed a knock at the door. Housekeeping. No, thank you, they didn't want the room made up. Fresh towels? Yes. Leave them outside the door, please.

'Tell them to leave sufficient for two,' he whispered.

Whether it was the arrival of the towels or the fractious conversation that preceded them that made her decide to take a shower, she couldn't have said. He decided not to join her under water, disconsolate, pleading tiredness. Wives – just the very mention of wives – spoil everything.

She came out of the bathroom smelling of all the spices of Arabia, abashed and yet brazen, with a towel tied round her head. He was snoozing when she left him and she thought he'd be asleep when she returned, turbanned, looking like a wife herself. He sensed what she was thinking and let himself drift off; when he opened his eyes again she was on the phone to the Pueblo authorities in Taos, pacing the bedroom, trying not to lose her temper. She looked unassailable, turban or no turban. From a knot in her brow a dark shadow, like a storm cloud, formed. Could someone so solemn and significant have been in his arms half the night? After each call she paused to write something down in the blue notebook she was never without. Had the blue notebook been in his arms half the night too?

Years later he will cherish this fond, almost domestic memory of her, which is also a fond domestic memory of himself, part husband, part father, part son, part petitioner, part Ptolemaic holy man. But at the time, as he dozed twitching like a pensioner, he feared he may have taken his foot off the pedal of passion too soon. What if she, coming out of the bathroom, had seen what life with him would be like when the bloom of wrongdoing had faded? She told him she hadn't had that many lovers, but he assumed that, whoever they were, many were younger than him. A critic had called him boyish but he was more than halfway through any reasonable expectancy of life. Yes, tonight felt like beginning all over again but that was bound to be illusory. He thought he caught her looking at him affectionately, a fond used-up lover already, someone she might mention in passing to the next man she stayed with in a foreign hotel.

She'd shown him her steeliness after he'd been fool enough to warn her against camping out on his doorstep. Well, he'd rather she wanted to kill him than console him.

At last night did come. This time he took the shower and when he returned she was lying disrobed like Manet's Olympia, a flower in her hair, a delicate leather lace tied around her neck, one black stocking on, one black stocking off, her hand covering the part Miss Gore presumed the poet Marvell meant by the 'rest', her gaze too direct for him to meet. Was she staging an ironic pantomine about male desire? Showing she knew? Knew and didn't mind? Showing she could live up to the fantasy, however preposterous? Or was the smile more collusive still? Was she saying 'This is my fantasy every bit as much as yours'?

Is he dreaming? Should he pinch himself?

It was no dream: I lay broad waking.

The Wyatt. How he loved that poem. He could not remember a time when he had not loved that poem. It had been an education to him, a prefiguration, a promise. So it would one day happen, when – a 'when' to trump all other dreamed-of 'whens' – *When*

> *her loose gown from her shoulders did fall,*
> *And she me caught in her arms long and small,*
> *Therewithal sweetly did me kiss,*
> *And softly said, Dear heart, how like you this?*

Long before he'd known a Lily he'd encountered her, for those 'arms long and small' were Lily's arms exactly. Long and strong enough, those narrow arms, to reach up to him and ensnare him but, in that very act of ensnaring, submitting – smally? – to his gaze and desires. Dear heart, how like you this? Was that sacrifice or seduction? Not good enough to say both. For it was as though the one could not be possible without the other.

Dear heart, how like you this?

For once, he didn't have the words.

She looked at him and at last he found the resilience to look back, their eyes meeting in mutual appreciation of her bold gesture, her high-class, educated whorish joke, the hellish and hilarious path from which, if they held their nerve, they would never have to deviate.

It was like a children's staring bet but with more at stake than any child could have wagered.

'What?' she mutely asked.

'What?' he mutely asked in return.

They stared, interrogatively, so hard into each other's eyes throughout the night, in a darkness made even darker by their staring, it would have been a miracle had they seen anything else for a week. Which, he would insist forevermore, they did not.

In the morning their eyebeams were still crossed.

'What?'

'What?'

TAOS: THE SHOOT, DAY 1

Taos is a tiny place, 30 miles from the railway, high up – 6,000 ft –
in the desert. I feel a great stranger, but have got used to that
feeling, and prefer it to feeling 'homely'. After all, one is a stranger,
nowhere so hopelessly as at home.

D. H. Lawrence to E. M. Forster, from Taos, 20 September 1922

The camera pans down from the Sangre de Cristo mountains,
into the cayenne-red dust of the pueblo, and finds him in an oatmeal linen suit reading from a collection of the letters.
Exterior – the Square

Take One.

'Writing to the novelist E. M. Forster, in 1922, Lawrence said—'
The cameraman steps back from the camera and looks to Lily.
'Can we lose the book?'
'Let's lose the book, Sam,' Lily says.
'Is there a reason?'
'It looks a bit too studied. This is the first time we see you.
We want to look straight into your face, not down on the top of
your head.'

Take Two.

'Writing to E. M. Forster, not long after he arrived here in 1932—'
  'Cut. That should be nineteen *twenty*-two, Sam.'
  'Bugger.'

Take Three.

'Writing to E. M. Forster, soon after he arrived in 1922, Lawrence said he felt a great stranger here, but preferred that to feeling lonely—'
  'Cut. *Homely.*'
  'Christ. Are you sure it wouldn't be better if I read it?'
  'Let's try it again.'
She is a different person from yesterday, in camel chinos and a Levi's shirt, her hair pushed back into a baseball cap, holding a clipboard. The crew attend to her orders. Can such a woman even own black stockings?

Take Four.

'Writing to E. M. Forster, not long after he arrived here in 1922 . . . Oh for fuck's sake.'
  A small crowd of children has gathered to look at him.
  'Shoo!' he says. But they don't move. 'Shoo. Shoo! What's Spanish for shove off?'
  'They're just curious. Imagine they're an audience.'
  'Shall I tell them who E. M. Forster was?'
  'They might be interested, but I think get straight on to Lawrence's strangerliness.'

'Shoo! Shoo!'

'Sam, it might be best to leave them alone. We need to respect the pueblo. They're not all that keen on our being here. They could easily tell us to shove off.'

'I can't concentrate when I'm being looked at. I'd be happier behind the book.'

'Just have one more go.'

Take Five.

'Writing to a fellow novelist, Lawrence said he felt a great stranger here, but preferred that to feeling homely. After all, he wrote to a fellow novelist, "one is a stranger, nowhere so hopelessly as at home".'

The cameraman lowers his camera. 'Repetition of "fellow novelist",' he mutters to Lily.

'Lose second "fellow novelist",' Lily says.

'Christ! Lose this, keep that . . .' He walks away. 'This is driving me to distraction,' he says.

Lily is annoyed – not with him but with herself for not picking up the repetition. Her attention had been taken by a young Indian girl standing in a corner of the square, ordering a dog at her feet to sit, lie, beg, before lifting it in her arms and cradling it. No sooner did the dog begin to lick her face than she dropped it, ordering it to sit, lie and beg again. And so on, again and again, until the dog could not tell what was love and what was cruelty. Unless a dog, of all creatures, knows the falseness of any such distinction. The girl laughed. Lily had never before seen one living thing so completely in the control of another. Observing her looking, the girl smiled at her. Lily smiled back.

TAOS: THE SHOOT, DAY 2

Take Six.

'In March 1924, in the company of his wife Frieda and the latest of his hysterical devotees, Dorothy Brett – he always needed a spare wife – Lawrence made his second trip to Taos.'

'Cut. Sorry. I don't think we need to know about Dorothy Brett quite yet and I think we should concentrate on Lawrence's first trip to Taos before getting into his second.'

Quaid slaps his thigh with the volume of Lawrence's letters he is loth to 'lose'. His nerves are shredded. He has noticed Lily and the cameraman exchanging looks, as though one of them has laid a bet with the other that today will go the way of yesterday when they'd had to give up pieces to camera in favour of shooting him wandering round the pueblo, though even this he found difficult to do without self-consciousness. 'Don't look at us, Sam. We're not here.' Then things had conspired to stop them getting adjoining rooms in the motel, and she didn't want the crew seeing him creeping into hers. 'Would that matter?' 'Yes.' So he'd sat up half the night in case she changed her mind, reading Lawrence, Lawrence, Lawrence, and more Lawrence. You can grow heartily sick, even of genius. Of Lawrence's evocative powers – overblown and consummate – he was simultaneously contemptuous and jealous. And as for the asexual magnetism or whatever it was, he couldn't have been alone in finding it galling. No man likes reading about another's successes with women, no matter who the women or how unsatisfactory the success. In the end, the only way out of this absurd envy is to blame womanhood itself.

67

Which means he is testy with Lily when they recommence shooting. 'I did tell you I had no flair for this,' he reminds her over breakfast. 'I am a writer not a performing monkey.'

She reaches for his hand under the table. It's a good job you just did that, he thinks. I've been a whole night alone. I was beginning to forget what being touched by you was like.

'Yesterday was your first time in front of a camera,' she says. 'It's a difficult art. You'll get better. Just relax.'

So he takes a turn around the perimeter of the pueblo in the hope of just relaxing. He notices a group of Indian men standing talking outside the Old Spanish Mission church. They look at him suspiciously under their big hats – *like dark gaps in the atmosphere . . .* The phrase is Lawrence's. From the heart of envy, Sam concedes the genius – one dark gap in the atmosphere to another.

He beckons Lily. 'Can we shoot here, with the Indians behind me?'

'If they don't mind. I did give my word we wouldn't trouble anyone.'

He goes over to the men and tells them he is making a film about the pueblo. They look through him.

He decides that means they don't mind.

Lily would like him to walk into the shot.

'Looking at anything in particular?'

'No. Just walk naturally.'

'I'm not sure how to do that.'

'Walk the way you normally walk.'

He doesn't know how he normally walks.

'Try not thinking about it,' Lily says.

Quaid walks into shot like a drunk.

Does she roll her eyes at the cameraman? He is lean, high-shouldered, ironic and ageless. Thirty? Fifty? A man who's seen all of life through his collection of lenses and so finds nothing surprising. Is she having an affair with him? Is that why she didn't want the crew to see them nipping out of each other's rooms.

He goes for another short walk, then clears his throat, coughing up dust. I've swallowed half this fucking pueblo, he thinks. And the half I've not swallowed is all over my suit. His shoes too, he notices, look as though they're bleeding. He kicks his toes against the church wall, angry and futile.

Take Seven.

'D. H. Lawrence was one of those fiercely argumentative Englishmen whose argument is first and foremost with themselves. To a man forever alienated from everyone and everything, forever at war with the constituents of his own spirit – his psyche, his pneuma, the breath of life itself – Taos, with its Catholicism grafted seamlessly on to a far older religion, must have held out a promise of impossible wholeness.'

He waits.

'Nearly there,' Lily says.

'You want me to lose "pneuma", don't you?'

'Yes, lose "pneuma" and then walk out of shot.'

'Must I? Walking out of shot always looks so artificial and peculiar, as though the presenter has just remembered he has somewhere else he needs to be. Can't I just lose "pneuma" and go on looking towards the horizon after "impossible wholeness"?'

The cameraman sighs loud enough to scare off a bird that's been keeping half an eye on the shoot all morning.

Quaid does a perfect take, then rigidly outfaces the middle distance, like a man expecting tragic news, waiting for Lily to say 'And . . . cut . . .'

'Great shot of the eagle,' says the cameraman.

DELIGHT MAKERS

'Sam Quaid,' Quaid says, entering the room and extending a hand. None of the clowns get up to shake it.

He is here to interview the Koshare – the sacred clowns whose irreverent antics had shocked and fascinated Victorian anthropologists. Lily had hoped to persuade them to be interviewed in clown regalia, naked but for their loincloths or ragged breechclouts, their bodies painted white with black stripes like zebra crossings, their mouths and eyes exaggerated with black circles to make them appear other-worldly and even childlike, with corn husks sprouting from their heads like horns. But she had never been able to get to them directly, only through pueblo elders who haven't wanted them to be filmed. It's one of the elders who's sulkily agreed to loan them his prefabricated house to meet in. But only for half an hour, and there are to be no questions about secret ceremonies. Those who refuse to shake Quaid's hand, or are simply uncertain what to do with it, are wearing cotton shirts and discoloured trousers and could be mistaken for furniture-removal men awaiting instructions. They smoke absently, look dull and incurious. They listen neither to Quaid nor the interpreter. Anthropologists christened them The Delight Makers. Ha! That they are clowns of any sort Quaid finds hard to believe. Nothing in their lugubrious expressions suggests mirth. But then people have said that about him.

He is as poor an interviewer as he is a presenter. He waves his hands about, asks verbose and not always penetrable questions, and would plainly be uninterested in the answers if there were to be any. Two of his favourite words are inchoate and chthonic.

These people are inchoate and chthonic, he thinks. As well as fucking rude.

Well, Quaid has to respect their reticence. Art does not have to explain itself. But they aren't welcoming him, either, to one of their festivals where he can see what they do for himself. He is all for staying on in the hope of finding just one clown with more delightful manners he can interview, Delight Maker to Delight Maker.

But Lily can't pay the crew to stay on in New Mexico indefinitely on the off-chance of finding one amusing and personable shaman. After four more days filming the Sangre de Cristo mountains, assorted cacti, Lawrence's farm, and people who have third-hand reminscences of the novelist to relate, she sends the crew home. She and Quaid will spend a few more days in Santa Fe, at their own expense, without a camera or a crew, eventually forgetting all about sacred clowns and doing what they have come to think of as what they enjoy doing most – shopping, talking, showering, kissing, coalescing, staring.

And of course historicising.

The myth of their first encounter, the suddenness of their attraction, how they differed in this regard and in that and yet how out of both their control everything felt, excited them almost as much as the encounter itself had. They couldn't stop talking about themselves, much as adherents to a faith go on marvelling about the miracle that brought them to the truth.

Adulterers are not like other lovers. Their desperation to devour each other – intensified by difficulty of access, exaggerated caution, fear of exposure and happiness coming to an end – finds expression in a compulsion to go over and over the circumstances that brought them together. At first they thought it profligacy to expend the little time they had in conversation instead of love-making until they realised the conversation WAS the lovemaking.

He eased himself into her in words.

71

And if the words were sometimes more Shakespeare's than his, well, Lily, who had never slept with two men at a time and didn't want to, was not of a mind to complain.

They coupled gently and with consideration, and she would wrap her arms around him, much as she had once wound herself around her favourite stuffed rabbit, as though to keep both of them safe from harm.

She couldn't have said what that harm was. 'Why do I feel I am saving you?' she asked one especially lovely night in Santa Fe, after they'd looked in the window of every artisan jeweller, after he'd bought her a starry gold chain, after they'd walked back to the hotel, hand in hand, under stars that shone even more brilliantly than those he gave her.

'It can only be because I want to be saved and you have a pre-ternatural gift for knowing what I want.'

'But what do you want to be saved from?'

'Not being with you for all time.'

Darkness fell on their last night together and their eyes were beacons. Of hope, of desperation.

'What?'

'What?'

His wife did not ring. He had been tensed for her call and feared the not ringing presaged an intensification of her anger. She had reason to be annoyed. Why, so many days after he was due home, wasn't he? And why didn't he have a convincing explan-ation of what he was staying behind for?

Something about clowns. Well, she could tell him who the clown was.

He and Lily did not leave New Mexico together. Hal, about whom she thought it tasteless to talk at any length, had noted that there were ski slopes not far from where she'd been filming and suggested flying out to join her for 'a longish weekend' and while there trying out a new light ski pole he'd invented. Though she pictured herself having to sit in the snow on a toboggan without her shirt on to keep him happy, she could hardly say no.

Quaid was relieved she was staying on. He was bad at partings and knew this one would be like a death. But by her staying, it wouldn't quite feel they'd separated. He wept in her arms for all that, insisting she should not accompany him to the airport; wept in the car as he saw her wave and walk away, normally so quick in her movements, now agonisingly slow as though trudging through mud; wept on the plane, remembering.

His eyes must still have been wet when he saw Selena waiting for him in the arrivals hall. Meeting him off a plane was not something she had ever done before. He blinked. Could this have been a vision cranked up by the engines of his remorse from that cellar beneath the stage reserved for ghosts which actors know as 'hell'?

She shouted his name. 'Sam, Sam.' And ran towards him, and threw out her arms, and kissed his face fervently, and looked as elegant, in a long Spanish Riding School coat and an insolently tilted trilby, as he had ever seen her.

PART 3

COME LIVE WITH ME AND BE MY LOVE – JUST NOT YET

'EUGH!'

Selena's daughters had argued the case for and against their step-father. Janine, the younger, who played the violin, thought he should be forgiven his trespasses on the grounds that he was an artist and artists had to familiarise themselves with everything loathsome in their own natures. Eleanor, who was a housewife long before she had a house or a husband to put in it, thought a plaque saying World's Greatest Living Playwright: World's Shittiest Dying Husband should be nailed to the door of the room in which her stepfather worked and which he should never again be allowed to leave.

'If he can't keep it in his pants, Mama, we should wall up his pants.'

'All well and good,' argued Janine, 'but locked up in his room he would soon cease to be a playwright of any worth at all. He writes about horrible things and has to go on familiarising himself with them.'

'Incarcerated with himself,' said Eleanor, 'he would be granted constant access to the most horrible thing of all.'

'All this,' said Janine, 'fails to take account of what you want, Mama.'

'Revenge,' Selena said.

'A dish best served cold, people say.'

'I've tried that. I'm ready now to serve it scalding hot.'

'So how recent,' Eleanor wonders, 'is the crime you want him boiled alive for?'

'Well here's the thing. He's on the plane back from committing it even as we speak.'

'Eugh!' said Eleanor. 'This minute?'

'Well . . .'

'Yet you'll let him back into this house?'

'I can hardly keep him out. He does live here.'

Eleanor threw her hands in the air. 'Mama, we go through this every time he goes away. Do you want him back?'

'I don't know.'

'That means you do,' Janine said. 'It's not as though you don't subscribe to the lawlessness of the artistic temperament yourself.'

'What's that supposed to mean?'

'Look into your own heart, Mama. You're two of a kind. You should be together.'

'That's all well and good. But what if he doesn't want us to be together?'

'Well he's never left you yet.'

'He degrades me, which is worse.'

'Love degrades all parties to it,' Janine said. 'That's its universal appeal.'

'Does it help me to know that?' Selena asked.

'Yes, if it brings you to a decision. I say give him the welcome-home-with-open-arms treatment.'

'And then put a bullet through his skull,' Eleanor added.

Selena wondered what a son might have added to the conversation.

WOMEN IN LOVE

Alone in the snow, while the man with whom she played Scrabble tried out his ski poles, Lily went over what had happened. 'How do you know when you're in love?' she'd asked her mother thirty years before. Her mother's answer had been unsatisfactory and she never asked again. She'd worked it out for herself, anyway. 'You aren't until you can bear to hear yourself say you are,' and now, at the age her mother must have been when she sought her advice, she still couldn't bear to hear herself say she was.

That was partly out of respect for language. She had never been above swooning in some clever man's arms when the lights were dim and the music smokey. There'd been times when she'd even wondered whether that sensation of liquid abandonment wasn't the thing all her girlfriends had talked about and in whose name they'd had themselves measured for wedding dresses. But to actually tell a man she loved him without experiencing something more exceptional than a swoon in his company, without a momentous upheaval of the spirit that could alone justify momentousness of expression, was impossible to her. Some words had to be kept in reserve for when life merited then.

She didn't exactly tell herself she was saving them, but it appeared she was. And if a time never came when they were needed? Well, she was no more prepared to cry over what might not happen in the future than she was over what had not happened in the past.

The words she had never before spoken had not risen to her lips once in the ten days with Quaid. But down there where words of that sort were minted, it seemed to her quite possible that the process of forging them – yes, she heard the pun – had begun.

So how much of a fool did she feel now? Put it this way: after a week in the snow without hearing a word from him, not so much as a rushed and whispered 'Can't speak now, miss you!', a cold dread descended on her. How could she have been so wrong about him? Had she misheard or misread every word he'd spoken? Had she been acting like a girl half her age? Had she been wrong about herself?

On the plane back she believed she had begun to tremble. Out there in the snow, so far from London, she could find a thousand practical, explicable, forgivable reasons for his silence. The closer she got to home, the fewer of them remained. By the time she was inside the house, where no letter from him or message on her answerphone awaited her, she was ready to begin the process of wiping out all memory of him.

Sad, very sad, and ugly, very ugly, but she believed herself to be made of strong material. Her mother had kicked out her lubricious, lying, lice-infested husband, and gone on to lead a life that was interesting if lonely, useful if forlorn. She would do the same.

The hard part was not being able to rid herself of him entirely. They had a film to finish. There was still archive to sort. There were distinguished Lawrentians lined up in Midlands universities for him to interview. There was a script to write. Like leaves in late autumn, scraps of him continued to fall around her.

After a fortnight – was it only four or five weeks since they'd begun whatever it was they'd begun? – she rang him. She had to, hadn't she? What if he'd died? What if I'd died, Quaid?

His wife picked up the phone. Of course she did. The wife picking up the phone is as integral to the saga of illicit love as a fat man dressed as a widow is to pantomime. As is the distraught mistress unable to go on a moment longer not knowing what's afoot.

She asked to speak to Quaid. The wife did not ask her name. It wasn't necessary. She'd been to enough pantomimes.

His voice was alarming in its brightness. 'So how was the skiing?' As though skiing had been just yesterday.

'Hal enjoyed it. Until his ski pole broke.'

'And you?'

'I don't ski.'

'Of course you don't. You told me.'

'I'm surprised you remember.'

The slightest pause. 'I remember everything. Anyway, how's the film looking?'

That was a painful question. It looked as it was: a touch amateurish on his part, a touch obsessive on hers. 'There's a lot of him,' the editor had wryly commented when he saw the rushes.

'There's a lot of dross,' she'd admitted. 'But we had to give him time to learn. He's raw but compelling.'

'I can see you think that,' the editor said, looking at her evenly. He knew her. They'd worked on many films together. He saw what she saw through a lens. And he saw that this had been more than usually intense.

That it showed, embarrassed her. But she couldn't hide the fact that she found looking at him, foolish and fierce in the suit they'd bought together, raffish and reddened by the pueblo dust, raging against the camera, furious with his own shortcomings, compelling still.

Explain that.

She can't.

Love remains the last of all inexplicable phenomena.

'So when do I get to see it?' Quaid wondered.

'After the editor's licked it into some sort of shape. You won't want to see all we're throwing away.'

'Ah, there's a lot of that is there?'

'Just the usual amount.'

She didn't tell him – though she should have told him, because why spare him? – that while in New Mexico she'd had to beg her commissioning editor to send out more film, so much wastage was there.

There was a pause between them. Where was he taking this call, she wondered. Within earshot? Then she thought, I don't care, I will say my say.

But she couldn't say her say, which was 'So are you back with your wife?' For he hadn't, had he, ever said, in so many words, I am leaving my wife.

She resigns herself to more anguished waiting. She will know when they meet, when they look at the rushes together, when they discuss and record the script, she will know then, oh yes, she will know then all right, but until that time she must resign herself to the torture of knowing nothing.

'If I am suffering minute by minute,' she thought, 'imagining that each of those minutes marks his stately progress, not back to her but away from me, my suffering is no more than I deserve. I can be forgiven losing my head as I did; what's unforgivable is trusting as I did. But that, too, isn't the worst of it. I am a moral being. I slept with another woman's husband. By the measure I have meted will it be meted out to me. I know I am where tens of thousands have been before me, but my crime is not alleviated by its being common. If anything, it is the worse for it. Mistress loses husband to wife. Ha! It is so obvious and so tawdry it barely excites curiosity, let alone pity.'

The spectacle of one who takes what doesn't belong to her being taken from in turn satisfies our craving for justice – in this case it even satisfies her own liking for irony – but it doesn't exempt her from tragedy. She has made it the business of her life to be in charge of herself, to look to no one else for help, certainly no man, to be the author of her own happiness and distress. 'No,' she wrote to tell her long-estranged father when, on her sixteenth birthday, he tried to crawl back into her life, addressing her as his long-lost beautiful daughter, 'no, I neither want to see nor hear from you. There is nothing you can give me and there is nothing I want to give you.' I will be as a man, she had vowed long before. I will be all woman and all man to myself, in that I, and I only, will control what happens to me. *Control.* The word enjoys a bad reputation in our take-it-easy age. A control freak is someone of quick temper and rapid movement, who leaves nothing to chance or other people, who endeavours, in any battle of wills, to make her will prevail. But why do we look askance at such a person, especially when that person is a woman? Why do we call her ambition to negotiate life at the speed she prefers, giving and taking by her own lights, unbeholden to others, *instability*? She saves the state some money; though she would shape the world to suit her, she is a drain on none of its resources. If anybody suffers on account of her unrelenting self-reliance it is her. As witness how unprotected she is the minute she trusts someone else to regulate her heartbeat – a woman lost and bewildered, unmoored, cast down, as the hours tick by without a word, into blinding grief.

There is no point in her trying to categorise Quaid's sin precisely – whether as abandonment, exploitation, disloyalty, apostasy, spinelessness. What counts more than any list of his delinquencies is that her happiness is in someone else's hands. And she a woman entirely without patience. If he means to pay her back for something – for causing him to lose himself, for causing him to say what he didn't mean or cannot go on meaning, for causing him to lose all reason and forget all vows – he could not have chosen a more cruelly effective means. The silence of a man who might as well have fallen off the end of the world. A silence that denotes everything and nothing, leaving it to her to decide which. They'd spoken each other into

83

adoration, and now he has gone off with a thousand sentences unfinished and abandoned her to a solitariness as wordless as a desert.

It is like an extinction. But without the consolation. Extinct, you don't hear your nerves stretch. How long must she wait before she hears herself snap?

So forget him, Lily. Do yourself a kindness. Consign him, as he has consigned you, to oblivion.

Good advice. But first she has to unlove him.

There! – albeit in negative form, she has said it.

WORK IN PROGRESS

More weeks go by before the film is in any kind of shape for him to look at, or before she is in any kind of shape to look at him. They arrange for him to come to the cutting room. Take it as a sign or not, but three days before the due date he breaks an ankle falling over his own shoelaces outside a homewares store and cannot leave the house. On the phone, explaining it, he makes a joke in such bad taste it takes her breath away. 'You seem to be having bad luck with men,' he says. 'Your partner breaks a ski pole, I break an ankle.'

She doesn't ask him to consider what else he's broken.

She has a portable viewing device she can bring to him. Not ideal but better than nothing. And so she returns to the house where she first saw him and went *kerpow*! It no longer feels daunting. Why did it ever? What had she been expecting? This? Had she known this was sure to be the outcome all along? Selena, prepared for the visit and dressed as though to bid at Sotheby's, opens the door Lily should never have knocked on. You must be, yes; you must be, yes; and thus they are acquainted. Hmm, Selena thinks. I see, Lily says to herself.

The lubricious lovers of Albuquerque, Taos and Santa Fe embrace chastely, ear to ear. He is struck by how pale she looks. How lustreless her eyes. How narrow her mouth. As she puts her lips to his cheek, she tastes what is either the remnant or the fore-runner of a tear. He loves me not, either way. Farewell, my lovely.

The film is no worse than Quaid feared and no better than he hoped. The pueblo looks grand and mysterious. She's found interesting stills of what it would have looked like when Lawrence was there. The pieces to camera? Cut savagely.

'You've got rid of most of my words,' he complains.

'You'll thank me for it,' she says.

She can barely speak. If she swallows, the sound will reverberate through the hated house.

He tells her what he would like her to put back. She tells him she won't. 'No one but you will miss that,' she says. 'No one else will ever know it was there.'

'But I do.'

She is short with him. 'I would never dream of telling you how to edit a play,' she says. 'Film editing is a ruthless business.'

Her words hang in the air. Is she implying his plays could do with some ruthless editing? Is she implying *he* could?

'Without the clowns it's a bit flat,' she goes on, 'but a good script will save it.'

What, though, Lily wonders, will save me.

I can hardly be surprised she's angry, he thinks. I have not dealt decently with her. I love her, but that doesn't excuse me.

So what explains his behaviour? Why does he treat a woman he loves less considerately than he would treat a woman he doesn't? Must he punish a woman for loving him? What sort of sickness is that?

Who did what to him when he was a boy?

According to his reading of himself, psychology will get you nowhere. Only evolution can explain him; he is somewhere on the ladder, maybe not very high up the ladder, of emergence from the primal myth of men marrying their wrathful, all-consuming mothers in order to redeem their maleness in incest, perfidy and rape. Anthropologically, he's work in progress.

'My mother called me Sam to make up for my not being the Samantha she'd wanted after a run of three boys,' he had confessed to Lily in those far-off days in New Mexico when they laid their naked anima on the table to prove there could be no way back for either of them.

'Ah. She had a pretty frock waiting for you. And you think psychology will get us nowhere. Presumably you were a disappointment to your father too?'

'Everything was a disappointment to my father. But if it's all right with you I'll give him a skip just now. One day when I am confident you will not hate me for who he is, I will tell you about him.'

'Hate you for *who he is*? Why, what is he?'

'A philosopher. Now can we drop him? Move me forward, not back. I am more yours than his. The way I am with you is the consequence of my being *with you*. Another time, with another woman, I may be someone else. The man you see before you is the man you have just made.'

In so short a time?

Lily, Lily, how long do you think it takes to make or change a man?

It's a recurring theme in Quaid's work that our sexual natures are not pre-fixed and immutable but, chameleon-like, find themselves anew each time they change their habitat. It's partly on these grounds that his plays have been charged with immorality and even maculinism – they seem to scorn constancy and to justify infidelity on the grounds that regularly changing a wife (he leaves it to other playwrights to tackle regularly changing a husband) promotes personal growth. In fact Quaid subscribes to no such philosophy. He's a playwright. He doesn't have a philosophy. Philosophy was what his father did.

'I don't fight my corner as a man,' he once said in an interview for *Esquire*, 'I just retreat to it and cover up. In the late twentieth century, no man dare come out fighting.'

Does his belief that *a man is who he's with* mean he ceased to be Lily's the minute he once more became his wife's?

That begs the question of whether he did indeed once more become his wife's.

★

If it stirred old desires in him to see Selena at the airport – dressed as she knew damned well he liked to see her dressed – killingly and allusively, as though she could be all his heroines to him at once, Anna Karenina, Salome, Clytemnestra, the Wife of Bath, Molly Bloom, Miss Gore even, and a thousand more – the very fact of her coming at all stirred an old tenderness. How lovely of her to take the trouble to come to meet him. How sweet of her to show him that she'd missed him, and how courageous, too, given that she'd never been enthusiastic about his making this film – Lawrence in Taos for fuck's sake! Who cared? – or his going away with another woman about whose existence she'd very pointedly chosen to express no curiosity. All forgiven, was what her presence at the airport announced. All doubts and suspicions hereby annulled.

That *she* was making up to *him*, when he had so grievously wronged her, wronged her still more.

He did not know what to feel or how to comport himself around her. He kept his head sufficiently not to beg her forgiveness, not to fall to his knees and kiss the hem of her coat. Some men, at such moments, confess everything. At least, Quaid thought, I am not so far gone in wretchedness as that. I will not trouble her head with the truth in order to lighten mine of guilt. The more honest the man, the more secrets he keeps. In marriage, if not in public life, only scoundrels admit everything.

They had been sleeping apart for years. That night – companionably, no more – he visited her bed. 'Don't say sorry,' he reminded himself. So he said, 'It's good to be home,' instead. She took his hand and put it to her mouth. He did the same to hers. Kissed her wedding ring. Neither wanted more than that. He would not tell Lily they had kissed hands. A confused consciousness of universal wrong stirred in the bed like an orphan looking for love.

So, Quaid wondered, must I learn to manage this for all time – the moral equilibrium from hell?

THE SCALES OF LOVE

'Yes, it ought, I know, to have been possible for me to feel all these things' – leaving out some of them – he told Lily over a bottle of American wine (she noticed the allusion) in a bar round the corner from the cutting room, 'and not treat you so contemptuously.'

By *all these things* he meant the commonplace abstractions of delinquency he had cobbled together, not the tenderness akin to love his wife had reawakened in him. For to have told Lily of that would have been no different to telling Selena of her. Each was now to be kept secret from the other.

Not that things weren't hard enough already for Lily. She couldn't meet his eye. 'Yes, it ought. It ought. You could have rung.'

'And said what?'

'"Hello."'

'*Hello, I'm trying to sort my feelings out vis-à-vis my wife?*'

'Exactly that. Why not? I might have asked how come you hadn't done that already. Or what you thought you were doing with me since you hadn't. But yes, you could have said that and I'd have understood.'

'But I didn't dare risk talking to you, Lily. I was frightened of hearing your voice.'

'Why, were you so vain as to suppose I'd try to inveigle you back?'

'Of course not. It was the music of your voice I feared hearing again. I couldn't think unless I could clear my mind of you. I don't mean forever—'

'Get away.'

'I mean it, Lily. I had to give my conscience air—'

'And I mean *get away*. Go!'

And because he was unbearably, vainly slow to realise she really did mean it, she rose and got away herself.

Which left the film in limbo. She called in sick to her editor. OK, yes, there was stuff he could get on with without her. The only pity was he couldn't do everything he'd have liked. Such as edit out Quaid.

Then Lucasta, whose husband had run off with an older woman, rang to say he was back. 'He's come to his senses,' she said. 'Just as I said he would.'

'I thought his senses were the reason he left you,' Lily said.

'Christ, Lily, that's a cruel thing to say.'

'I'm sorry. I didn't mean it to be. I'm a little disillusioned with men at the moment.'

'What do you mean at the moment?'

'I don't believe them, that's all. But if you're happy to have him back . . .'

'Of course I'm happy to have him back. If I don't have him back I watch television on my own.'

'Then I'm delighted for you.'

'But you aren't, Lily, I can hear that. I'm sorry I can't be more like you.'

'What does like me mean?'

'Self-motivated. True to yourself. Cynical.'

'Cynical? Lucasta, I'm made of jelly.'

'Well it doesn't show.'

'The worse for me.'

'You mean the worse for me. I can hear your disapproval.'

'If you hear disapproval, it's your own. I wouldn't dream of judging you.'

'Look, Lily, I know what you're thinking and I agree with you. But if we don't cut these lying swine a bit of slack – which is no more than we are always asking them to cut us – we'll die lonely.'

'Christ, Lucasta, that's a cruel thing to say.'

'I don't mean you.'

But Lily decided she did mean her.

They can't go back into the cutting room together without returning to the whys of what he'd decided to call his tergiversation.

'That enables you not to call it what it was.'

'So what do you call it?'

'Spinelessness.'

'I'll take pusillanimity.'

'You'll take what you get. You can't word your way out of trouble with me. Pusillanimity, indeed!'

He loves the way the word explodes on her lips.

Yes, he is admiring her again. A rush of tenderness over-whelms him. All right – it was a rush of tenderness for his wife that overwhelmed him into forgetting Lily. Can't a man show tenderness to two women? He feels morally weightless, as light as a pin hovering between two magnets.

'What was I to do? Walk past her in the airport? Wasn't she entitled to an explanation?'

'And did she get one?'

'Not in so many words. It's hard. I felt a heel. I still do.'

'Heel! You feel a *heel*? I think I prefer tergiversator. But can we get one thing clear? I am not talking about your wife. I have no business talking about your wife. I am only asking why, however much of a heel you felt about her, you couldn't squeeze in a quick call telling me you were all right and asking, if only out of politeness, how I was.'

'All right, all right. I wanted to punish you.'

'Now we're getting somewhere. You hated yourself and so you had to wound me as your accomplice.'

'No.'

'Yes. Dropping me like a stone and not bothering to find out if I'd drowned was your way of punishing me for your guilt.'

'No, it was not as bad as that, unless it was worse. I thought the more I neglected or, if you like, disrespected you, the less I'd be neglecting or disrespecting her.'

'So your guilt was a shuttlecock that you batted to and fro between us?'

'I'm talking about more than guilt.'

Lily pricked her ears. If he were to talk of love in this context he would ruin all mention of it forever.

'Others have their rights to you, Sam. I have none. But I will not be weighed out as on a set of moral scales, wondering every time I see you, or don't see you, on which side the pan happens to be tilting that day.'

'Lily—'

But she wouldn't be so easily Lilied.

SHE WHO STRIKES THE FIRST BLOW
WINS THE ARGUMENT

Was it soon after that, or was it long after that, that she struck him?

Almost wordlessly, as though the decision would not have survived shame had they spoken it, they found a way of meeting in a hotel room in Whitehall. Why Whitehall? Quaid guessed that a hotel in Whitehall must cater for cheating politicians and so know how to keep their guests inconspicuous. They didn't go to the room together. She'd go first. He'd follow fifteen minutes later and knock three times. Neither could quite explain why it had to be so cloak-and-dagger. It wasn't Albuquerque, that was all. And because it wasn't, and because this was the first time since New Mexico they'd dared to be intimate, they felt they had to start over again, shyly, uncertainly, furtively. How dispiriting the change felt to them both. They had got to where they were without having had to start out as afternoon adulterers. They had gone from fancy to effectuation as though on the wings of a wish. Now they were having to resort to scheming and contrivance to be together. Each, independently of the other, regretted bitterly this retrogression into something less exalted.

Her lashing out at him had many causes, among them, surely, this new reality. She could have been hitting them both.

In the novels of Lawrence, Quaid thought as he bowed his head beneath her blows, women try to brain the men who wrong or jeer at them. The grandiosity of Lawrentian man resides in his believing that only his death can purify the outraged soul of womankind. Quaid doesn't consider himself to be quite so important. Though Lily wishes him to have behaved differently, she doesn't need him to be dead. New Mexico had been an idyll. In New Mexico they'd been as innocent as children. But the idyll had been betrayed. It was incumbent on them thereafter to act as adults. Yes, the drum roll of thumps and kicks and mis-directed slaps had something of the nursery about it still, but it was necessarily transitional – she wouldn't have dared lash out at him in New Mexico, nor he her, for then they shut the world out, protecting each other from its violence, whereas now the source of violence was her, and the reason for it him.

He lay back on the bed and offered no resistance. Had she attempted to claw his eyes out he'd have let her.

'It's possible,' she said between blows, and with an illogicality he couldn't account for, 'that you are more moral than me. I think you are. I don't suffer your remorse. I would like to but I don't. What can I say? Somewhere, a woman is always taking a man from someone. It's how life progresses. That being the case, you should have discouraged me. You should have kept the door locked against me. That isn't blame, it's description. We need to wise up to who we are.'

Then, precisely as though to close all the exits on them for-ever, she did something that was at once in perfect accord with her pitiless Darwinian account of life, and utterly bewildering. She stopped hitting him, rose sinuously like a genie from a lamp, vanished as though in a wisp of incensed smoke into the bath-room, and returned with a narrow girdle around her waist.

'Do you recognise this?' she asked, taking it off.

He didn't, then he did. It was the plaited leather belt with the snake buckle she'd bought him in Albuquerque to go with his oatmeal linen piece-to-camera suit.

'How come you have it?' he asked.

'I stole it from you before you left. You obviously didn't miss it.'

'Why? Why did you steal it?'

'Why do you think, you fool?'

He couldn't bring himself to say 'To remember me by?' And anyway, as she wound it round her small clenched fist it resembled more an instrument of vengeance than a token of love.

How did he know what to do? How did he know what she wanted?

He could have held out his hand as he had at school, when the cane or the slipper came out. He could have rolled over and let her thrash him as his father had once done. He could have offered her his neck. Alternatively, he could have said, 'No, Lily' – 'No you don't,' in Lawrence speak – and jumped to his feet. But he did none of these things. Instead, keeping his eyes on her all the while, he put his hands behind his head and made a cross of them as he had seen hostages and other frightened supplicants do.

She made a sound at the back of her throat that could have been exultant or could have been appreciative. Why not both? *It becomes you, Quaid, to be at the mercy of my resolve.*

'Raise your head,' she said.

'This much?'

'More.'

Then she straddled him, driving her knees into his sides, and bound his wrists with the belt. Not tightly. He could easily have slipped his wrists free had he wanted to, but there was nothing he had ever wanted to do less.

Though the room was light, their eyes that had not met for months until tonight were suddenly as two black craters, unfathomable and empty, each a silent menace to the other.

'Now what?'

'Now what?'

A MAN'S A MAN

You never know what's going to make everything all right again. A good night's sleep, an aspirin, a plaited belt . . .

In so far as it paints her as the instigator, Lily will contest the foregoing history of the belt's role in reuniting them. She wouldn't be in the slightest bit ashamed to admit it were it true – shame plays a very small role in the drama of Lily's conscience – but it isn't how she remembers it. And in so far as it shifts the responsibility on to him, Quaid, too, will raise an objection. But since shame plays an overwhelmingly large part in his moral consciousness, both as the son of a father in whom he can take no pride and the pupil of Miss Gore, he isn't trustworthy.

'Why don't we agree that the only entirely innocent party is the belt itself?' one of them says when it comes up for discussion in later years.

It doesn't matter whose words they are. At some point each of them will speak them. But Lily knows the truth and allows Quaid to bend it to save him embarrassment. A man is a very thin-skinned creature, she has learnt. If it falls to her to be his scourge, it also falls to her to be his salve.

Salve/slave . . .

The anagrams will have to wait until they are a lot older, when words are to play with, not tremble before.

But for those who like to picture the practicalities of a love affair, there are other questions to be answered. Such as: did the plaited leather belt with the snake's head buckle become a fixture in the passional life of Quaid and Lily?

If yes, did Lily carry it around with her and produce it of her own accord most nights, or did Quaid request it, if not in so many words then by intimation of the sort lovers become adept at communicating? Such as – to make a jest of it – by crossing his wrists behind his head the minute that head touched the pillow. But all jests are facile, heartless and dishonest when it comes to the erotic goings-on of men and women. Act out any desire, and there will always be someone who finds it laughable – no matter that many of those who laugh are performers themselves when darkness falls.

If no, if the plaited leather belt with the snake's head buckle was brought out only on special occasions, was that because Quaid and Lily were alert to the dangers of normalising a fetish? Did they know how perilous to arousal routine was? We must assume that as mature fugitives from staleness they put their minds to that. But so long as the routine is working, it is as hard to recall, as it is to foresee, what the tedium of sex is like.

Truth to tell, it was not routine that caused Quaid concern in those first prickly days of their rapprochement but the confused trajectory of his self-esteem. That the belt bespoke submission was not discussed. Precisely because words were their medium, there were some that dared never be uttered. The belt was a totem. It radiated a magic silence. But within the force field of that silent radiation Quaid grew anxious. So long as he, a playwright, could think of what he and Lily had begun to brew up between them as 'play', he was on secure ground. They were still relatively new to each other. There was still a lot of sparring and finding-out to do. Men in his profession, both on the stage and off it, not uncommonly dressed as women. And vice versa, of course. Roles were not so fixed they couldn't be interchanged. Love the same, surely. It had to be allowable to shape-shift in the arms of someone you loved. To swap characters even, in the knowledge that you would eventually swap

97

back. But didn't the noun 'submissive', at least in the tacky literature of S&M, denote a near-pantomime rigidity of preference? Submissive, by this understanding of the word, implied a state of total sexual capitulation, a kitsch renunciation of authority, assertion and, if the submissive were a man, everything that made him manly. Would he be lisping next?

And yet, yes, Lily ran things. In Taos he had marvelled at the assurance with which she superintended the shoot; her calm, always polite but never less than firm way with the crew; the decisiveness with which she changed a plan and indeed a script, no matter that he – Sam Quaid, distinguished, prize-winning playwright – had written it; the clear sense she always gave of where she wanted the film to go. Quaid, who never knew where anything he wrote was going, and took fright the minute a direction suggested itself, was awestruck. And not only by her assurance but by her authority. When Jeep Number 2 from which he was being filmed driving Jeep Number 1 broke down between Taos and Santa Fe, she flagged down a passing motorist and suborned his services for the rest of the day. 'I have to pick my wife up,' the motorist complained. 'And I have a film to make,' Lily said, all but threatening him with the camera. But she did agree to ring the wife.

Back in London she was equally overweening. They cooked up schemes to make more documentaries together but always under her direction. Yes to this; no to that. During absences dictated by his periodic fits of marital compunction – absences which she would not have dreamed of questioning – she ran the diary of their amorousness: where they could look forward to going when he was in the mood – for she read the fluctuations of his moods with uncanny accuracy – and how long they would be able to stay before he felt bad again. Which meant that yes, she ran him. So long as no one outside the two of them was aware of this evolving hierarchy, he was and looked happy – a successful, haughty dramatist who ruled the roost, who took plaudits from audiences and awards from critics as though they were his by right (if not so frequently in recent times), intellectually under the thumb of a clever, discreet, austerely beautiful – and, all right, exacting mistress. *Mistress*. The belt she wielded made the very word shudder. Whisper it, but she was his mistress in every sense.

So where did this leave him?

Paradoxically, it solved the issue of his fearing he had gone downhill since his legendary starred first and become yesterday's man. Yesterday's man could not have consented to this intimate arrangement with Lily. Yesterday's man would not have had sufficient confidence in his virility – his ruggedness, let us say – to allow it to be compromised in this way. Thus, the less of a man he became, the more of a man he felt. To employ a figure from a greater dramatist than him – a concession he didn't find it easy to make – he was bound upon a wheel of contradiction: richly rewarded in the very actions that demeaned him.

Of those rich rewards, the richest, precisely because it could have been the most unmanning, was Lily's subjection of his 'person' to her will. In matters relating to sex, Quaid favoured biblical circumlocution. By 'person' he meant that entity he was not prepared otherwise to name. His veneration of Lily was of such a kind that he could not envisage her in the neighbourhood of that entity in language other than Old Testament. From the first moment that she (the woman), took possession of him (the entity), he (the man and the entity) passed into her possession. Her hand was small, her touch was of the lightest. But it was as though she had, once and for all, laid claim to him.

'I feel,' he told her, his wrists lashed behind his head, his body open to her invasive gaze (and whatever else she chose to invade him with), 'as though just one of your fingers could—'

How did the Bible put it?

This wasn't a time to consult a concordance and, besides, she didn't need the Bible, for lo, miracle of miracles and praised be the Almighty, just one of her fingers did as he foretold it could.

'I can well imagine that one day,' he said, 'even your touch won't be necessary. Just your command.'

Having said which, it has to be conceded that he sometimes fell back into shame. Would the time come when all his functions operated by her will alone? God forbid any member of his audience – naturally, he hated the word 'fan' – got to learn of it.

He was proud, invigorated, elated, exultant, but he wasn't out of crisis yet.

Lily, as might have been guessed, was not in the slightest bit troubled by any deviations from the straight and narrow of love. If it pleased him to be mistressed, it pleased her more. She could do pliancy, in its time and place she could positively enjoy pliancy; but assertion suited her better. She was no less a woman for playing the man, and in her eyes Quaid was no less a man for playing the woman. Who originally assigned those roles anyway?

What passed between them as she tightened the belt and rose above him was an exchange that didn't stop at he becoming her and she becoming him; it was a dissolution of what 'he' and 'she' meant. It could be said that they were pioneers in the probing of pronouns.

From the beginning, her nerve had been stronger than his. He blinked first. Or rather, wherever this was going to take them, she wouldn't blink at all.

Thus Quaid, long and widely lauded as supreme puppet-master and magician of the English stage, embarked upon a covert life as puppet and magician's pretty assistant.

'Am I absurd to you?' he asked her.

'No.'

'Am I a disappointment to you?'

'No.'

'Would you rather—?'

'I wouldn't rather anything.'

'I'm sorry.'

'What for?'

'Everything.'

'Who are you apologising to? Me or yourself?'

'You,' he said.

'And why do you feel the need to apologise to me?'

She knew perfectly well why but among her many jobs was that of confessor and exorcist.

'I don't have the words to explain it.'

'Ha! Don't have the words, you! The time you don't have words is the time the world will have run out of them.'

'Now you're just trying to make me feel better.'

'I can make you feel worse if that's what you want.'

'I want everything.'

She was supporting her head on one elbow, looking down on him. 'You've got everything.'

'But have I?'

'Haven't you?'

'Yes, but how did I come by everything?'

'Luck?'

'What if I didn't "come by" anything? What if I insisted my desires?'

'On me? Don't flatter yourself.'

He flushed and looked away. Then, 'Do you know what I most fear?' he asked.

'What do you most fear?'

'Coercion.'

'I thought our working assumption is that you love coercion.'

'I don't mean that you have been coercive. I mean that I have.'

'You have not coerced me. Groomed me a little, maybe . . .'

'Oh, God. I'm sorry.'

'Don't be. I'm not. I wouldn't have gone anywhere I didn't want to go. Not everything's for you. This' – she opens her hands wide to suggest the panoramic spectacle of his abnegation, Samson before Delilah, John the Baptist decollated on Salome's platter – 'is as much for me.'

'But if I had not somehow signalled . . .'

'Yes, yes, and if I had not not known how to interpret it . . . And if you had not known what you dared or dared not communicate . . . And if I . . . And if, and if, and if . . . Quaid, don't you think we are too far in to trace the origins of things? Of course if you are wanting to bail out . . .'

He looked startled. 'Not ever,' he said. 'Not ever, ever . . .'

Now it was her turn to look away. 'Don't make promises,' she said. 'I know you to be a man who breaks them.'

Man. He took her in his arms. At least she called him *man*.

TO THE LIGHTHOUSE

Notwithstanding her assurances that theirs was a democracy of strange desires and that all happened between them happened as much because she wanted it to as he did, there were moments when she felt cheated of more conventional ways of expressing tenderness.

On what must have been the tenth or twelfth time she bound him – she later recalled that they were staying in a seaside bed and breakfast and were kept awake by the flashes from a nearby lighthouse – he so far consented to powerlessness as to say 'I am in love with you, Lily, but accept that you will never be in love with me.'

Could there have been crueller timing! Lily had at last come to believe (and to trust her belief) not only that she was in love for the first time in her life, but that for the first time in her life she could without falsity shape the words to say so. And now—!

He was hungry, hungrier that night than ever, for immolation. The lighthouse could have been his inquisitor, refusing him sleep. Confess, Quaid.

He rose up, straining against the belt, and offered his face to her. He was alarmed to see that she could not meet his usual implorations with her usual sternness of expression. Was that sorrow in her eyes? Were there tears even?

What had he said? He hated to see a sign of distress in her or to think that he was its cause, and at any other time would have called a halt to this flummery – *La commedia è finita!* – and apologised so obsequiously as to begin it all again. But ritual is selfish and the transpiercing of his soul had barely begun.

Closing his eyes so as not to see what was in hers, he told her he did not presume to believe that his love for her gave him any right to comment on where she directed hers. 'Even to discuss it with you is unpardonable.'

He pushed his face still closer to hers. What did he want? Normally she knew. But the light from the lighthouse was flashing in his eyes . . .

'Slap my face,' he said. 'Hard.'

Years later, abashed, he will deny saying it.

'I couldn't have.'

'You did.'

'And you?'

'And I what?'

'What did you think?'

'That your timing was crap.'

'I'm sorry.'

'Don't be.'

'What did you say?'

'Don't be.'

'I mean what did you say *then*?'

'I said nothing. I would have found it hard to say anything. I had the words "I love you" ready to deliver and you said "Slap me".'

'So what did you do?'

'You're telling me you forget?'

'If I forget I must need to forget.'

'Then you must be doing a lot of forgetting.'

'Just tell me what you did.'

'What do you think?'

'You slapped me?'

'I slapped you.'

'Hard?'

'How can I know? I doubt it. I struck you across the face. You winced and said "Again".'

'And?'

'Did I? Yes. Still probably not hard enough. I loved you, remember, and precisely because I loved you, I had to give you what you asked. But also because I loved you, I couldn't bear to hurt you . . . Or not to.'

He thought that were they to make it to the end, that should be her memoriam to him. *I loved you so I hit you.* Unless it should be, *I loved you, so I didn't.*

And his to her? *I would not have survived without your blows.*

For her part, Lily, at one and the same time didn't recognise herself and did. She was not a violent woman. She did not come from a violent family. Her mother had told her father to leave and he'd left. If there'd been anything in her background to be alarmed by it was its well-mannered compliance. She did have a jealous streak and had once struck a man who had cheated on her, but a single slap in forty-odd years did not make her a brute. And yet she knew from dancing that she could forget herself, the wilder the music the more fierce and freed it made her feel. Did the dancing create an entirely new euphoric her, or did it simply restore what had somehow and somewhere been lost? She had asked that question of herself before. Now what prompted it wasn't dance, it was Quaid.

Since returning from Taos Pueblo she had not been able to clear her mind of the scene she'd witnessed of a young Indian girl alternately adoring and tyrannising her dog. The girl had noticed her watching and smiled at her. Collusively? Could a fourteen-year-old New Mexican girl recognise a bond of blood with a woman in her forties from Muswell Hill? That question aside, what was it about the girl's sadism and the dog's total capitulation to it that roused her? She laughed at her own question. What excited people about blood sports? Blood, you fool!

But as she went on thinking about it, the more precise in her understanding she wanted to be. Was the girl's exercise of power exciting simply in and of itself? Or was the sight of the cur she whipped and kissed, kissed and whipped, necessary to the composition? Close your eyes, Lily, and say what you see first. The girl smiling at you in shared knowledge? Or the dog shrinking from you in utter abjection?

There was a third possible answer to that question. Quaid.

The following week, on a day off from filming, they had strode hand in hand through Santa Fe, checking out the handicraft stalls, admiring Indian rugs they had no intention of buying and ceramics that would never fit into their luggage. A shop selling silver and leather specialised in wristbands and anklets and chokers for both sexes. If you waited they would spell out your name on a choker in metal studs.

'Would you like one with your name on it?' Quaid asked, good-humouredly.

'In case I get lost? I'll find my own way home, thanks.'

Then it occurred to her, as Quaid continued to sort through the variety of designs, that what he was really thinking about buying was a collar for himself.

'Where would you wear it?' she said, showing she had read his mind. 'Crufts?'

He flushed the brightest scarlet. 'I think I can find my own way home too,' he said.

Yet still he lingered.

'Let me buy you one,' she said. 'For fun. It doesn't have to have your name on it. You could have mine. L.I.L.Y.'

'For that to have any meaning,' he said, 'it would have to be L.I.L.Y.'S.'

Then, just to be clear, he led her out of the shop.

★

106

Many months later, coming back late from a cutting room in Soho after a long day's edit, they saw a boy in a studded dog-collar being led on a chain by a much older woman.

'Remind you of anything?' Lily asked.

He shook his head. 'Should it?'

'Just some silliness.'

She was surprised to discover she was the tiniest bit hurt he'd forgotten.

Not that he had.

'Do you know,' he said to her over scones in a discreet corner of the Randolph Hotel in Oxford, Selena having grown more than usually suspicious, and Oxford having become their bolt-hole, 'that James Joyce wrote to Nora Barnacle before he married her asking her to pass wind in his presence . . .'

They had not met for several weeks; work keeping Lily away, his monthly bout of marital remorse detaining Quaid. Lily never knew what manner of man she was going to find when-ever they reconnected. So to find him engrossed in the bathroom intimacies of James Joyce and Nora Barnacle was only mildly startling.

'Thank you for ruining my scones,' Lily said. 'Yes, as it hap-pens I do know what Joyce asked his wife to do. I too have read the letters. But he was less squeamish than you and called it fart-ing. And it wasn't in "his presence" that he asked her to do it, it was in his face.'

Quaid returned a cucumber sandwich to his plate and buried his face in his hands. 'I am sorry I brought it up,' he said.

'You should be. But I don't understand, since the very word disgusts you, why you did bring it up. I'm assuming you weren't proposing—'

'God no.'

'Because—'

'No, no, absolutely not. I was reading his letters, that's all.'

'Are you still wishing you'd done him instead of Lawrence, who didn't, that I know of, ask his wife to fart in his face?'

'All right, don't rub it in.'

'So is that a yes or a no?'

'It's a maybe. I'm more at home with Joyce constitutionally. Not because of *that*. God forbid. But because he lets me be. Whereas Lawrence has been lecturing me about being a man for years before I was one. He put the fear of God into me about my body and what not to do with it when was I eleven. *In sexual intercourse there is a give and take . . . But in masturbation there is nothing but loss. There is no reciprocity . . . The body remains, in a sense, a corpse, after the act of self-abuse.* Fancy me still remembering it.'

'Who gave you that to read?'

'Probably my mother. It doesn't sound like my father's philosophy.'

'And she gave you that when you were eleven?'

'I'm only sorry she didn't give it me sooner.'

'Sooner! How old were you when you started masturbating, for God's sake?'

Quaid turned pale, looked around the room, and returned another sandwich to his plate. 'I might be exaggerating a little,' he said.

But she can see he finds her language upsetting. 'Forgive me,' she said, touching his arm. 'I forget how many words make you uncomfortable. I should have asked how old you were when you first became a corpse.'

'Laugh at me all you like,' Quaid told her. 'It behoves one of us to be puritanical.'

Whereupon they fell silent and finished their tea. But before they rose to leave he returned to James Joyce. 'You know, passing wind in his presence wasn't all he expected of Nora,' he said.

'I should hope not,' Lily said. 'That would not have been much of a marriage.'

Quaid decided to keep what else he knew of James Joyce's marital expectations to himself.

Joyce in Trieste was no longer on the table anyway. No one was in any hurry to commission a second series of *Writers in Exile*. 'Lawrence in Taos' was enjoyed by the people who were to be relied on to enjoy such things, and not by those who weren't. The photography was admired. Lily's 'nerveless' direction was commented upon, and one reviewer, noting her reputation for getting the most out of unappealing presenters, wondered if she'd met her match this time. Quaid accepted that he was on the verbose, meandering and unlikeable side for television. Since likeability was a gift he didn't value, he could hardly complain when critics said that by and large he didn't possess any. As for D. H. Lawrence – a consensus thought it a pity he hadn't been available to present the programme himself. That was the only criticism Quaid found hard to swallow – that he wasn't even as good a television presenter as D. H. Lawrence. But as someone who offered to scorn television, he readily allowed that television had a perfectly good right to scorn him. All things considered, he acquitted himself just well enough in the eyes of those who had commissioned him, not to be rejected out of hand when Lily proposed a six-part series on *Islands and Their Significance to the Human Imagination*. When quizzed by her bosses as to Quaid's qualifications to present such a series, she told them he shunned human society and had as good as lived on an island all his life.

'You told them that?'

'Well maybe not in so many words. Do you mind?'

'I mind everything and nothing.'

'There you have it. You would mind more if you lived among us and not on Quaid Island.'

He bowed his head into the rebuke. She was right. She was always right. And that included right to love him.

'So what chance?' he asked her the next day. Living on Quaid Island meant that communication could be slow.

'What chance they'll give us another series? Slim, but I think I'll be able to get some development money out of them and we might enjoy developing it.'

'In the British Library or on Robinson Crusoe Island?'

'Where's that?'

'Some 500 miles off the coast of Chile.'

'Pack your swimming trunks.'

Suicidally, he mentioned it as a possibility to Selena. The idea was to prepare her for his absence.

'I wouldn't be wrong in thinking, would I,' she wondered, 'that you will be working with your precious Emily again?'

'Emily. Who's Emily? If you're talking about Lily, her name's Lily.'

'Am I supposed to remember the names of all your women?'

'She isn't one of my women. She isn't even my type.'

'Since when did that stop you? I know you by now. You're such a preverted bastard you *prefer* women who aren't your type.'

'If you don't want me to do it I won't do it,' Quaid said.

'Oh yes, and hold me forever responsible for ruining your career. Though what you think you gain by looking a chump on late-night television, I am fucked if I know. Isn't it time you wrote a play? Let me suggest a theme. How to Throw Your Life Away? Oh, I forgot, you're too grand for "themes".'

She had a point. Where was the latest play?

Soon. Soon. You can't force these things.

As for a theme – it turned out he had one: Modern Man in Search of His Manhood.

Unless he'd already written that.

SIREN SONG

The Hotel Punta Tragara enjoys a beetling view of the Faraglioni rocks at the south-eastern tip of the Isle of Capri. That stiffest of architects, Le Corbusier, lent a hand in its design. Quaid isn't sure he likes it, but its stucco is almost as red as the pueblo at Taos, which is why he has chosen it for a surprise holiday for Lily. Capri is one of the islands he imagines they'll be filming on if their series ever gets off the ground, so their coming here is a salute to their past and their future. They are standing on the terrace of their room, looking out over the Tyrrhenian Sea, named after the Tyrsenoi, or Etruscans, whose creative energy Lawrence so admired. But that's just a coincidence. They aren't following Lawrence around the globe. 'It's just,' said Quaid, 'that the little bastard went everywhere.'

Quaid has brought Lily to Capri to celebrate their first anniversary. Just the two of them. For this is said to be an island for romance. For risky romance at that. It was hereabouts, on the Faraglioni rocks below, that the sirens sang.

'Sing to me, Lily,' he said.

'I can do a passable Gracie Fields.'

'Then don't sing to me.' The snob he was.

'Is it really a year already since we met?' Lily marvels.

'Not met. Kissed.'

They will always argue about the date 'they' began. To Lily it was the moment of her setting eyes on him. To Quaid it was the moment they touched. But they kiss again, anyway, Quaid enfolding her so possessively and not letting her go for so long that a group of sightseers in the little square outside the hotel look up and applaud. They are gathered for a plein-air poetry event. A couple of Neapolitan poets who are over for an arts festival sponsored by an amaretto bottler are giving free readings from their work all over the island. Quaid is envious. If he weren't up here holding Lily he'd like to be down there reading with them. Could there be a grander arena for a recitation? Capri is the posing capital of southern Europe, but even the fashion models pause from their loping llama promenades to listen. When Quaid remembers the scene decades later the models will all have Donald Duck mouths. But this was a more innocent time, before ugliness mistook itself for beauty. Softly and mellifluously the poets' words drift out like soft-bellied birds over the gulf. Quaid and Lily, locked in an embrace, oblivious to the great basin of heaving blue water, could be effigies embalmed in poetry – Dante and Beatrice, Petrarch and Laura.

'*Buon compleanno, più affascinante delle donne*,' Quaid says, raising a glass to her. 'We are One.'

Lily appreciates the conceit. They met and they were born.

Quaid wants to go on toasting. 'To us,' he says, 'and the extraordinary fortune we've enjoyed from whenever we date our waking.'

Quaid's second-favourite poem. *And now good-morrow to our waking souls* . . .

Lily puts a finger to his lips. 'Hush,' she warns, citing her second-favourite poem, '*'Twere profanation of our joys / To tell the laity our love.*'

'These aren't any old laity,' Quaid says. 'These are Italians.'

Lily hasn't the heart to tell him they are Americans.

And the evening and the morning were the First Day . . .

. . . which is where, if we had a grain of narrative decency, we would leave them.

But it takes decency in the principals of a tale to beget decency in the teller, and Quaid and Lily are poised to throw decency to the wind.

PART 4

THE GARDEN OF EARTHLY DELIGHTS

THE LAST DAYS OF MAN

There's a tide of impropriety in the affairs of lovers – lovers in the true, ravening sense, not mere chaste partners in the business of starting a family – that taken at the full sweeps them to perdition.

That's Quaid's way of putting it. He's been waiting to be swept to perdition ever since playing Othello in a classroom reading of the play and swearing devotion to Desdemona with the words 'Perdition catch my soul, but I do love thee.'

'You could try saying that less hungrily,' he remembers Miss Gore advising, piously pressing her fingers together. 'He says "I do love thee" not "I do devour you".'

'I'm trying to do justice to Shakespeare's genius, Miss.'

'And I'm trying to save him from yours,' Miss Gore said, giving the part of Othello to someone else and Desdemona to Quaid.

The someone else turned Othello into a kindly uncle who wanted nothing more than to sit down in the evening with his wife over a green tea and show her holiday snaps of his time with the cannibals. Quaid knew the words should not be delivered other than as he had delivered them. *Perdition*, Miss Gore. You don't expect perdition to make a grab for your soul just because you quite like a girl. Inordinate love invited mortal ruin, indeed half the time a longing for mortal ruin was the only available explanation for loving inordinately at all. He knew that at fifteen? Not in so many words, but fifteen is the first staging post of sexual desperation and he had a feeling that a longing to possess was not always to be distinguished from a longing to throw away.

Or be thrown away, come to that. At fifteen? When else?

Still waiting, in his almost-fifties, for the flames of hell to consume him, Quaid believed fate had at last delivered him into the hands of a woman who had the nerve to pitch him into them. How many times has he told her he wants her face to be the last face he sees, to ensure which she must cut his throat or tear his heart out? Does he mean it? At the time he says it, yes, he means it. And let perdition catch his soul.

Lily employs a more temperate vocabulary of desire, but she too cannot claim to be in control of events when she is with Quaid. Will there be a time when she takes him at his word, presses down on his chest, binds his wrists, looks into his pleading eyes, and shuts off his air supply once and for all?

But won't such an act damn her too?

Perdition catch them both.

But not yet awhile. They proceed slowly, even cautiously, on their return from Capri, settling at once into that routine of subterfuge and depression well known to adulterers.

Quaid wonders if it was such a good idea, after all, to name and number the time he and Lily have spent together. Does it not throw into harsh relief the question of what-now to which neither of them has an answer? They both feel they have returned to school after the holidays. Unable to shake the chill of Sunday evenings from their souls, they fall silent with each other, in case sharing the despondency of indecision will only make it permanent. That to which they don't refer, they hope silence might remedy – which is exactly what the knowing but forgiving Hal, and the only half-knowing but not at all forgiving Selena, also hope will happen, though of course to different effect. A nerve-wracking stillness descends on both households, reminding Quaid, who played Henry V as well as Othello in the Literary Sixth, of the creeping murmurs that hum through the French and English camps on the eve of Agincourt. One doesn't have to be a soldier to be afraid. Illicit lovers, too, fill the wide vessel of the universe with their apprehension. Every day in which they go undiscovered might be their last. Their superstitions, bred from alternating convictions of entitlement and guilt, haunt the quiet of drowsy morning. No one knows who the wounded will be or where they'll fall.

Or who will be the first to ring the other. It doesn't matter. They feel as one, so that when the call does come neither can say who made it. This is the enforced pattern of their lives before they jump once and for all into the furnace, while they wait for a pretext to spend every minute of every day and every second of every night together. Times passes without any word about the series. Commissioning editors die. Winds of change blow through the corridors of broadcasting. And Lily has still not got her hands on development money. Sometimes, buoyed by something Lily thinks she's heard, or Quaid thinks should happen because he wants it to, they believe they are on the cusp of favour and spend a morning buying books for research they probably won't get round to undertaking, and then the afternoon in a hotel. Otherwise, they live like rats in the interstices of mundane existence, seizing whatever opportunities for ecstasy are dropped for them to gnaw.

'We could,' Lily suggests, 'travel on our own money in expectation of its coming back to us.'

Quaid is hesitant only because spending money to be with a woman not his wife strikes him as a betrayal too far.

'Some morality,' Lily notes. 'What's in your bank account is more Selena's than what's in your trousers.'

She's right. When he isn't offering Lily his throat to cut, Quaid is governed by a quaint old-fashioned morality. Without the justification of a joint enterprise, he feels bound to withdraw periodically from the woman he thinks of as his mistress in all senses. It's as though working together licenses their doing everything else together, no matter that the point of their working together is that they can do everything else together. He can't explain it.

Lily goes along with it. You have to honour another person's sense of decorum, even if you think it's claptrap. She fears examining it too closely. What if it is just another word for indecision? What if it simply means keeping every option open? Is she merely one of several he might one day decide to take? Who knows better than she how pliant and biddable he is? She has to be steadfast and ruthless for both of them. On the other hand she no more wants to scare him off than steal him. At no point does she ask if he has any intention of divorcing his wife. As for him, he never asks about her situation. Is that because he doesn't care or is insufferably confident of his power over her?

She has no other choice she can bear to countenance but to sit it out. Like Penelope, she listens, waits and weaves.

And are there suitors? It isn't for Quaid to ask. Best – to beg a phrase from James Joyce on the subject of jealousy – to live in 'wounding doubt'.

They can sustain three or four weeks at a time without meeting. Any longer and Lily goes into a decline. It isn't only Quaid she misses, it's her own resolution, everything she's lived by since she was a girl, the authorship of her own actions. She has never had patience. Waiting on another person's strength of mind robs her of her own natural robustness. Her face drains of colour. Her shoulders droop. She is subject to mystery pains. She begins to shake. Hal tells her she should see a doctor but fears what she might be diagnosed with. Her friends the same. Because she hasn't told them that she and Quaid are lovers they can't help her and, like Hal, dread the early onset of those ailments that stalk ageing women and which, for that reason, ageing women don't dare name. 'I'm not yet fifty, for fuck's sake,' she reminds them. She is a magnificent liar. None of her friends guess what's wrong – that she is ill with the magnificence of her lies.

Over the years, Quaid has kept himself fit. Not in the gym, though he has a workout machine in his bedroom and keeps weights under his desk, but in nearby parks where he has always walked at a good pace and thought up ideas for plays which only take wing or die when he is back at his desk. Nature has been no muse to him. He needs stale air and oppression to write. Just as he needs an absence of air altogether to love.

Loving Lily makes him feverish. When he has not seen her for a while he can spend whole afternoons on a bench in the rose garden absorbed in thoughts of her that are so fantastical, adoring and obscene that he wonders whether, if the real her were suddenly to join him on the bench, he would recognise her. He is never – not for a single second of recorded time – not thinking about her, though he'd be the first to admit that it isn't exactly by thought that he summons her. She just bursts into his mind. When he sees her face he smiles. She possesses an extensive collection of dressing gowns – Javanese, Chinese, Fijian, Arabic, Inuit – and, in so far as he can recall, has never worn the same one more than twice in his company. Her Japanese robe with its swirling pink dragons pleases him in particular – he cannot say why – and he can sit for an hour at a time recalling her strolling out of a hotel bathroom in it – girlishly, somehow, as though wearing this robe makes her feel she is dressed up for a party. What begins in a wolfish trance often ends in this almost fatherly appreciation. Because he has otherwise never felt fatherly in his life, he ascribes this unfamiliar sensation to her capacity to awaken in him forms of manliness – his word: always assume that when the word manly arises, it's at Quaid's summoning – of which he never knew himself capable. How do I love thee? Let me count the ways. Though quicker will it be to count the ways I don't.

And then, after the fatherliness, the reversion to feelings no father should know anything about. He may have violently capitulated to Lily's will, but when such a capitulation is welcomed to the degree that Quaid welcomes it – welcomes it even as it shames him – who can truly say who it is that is ceding power to whom?

On his bench, Quaid farewells the man not just in him but in all men. As a species we are over he says, but doesn't feel over as he says it. Love has unmanned him and he isn't sure how much more man he has left to lose. On the other hand, love has filled him full of man. New man? He wouldn't go so far as that. Better to think man as differently conceived. How is he able to be replenished by what he's lost? But since he is, he wants to lose some more.

He sometimes thinks he would like a friend to discuss this with. A good listener like Horatio.

Friends? Did someone mention friends? He'd settle for an acquaintance, some man with whom he could exchange thoughts on the subject of man. Some Horatio who'd know exactly what he meant. And then agree with it. 'Aye, my lord . . . E'en so, my lord.'

It had always bemused and bothered Selena that Quaid had no male friends.

'It's not natural,' she told him.

'Friends aren't natural. Enemies are natural.'

'Then get yourself an enemy. Go out and have an armwrestle.'

'You should be pleased I have neither friends nor enemies,' he answered. 'It means I'm free to give all my time to you.'

'Except that isn't how it's worked out,' she told one of *her* friends. 'It means he's free to give all his time to other women. Whenever he's not with me he's with an alternative to me.'

Her friend thought she was overstating this. 'Do you have to see them that way? Couldn't they simply be alternatives to men?

I think it's rather nice that he treats women as friends. Not all men are able to do that.'

Selena shook her head. 'No they're not, and he's no exception. The women are alternatives to me because he only thinks in alternatives. He doesn't have the words "and" or "also" in his vocabulary. It's all "either – or". And if it's every other woman or me, I am bound to lose in the end because there are so many more of them.'

'What would happen if you invited some of these women over?'

'I'd have to cook for them.'

'No, I mean accept that they truly are his friends and not his women.'

'You mean believe him?'

'Is that impossible?'

'More than impossible. Unnatural. His word for why he has no male friends.'

'Really none?'

'Really none.'

'No male friend to watch football with?'

'He hates football.'

'Someone to go to a film with . . . the theatre?'

'He *is* the theatre.'

'Fellow writers? Directors? Actors? Scene-shifters?'

'He likes to keep his private and professional lives separate. Most of his directors have been women, coincidentally. And he sees himself as a bit above scene-shifters.'

'The pub?'

'He hates pubs.'

'Golf?'

'Golf!!!'

'Music? Opera? A rock concert?'

'He only likes music that makes him cry, and he prefers to be alone for that. But there's no point listing where he could go with a friend when the problem is he doesn't have a friend.'

'If he joined an orchestra or a choir he might make a friend.'

'Yes – one of the sopranos . . .'

He can hardly tell Selena that Lily is very nearly all the friend he needs. But Lily, too, worries that he has no one else to talk to, except of course his wife, and there are things a man who is cheating on his wife can't tell his wife.

She loves being all in all to him, but not every man wants a woman to be that. There are those who prefer it the other way round.

Can't there be a democracy of it? That, for the moment, is the big question of Lily's life.

So where have his friends got to?

Suicide had taken one, a drugs overdose had taken another, and then there was the family. Quaid couldn't share a friend's attention with the friend's children. It was him or them. Others emigrated or might as well have emigrated they became so consumed by campaigns and causes of a sort he couldn't take seriously, let alone support. 'A writer inhabits a different universe of discourse,' he told those who sought his signature on petitions. His Wunderkind years at Oxford hadn't helped either. He said friends treated him differently after his first play was staged, but Lily couldn't help but wonder, when she heard him talk of this, whether it was he who had treated them differently. Not out of arrogance but a sort of self-amazement that couldn't be replicated. If they weren't able to be as astonished by him as he was by himself – this quiet, easily buffeted boy now lauded by critics as 'a force to be reckoned with in the British theatre', what kind of friends were they?

Once in a blue moon he met up with fellow writers. Thrice-yearly get-togethers at someone's club or in private rooms at restaurants where the staff knew their names. In them he should have found the company and conversation he insisted he wasn't missing. Art, philosophy, the state of the culture, detested reviewers, tax – what more did he want to talk about? That was easy to answer. Lily. Would showing around her photograph have been so terrible? Yes. Uxoriousness was a quality no more revered by writers than by his father.

And then Tim Marchant pops up out of nowhere. 'Fine, Tim, thank you, yes,' Quaid says. 'You?'

Tim was an exact contemporary whose cleverness made Quaid feel banal, or would have done had Tim not admitted that Quaid made him feel banal. 'I'll never forget meeting you on the first day of term,' Tim said. 'You seemed to know by heart every poem written before 1650.'

'And you seemed to know every poem written after it,' Quaid had rejoined.

Tim and Quaid had moved in different circles at university. Quaid among theatre people. Tim somewhere else. But they ate together often, in Chinese restaurants and curry houses where they bewailed what T. S. Eliot had called 'the dissociation of sensibility', that's to say thought and feeling going their separate ways in the seventeenth century. They tried to locate the very poem in which that separation could be seen to begin, but couldn't agree on what they called the salient text.

They have not seen each other for years, but neither has changed much. Quaid is still dishevelled trying to look a dandy, and Tim is still a dandy trying to look dishevelled. As far as Quaid knows, Tim is living in Kent and teaching sixth-formers at a smart private school. That Tim knows what Quaid has been up to, professionally at least, goes without saying. In town to see lawyers about a divorce, Tim had rung Quaid's agent with a message on the off-chance he'd be in town himself. And lo – here they are at the American Bar in the Savoy. Quaid can't remember if he'd ever met Tim's wife. 'Yes, you have,' Tim says. 'Melanie. She was at Somerville.' Melanie, Melanie . . . No. He can't bring her to mind. I mustn't have fallen in love with her, Quaid thinks. Was that why Tim had? They were rivals after all. They even liked different poems on principle.

'So how long were you married?' Quaid asks.

'A lifetime, but thank God the tragedy is nearly over.'

'I'm sorry,' Quaid says. 'Do you have plans to marry someone else?'

'Marry? No,' Tim laughs urbanely. 'That's not possible. Not until the law changes.'

'Ah, is she already married?'

'No. *He* is.'

He still makes me feel banal, Quaid thinks.

Tim is evidently in a cheerful frame of mind. Sad that he didn't make a bid for happiness of this sort much earlier, but otherwise fulfilled, fruitful, productive. Quaid is bemused by how Tim manages to make not having written a play appear grander than having written a dozen. How does he do that? Gender, Quaid recognises. He makes me feel gender-inadequate. 'I too,' he confides, 'have fallen in love and am considering breaking out.'

'Out of your marriage or out of yourself?'

'Like you, I suppose. Out of the confines of my outdated masculinity.'

Go on, Tim, say it. *E'en so, my lord.*

Instead, Tim lays a hand on Quaid's sleeve. 'Just to be clear,' he says, enunciating as though to a child, 'masculinity has never been a problem for me. And isn't now.'

Having been talked to like a child, Quaid blushes sufficient for a schoolroom of them.

Though it's early evening, a time he imagines Lily to be *en famille*, however *en famille* works in her life, he rings her. She is surprised to hear from him. She wonders if he is all right. 'Yes,' he says, 'but is this a good time to talk? What are you doing?'

'Snacking.'

'Smacking?'

'*Snacking*.'

'Does that mean you're on your own?'

'Ish.'

What does 'ish' mean? Is she or isn't she?

'Can I come round?'

'No. Just tell me what's wrong.'

'Who said there was something wrong?'

'You never ring me at this hour, and so close to the last time, unless something's wrong.'

'I maligned you to a friend.'

'I thought you didn't have a friend.'

'Well I certainly don't now.'

'Because you maligned me?'

'No, because he thinks I maligned him.'

'What did you do?'

It's like pulling teeth, she thinks. Which can only mean he wants the comfort of staying on the phone to her. Well, comfort is one of the things she provides.

'Are you sure I can't come round?'

'Certain. Just tell me what you did to your friend.'

'I inadvertently questioned his masculinity.'

'How does that malign me?'

'I implied that you made me question mine.'

She laughs. 'I should hope so,' she says.

And that's all it takes. Can lightning strike from below? A forked flame ascends Quaid's body, as though from the fiery centre of the earth.

They spend the following day in a hotel close to the London Library.

THE PROGRESS OF A FLIRTATION

Was Lily on her own when Quaid rang to talk about his 'friend' Tim Marchant, or wasn't she? *Ish*! What did *ish* mean? And if she was – and there were many nights when she most certainly did have the place to herself, no *ish* about it – why didn't she invite him over?

He has been to her house on several occasions for a script conference, kissed Lily in her office, and once slept with her on the floor of the guest room. 'We can go to bed,' she'd said. But he was uncomfortable with the idea. 'I couldn't sleep with you in the guest room of my house,' he'd told her, 'so I can't in all honour sleep with you in the guest room of yours. Apart from anything else it would profane the idea of guest.'

'But you *are* sleeping with me.'

'The floor's different.'

'How?'

'It's a bedding thing. Floor suggests impetuosity. You can forgive impetuosity.'

'All right, then what about the floor in your guest room?'

'Selena's daughters use the guest room.'

'Your study then?'

'Lily—'

'I'm teasing you,' she said.

It pained her to witness his discomfort. But she wasn't going to throw open the portals of her house to a man who closed his to her. Was that petty of her? She didn't think so. She was ready to forgo the world for him. Let him just say the word. But he couldn't.

★

So what *is* holding him back?

Selena, too, would like an answer to that.

She has taken to saying, 'You don't have to be here, you know,' when Quaid falls into one of his trances at the dining table.

He apologises. 'I've been writing hard,' he lies. 'I'm tired.'

'You're never tired when you've been writing hard. You get tired when you've been writing nothing. What's biting you? Mistress troubles?'

'I don't have a mistress.'

'I suppose you tell her you don't have a wife.'

'What do you want, Selena?'

'You to go.'

'I live here. I must have a say as to whether I go or not.'

'You have a say. When haven't you had a say? But you don't live here, Sam. Your face says it. Your whole deportment says it. It's like looking at Peter Pan's shadow. Who do you think you're fooling? You left in mind long ago. All I'm asking now is that you leave in body.'

He doesn't think he's fooling anyone. But he knows what will happen if he takes her up on her offer and goes. She will make him speak the words, 'I do not love you. I am leaving you for someone else. Her name is . . . Goodbye.' And he can't. Too final. Too cruel. You can't look a person in the eye and tell her you are leaving her for someone else. Especially when that person is your wife. He has to find a more dishonourable way – slip out in the night, go off with Lily and never return, jump off the roof, be so vile to Selena that she will drive him out, take a knife to him, stone him. Then it's she who will have left him, the coward. But the words 'I am leaving you for . . .' are beyond him.

Is that because he could never bear to be the recipient of so final a rejection himself?

That, he believes, is banal psychology. Not every refusal of cruelty is rooted in the self. The reason he doesn't kick a cat in the street is not that he wouldn't want a cat to kick him.

Lily is in the weakest position. She has no one to complain to. She cannot allow herself to believe she is owed a future, or even a half-promise of one. This is the adultery deal. How much longer, though, she can go on abiding this strange stasis, in which all parties are frozen in fear of change, she doesn't know. Hal will let her go with good grace – they have had their time – but even he has begun to be affected by this infection of indecision. Leave aside the insult, it doesn't suit Lily to be sucked into the whirlpool of another person's wavering. Having to fuel Quaid's resources is draining of her own. The night he rang her like a dead man, wanting and yet not wanting her to invite him round, was a perfect example of what he was coming more and more to expect of her. 'Inflame me' – so she inflamed him. But what would happen when she needed him to inflame her?

Over breakfast after the impromptu night of arousal at the hotel by the London Library she broke her own promise to herself and asked, 'So how long, oh Lord and Master, before the next instalment of our flirtation?'

'Flirtation' had been his word for what they'd entered into. She understood its comic strategy. It was to take the heat out of things. Not minimise their feelings but allow the winds of irony to play about them, leaven infidelity with frolic. It did the opposite of course; they had only to say 'flirtation' to remind themelves how much more than that it was. But on those rare occasions when she felt it wasn't petty to feel slighted, she could still employ it as a reproach.

Flirtation, was it!

He knew what she was asking of him. When would he grow up and take responsibility? When did he intend to come out from the wings and stand centre stage? Play the Prince, Sam.

128

Playing the Fool doesn't become you. The trouble was, all the stage Princes he could think of were in a similar mental state to him. Yes, these were bad times to be a man, but when had been a good time?

'I rang you last night,' he reminds her.

'First time in a month.'

'Surely not.'

'Trust me. Four weeks is how long it takes for your system to recharge and for you to want me again.'

'System?'

'You can describe it how you choose.'

'My "system" wants you every day. I want you every day.'

'So what keeps you?'

'You know what keeps me.'

'Oh yes, you don't want us to get into a rut. You want me to be your always and forever alternative to routine. Has it occurred to you that I might occasionally want to be in a rut with you?'

'There'll be plenty of time for that . . .'

'When we're both in our eighties?'

'I hope the excitement won't have worn off as soon as that.'

'Trust me,' she says, 'it will have.'

She is of a mind to strike him. But tenderness gets the better of her. Imagining him starting from the blow, she turns her face as though to avoid the sting of it herself. Her own eyes have filled with tears. You never know when the gentle side of love is going to give you away.

She apologises. This is not where this conversation was meant to lead. No promises, no betrayals. She isn't his wife.

'If you want us to be lovers like everybody else, I suppose we can be,' he laments.

'I didn't say that. But what's wrong with everybody else anyway?'

'They're not us.'

'What's so special about us?'
He burns at her across the breakfast table.
'You look as though you've got indigestion,' she says.
'OK. Lovers like everybody else it is.'
'And how do you intend to fix that?'
'By ringing you every day.'
But she knows that's not going to happen.
Later she wishes she had struck him.

LET THE GAMES BEGIN

Perdition was taking too long. They had started to meander. In the absence of decisive action from Quaid to move things along – impromptu phone calls weren't decisive action – Lily had little by little begun to pick up the threads of her pre-Quaid life. She saw more of Hal. Not romantically – neither of them wanted that – but accompanying him to inventors' balls and conferences, making up the numbers at dinner parties, even complimenting him on the suits he bought. As regards the latter, he wanted her to know how touched he was. 'Thank you for noticing,' he said. Not with sarcasm or even hurt. Just thank you. You are a good man, Lily thought. Meaning Quaid wasn't? Quaid? Who was Quaid? For her part, she was grateful to be putting dates in her diary again. She had almost forgotten what a diary was for. The future? She did not know if she had any. You dread the future if you are an adulterer, you don't plan for it. The future is for ruby weddings and children's birthdays. As for Quaid, he was too susceptible to mood change, too given to sudden accesses of desire and then sudden accesses of guilt, to risk making plans with. How many times had she turned down a shoot so that she'd be available to meet him, only to discover that he was not available to be met? Now, she was saying yes without consulting him and he'd just have to manage without her for as long as the shoot took. And when she wasn't away filming or being Hal's companion, she resumed the regime of long walks – alone or with a girlfriend – that Quaid had interrupted. He'd told her he too was a walker, but he walked slowly with his head down as though in pain. 'The outside hurts me,' he said. When he walked he wasn't with her. To be with her he had to be looking into her face, seeing through her eyes until he penetrated the sanctum of sanctums, the matrix of electrical and passional awareness that was her intelligence. It was flattering, when it wasn't uncanny, to be seen this way. Following his example, she'd look back. Did she get as far into his head as he said he got into hers? She didn't think so. She wasn't entirely sure she wanted to. There was enough of him to love outside his skull, she thought – at least when he was there – enough of him to work on, if she could put it like that, without having to enter the engine room of his being. At the same time, yes, these exchanges of intense awareness, shutting out the whole world, overwhelmed her. He'd convinced her. To love was to annihilate everyone and everything but them.

But just occasionally she wanted to see a tree.

What Quaid was slow to understand was that the other thing she needed to see was him.

'You can't make yourself everything to me and then disappear,' Lily warned. 'And you can't suddenly appear again the minute you need a fresh injection of delirium.'

Why couldn't he?

It wasn't as though he were living a secret life. He wasn't such a fool as to suppose he could spread the bounty of himself evenly. The house he shared with Selena was no happier on the nights he was not with Lily. No other woman interested him. He was not giving any more time to his writing. It was more—

Well he didn't know what more it was. The ship of Passion had become becalmed, that was all. The winds of Madness that had driven them this way and that had dropped. No one's fault. These things happened. You just had to wait the lull out.

Lily had once told him that the time between their trysts could be measured by the time it took his semen to replenish itself. Like the cicada, in popular myth, he slept seventeen years before and after coupling.

An accusation, he declared, clutching his heart, that was more hurtful to him as a man than anything any woman, other than Edina Gore, had ever charged him with.

Lily was in skittish spirits. 'I'm sorry I never met her in that case,' she said.

But her words had the immediate effect of getting Quaid to ring her every night and proposition her. An enthusiasm – they were both sourly amused to note – that could not be sustained beyond a fortnight.

Becalmed, then, they were, waiting for the weather to change, Lily taking her solitary walks, Quaid thinking of her every minute God sent, but making a sort of sacrament of not seeing her, until one sweet night – 'sweet' is the clue: one night in which he did not look into her brain and she did not bind his wrists – she asked him if he'd like to accompany her to Amsterdam, whereupon the winds picked up again.

The mechanics of Amsterdam are easily explained. On the eve of the closing of the Rijksmuseum for substantial renovations, Lily was hired by the Dutch tourist board to make a promotional film highlighting what else the city had to offer beside wall-to-wall Rembrandt and Rubens. Quaid found himself enraptured as of old. He followed Lily and her crew around the city. He loved watching her work. 'And . . . cut,' she would say with an authority that made him shiver. He found himself mind-writing a screenplay about a man who falls in love with a documentary film-director, pursuing her around the world without her knowing it and succeeding in getting himself into at least one frame of every film she ever made. Just before his premature death of a disease he'd picked up while following her to the Sumatra rainforest, he sent her a composite clip of all his surreptitious appearances, telling her he'd been content to limit his devotion to her to being on the end of her camera, knowing that she saw him whether she knew it or not. Although she had never once been aware of him she now realised he'd been a permanent presence in her life. Was it possible that she'd all along been unwittingly in love with the image he'd secretly inserted into her life? This question haunted her as she lay dying of the very disease that had killed him.

'What do you think of it?' Quaid asked Lily.

'A bit Peruvian, perhaps?'

'Is that a bad thing?'

'Not necessarily. Will the film fade on her declaring "My God, I love him"?'

'Of course.'

'You are quite the sentimentalist.'

'But you knew that already. And this is a film not a stage play. Films are a sentimental medium. You sit in the dark, existentially alone, and weep. I thought I'd call it *Lily*.'

'Thank you, but do I have to die?'

'Two answers to that. Yes. And what makes you think it's about you?'

She scratched her head. 'Little clues.'

In a small coffee house by the Brouwersgracht Lily pointed to a poster on a message board for an upcoming Leather and PVC Ball. It showed semi-naked revellers one of whom, she maintained, notwithstanding the wire halo on his head, looked like a younger Quaid.

'There never was a younger Quaid,' he said. But he conceded the resemblance.

And there the matter might have ended had Lily not noticed Quaid's attention returning at frequent intervals to the poster.

'Fancy it?' she asked.

He took too long to say no.

★

As ever, it had fallen to Lily to make it happen, check out the dates, buy tickets, make enquiries as to dress code – as little as she dared for her; whatever could not be mistaken for street clothes for him – and then keep up his enthusiasm. Hell finally awaited, but Quaid would never jump of his own volition.

Quaid made the same joke whenever they passed a novelty adult fetish shop. 'Was ever the word "adult" more misplaced?' he'd ask. 'Could there be anything more oxymoronic than an adult doll?' But Lily would notice how he would hesitate a little longer outside these shops than the joke merited before walking away with a sniff. Once they'd agreed to give Amsterdam a try Lily registered a change in Quaid's shopping patterns; now the racks of chorus-girl corsets and rows of patent leather boots with spiked, hallucinatory heels transfixed him. 'If you want me to go to the ball looking like a tart at least let me go looking like a tart with taste,' she said, assuring him that shoes no less high and corsets no less dangerously cut could be bought in her usual shops in Knightsbridge for ten times the price, which, if that was all right with him, she was more than willing to pay.

As a rule she loved shopping with him because he loved shopping with her. She would come out of a changing room and there he would be, not reading the sports page of a newspaper, not rolling his eyes in impatient collusion with other men, but attentive only to her appearance and possessed of a vocabulary of fashionable appreciation rare in his sex. Given how refined and conservative a judge he was of what suited her best, it was a surprise to discover his weakness for pink fur, cheap satin and black PVC. 'I would appear to be the Dr Jekyll and Mr Hyde of couture,' he admitted, uncertain which of those men preferred what.

Lily apologised for not being able to satisfy the lowest of those longings. 'Like you when it comes to love,' she said, 'disreputable I'll do, plebeian I won't.' But he assured her he hated this 'sorry junk' every bit as much as she did. What he felt for it was a fascination born of horror. Not because it suggested all things infernal but because it didn't. 'I'm prepared to burn for eternity for my sins,' he said, 'but what's the punishment for sex-shop sex?'

'Susceptibility to it is its own punishment.'

Did he blush ever so slightly? He thought he didn't mind what she knew about him but he was wrong.

'Just you leave the management of the costume side of all this to me,' she said, stroking his hair.

In so far as there was a saving elegance to be found, she found it in a magenta metallic sheen bustier with semi-sheer panels purchased from a boudoir shop in Sloane Street, and something more obviously Moulin Rouge in soft black leather with French lace and a scarlet feather boa which she had made for her by a designer in a top-floor atelier on South Molton Street. She would only show herself to him in both outfits like a bride several hours before the ball. He could choose and then lace her into it. For him she bought a priestly cape from Ede & Ravenscroft, Doc Martens and a white Pierrot mask framed with soft white feathers that blew about his face. She had offered him a choice – he could be Pierrot or Arlecchino – a clown to whom everything had ceased to be funny or a heartless savage of misrule. He picked the Pierrot because it looked tubercular and wasted and seemed to remove him from the business of life. He could decide later whether or not to wear the leather choker studded with the letters L.I.L.Y.'S which she had – of course – gone back to buy from the artisan shop in Santa Fe after he had returned to England and the embraces of his wife.

In answer to the only question that really mattered to her, would she be the only woman over twenty at the ball, the organisers were non-committal when she rang them. But further researches suggested that while there were lower age restrictions, there weren't higher. Whoever could negotiate the corkscrew spiral of pitted stone stairs down into the vaults of the deconsecrated Lutheran church in spiked-heel boots, was welcome to participate. No mention was made of climbing back up again.

Waiting for the evening to turn into night – for no Leather Ball protective of its reputation opened its doors until sane people were asleep – was a torture of another sort to them. They sequestered themselves in their hotel bedroom and pretended to read, then sat with their heads between their legs, tensed and trussed, consulting their watches every fifteen minutes. Could time really pass so slowly or so silently? Though garrulous by erotic inclination, they knew they dared not speak or even look at each other. The longer the hours before the night itself dragged on, the more estranged they grew, like criminals waiting to be led to the scaffold, with nothing further to confess, no more blame to lay, no more guilt to share.

Negotiating the midnight cobbles – she in vertiginous French heels and shudder-making Moulin Rouge corset, he in the more chicken-hearted guise of fallen Quaker who had never seen the sun – did nothing to break their silent trance. An icy, fateful mutuality led them on. But whose idea was it – once they'd discovered how cold the stones beneath their feet were, how loud the torture music for the artificially intelligent, and how little in the way of good wine was on offer at the bar – to stay?

'Well?' Lily asked. She was shocked to hear her own voice.

'What do you think?' Quaid whispered in return.

'No, you.'

'No, you.'

They couldn't decide if the event was too wild for them or too tame. The former because guests were more overtly costumed for debauch than they'd expected, the latter because they'd arrived too early, still, for any actual debauch to have yet got going; but by the time they'd deferred to each other sufficiently and shared a bottle of lukewarm Dutch beer and fallen into further pre-execution silence, there was more of what they'd come to look at, if that indeed was all they'd come to do – more slaves and slave-owners, more Roman centurions in swaying studded skirts, more rubber-encased deep-sea divers breathing raspily through snorkels, more mixed-metaphor fishermen, unless they were airmen, in thigh-high waders and gas masks, more bodybuilders in posing pouches and dog muzzles, more Nazis in bus conductors' caps, more leather-harnessed clergymen, more bears, more vampires, more Hapsburg Empire courtesans, more men wanting to be dogs and women wanting to be their walkers, more of the gilded young and desperately not so young, the dissolute and would-be dissolute, the lost, the lonely and the louche, about whom Quaid had blithely written from time to time but never looked upon with his own eyes.

'Gosh,' he said.

'Seen enough?' Lily wondered.

'You?'

She wasn't sure. Her initial dread of mixing with the depraved youth of Europe looking like mutton dressed as lamb had subsided. Men appraised her lasciviously enough. Women too. A pair of identical twin schoolgirls of indeterminate age blew into her feathers to make them ruffle. Quaid shook his head over her appearance. 'Who'd have thought,' he said.

'Are you saying the woman you see tonight is not the woman you saw all along?'

'Only in my wildest imaginings.'

'Then your wildest imaginings are where you should expect to find me from now on. Just allow me to direct them.'

Was that a threat or a promise? He stepped back to look at her. Never mind where had she been. Where was she going?

Would she want to take him with her? And would he have the nerve to go there?

How had she done it? How, out of the reserve and propriety native to her had she manufactured such indecorousness? How, without losing her reserve, did she succeed in conveying abandon. Selena could have worn these clothes, laughed and let her hair down. But she would have looked ready for netball. Before marriage and a husband had ground the zest out of her, Selena could be counted on to be the life and soul of any party. For precisely that reason she was never shocking; she could never have communicated the idea, as Lily did, of a *fall*, of a solemn, even hallowed descent, from respectability and conscience into depravity. Quaid took great care never to compare the two women in his life, the artist and the documentary-maker. But in this instance he couldn't help it. Lily the documentary-maker was more reflective and withdrawn and on that account more libidinous.

'I don't know what the word for you is,' he said. 'I am bouleversed. Is that a word? You look as though you've stepped out of *The 120 Days of Sodom*.'

'Let no one say you don't know how to compliment a woman.'

But others were clearly thinking the same. A heavily made-up man in papal garb and a Medusa wig – just possibly those *were* real snakes in his hair; just possibly he *was* the Pope – genuflected before her. A passing stormtrooper whispered '*Schön*' into her ear and handed her his card. 'Ah, we're in the same business,' she laughed. He was the producer of porn movies, based in Berlin.

She showed the card to Quaid. 'What do you think?' she asked. 'Should I audition?'

The stormtrooper had good English. 'You won't need to audition,' he said, looking back at her.

And then the dancing started. Not waiting to find a partner – she knew not to ask Quaid: playwrights are no more inclined to dance than novelists – she let herself be sucked into the maelstrom.

'Be careful in those shoes,' Quaid shouted over the music.

'You're the one who wanted me to wear them.'

'Not to dance in.'

'You're beginning to sound like an old man. I can dance in anything. You just might have to carry me home afterwards.'

Quaid, who had begun the night fearing he might be recognised – yes, he was hidden behind a *commedia dell'arte* mask, but what if, in the true spirit of Carnival, someone plucked it off him? – feared he was going to end it not knowing who had taken Lily home.

He sought the safety of an apse which he thought might once have housed a saint, before he remembered that Lutherans didn't hold with saints, and strained to see her. He couldn't tell who she was dancing with but saw that she was waving her hands in the air and thought her breasts – two hundred years to adore each one – had escaped the confinement of her corset. Escaped or been released? Should he march out on to the floor to tell her? He caught her eye and tried to signal her, tapping his own chest and then covering his mouth in shock. Miraculously, she understood him and laughed. Yes, she was on show. Wasn't that why they'd come?

She'd never felt she lacked power. Yes, of course she'd had to put up with the usual spurns and insolences – the plumber wanting to talk to her 'husband' to explain the mysteries of the 'O' ring; the mechanic guessing she must have been a good girl to be allowed to drive a car like hers; the men who told her their life stories over dinner and never asked a single question about hers, the odd too-knowing stare and misplaced pat, but on the whole she'd been mistress of her life. She told the cameraman to cut and he cut. This, however, *this*, was different. Aware of Sam's eyes burning at her behind his mask, she danced with an abandon she had never risked, not caring what she looked like or what anyone thought, allowing her body the freedom to go where it wanted. And the more Sam's eyes burned, the more she burned – with the exhilaration of being someone she didn't recognise and yet somehow knew as from an earlier life.

After twenty minutes she returned to his side, perspiring. 'Don't look so alarmed,' she said.

'It's an inferno,' he said.

'I thought that was what you wanted.'

'I didn't know what I wanted.'

'You are always inviting hell to throw open its gates and then complaining when it won't. Well now it has. Come—'

She took him by the wrists – Virgil escorting Dante – and led him into the dancing flames, proprietorially as though the task of stoking them fell to her, deep into the great vacant church interror, smiling at dancers she seemed already to be familiar with, showing him where she'd been, what she'd seen, unimaginable religious tableaux in which congregants were nailed to crosses or flailed, and boiling wax from holy candles was poured on unholy flesh, and ropes disabled able bodies longing to be restrained, and lovers watched in fascinated devotion as one or other of them was sacrificed to the brute incursions of a third party, and on her knees a traffic warden who had issued tickets for more than half a century took parking offenders in her mouth, two, three, four at a time.

'Hellish enough for you?' she asked.

'It's a start.'

'Have you noticed something surprising?'

'This and that.'

'No, I mean how decorous everybody is.'

'Decorous!'

'Circumspect. Respectful. Well mannered. In all the depictions of hell I know Satan's security men drive sinners into the flames with pikes. Here, if anyone so much as brushes past you they apologise profusely.'

'So how is it that your breasts are on show? Did someone pass too close?'

'Possibly. But rest assured, whoever did so would have asked my permission first.'

Had wax from holy candles been dripped on Quaid's exposed flesh, he would not have stung and smarted as he did.

His eyes met hers.

What?

What?

Lily kept the card the Berlin-based producer of porn movies gave her. She couldn't have said why.

Back in London Quaid found it when she accidentally spilled the contents of her handbag on the floor of a taxi. That was when she understood why she'd kept it – to arouse and perplex him.

'Would you actually have done this?' he enquired.

She shrugged.

'Would you consider doing it now?'

'Do you want me to?'

This time he shrugged.

'Do you think I shouldn't?'

'It's not about what I think.'

'What's it about?'

'Why you think you should.'

'*Should*?'

'Could.'

'You don't think I could?'

'Might, then.'

She didn't answer.

WHAM BAM THANK YOU MA'AM

No good can come of this, Sam thinks, shaking his head. He has taken to doing that a lot. When he is not sitting with his head between his legs, waiting for the night to start, he is shaking it.

By 'this' – the 'this' that no good can come of – he means masquerading, which is his fancy word for 'clubbing', something they've taken to doing on a regular basis after Amsterdam, though he will go around the houses linguistically rather than join the riff-raff with words like 'club' and 'clubbing'.

As for 'no good' coming of it, when did good ever come of erotic thraldom, which is another of his fancy terms for how he feels about Lily after Amsterdam? What's happened to admiration, respect, awe? To Quaid, erotic thraldom encompasses them all. Erotic thrall is admiration heated up.

Amsterdam, Amsterdam, and the sight of her dancing in near-undress! Undress had been the norm there. A librarian in a cashmere cardigan would have attracted more attention than a woman with a bare chest. But these weren't the breasts of any woman as seen on a beach in Ibiza. These were Lily's breasts and they were exposed, not flagrantly but by suggestive mischance, on a crowded dance floor, as though to subtly intimate that there could be more to come, so long as the dance went on. There was, in other words, lewdness in the exposure and lewdness was not a quality he had until now associated with Lily, the most reserved and demure, the most dignified and genteel, of women.

Lily lewd!

No. No good could come of this.

★

Good or no good, they are soon slipping their domestic moorings and 'masquerading' wherever they can find a venue. They are selective at first – if not Amsterdam then Hamburg, and if not Hamburg, at the very least Prague or Paris – but soon, to satisfy Quaid's hunger, they are to be seen, by anyone keeping watch over them, in such Home Counties Sodoms as Woking, Dagenham, Slough, Maidstone and even Sevenoaks. There is, they discover, no town too provincial to deny its home-grown crazies a cosy place to take their clothes off and exchange velvet blows and a little boiling candle wax. Quaid and Lily still wait eagerly for news of the series that will enable them to island-hop across the globe, but in its absence they masquerade conscientiously, as though they will forget what they are for if they don't.

Aside from being recognised, the two things they have most to fear is hurt pride and a sense of the ridiculous. For all that he can't get enough of seeing Lily let her hair down in public, Quaid is unable to reconcile himself to having to go to Woking and its environs to see it. Datchet, where taxi drivers in PVC harnesses look them up and down the minute they arrive – the tall, mute, despondent Venetian masquerader who holds himself like an inquisitor, and the haughty society lady who never wears the same corset twice – and don't allow them to leave without giving them their number in case they ever again find themselves in these parts without transport. Dagenham, where Lily has to kick away the men who crawl to her on their bellies to kiss her boots and beg to be her home-help. 'Mightn't we need their services one day?' Quaid wonders. She doesn't say, 'For that I'll have you, darling.' And God knows, if they ever do set up home together they will require someone to make the beds and clean the toilets. But she is quick to picture the Dagenham degenerates in their lurex thongs, spreadeagled in her way whenever she wants go to the bathroom or make a pot of tea.

Quaid is sorry Lily turns down the chance to have her own lovesick seraglio of below-stairs staff, but then again he isn't. Everything in this world ministers to arousal and then defeats it.

He's always waiting for something to happen that hasn't yet. Does he know what that something might be? No, but Lily will be the centre of it. Whether the cause or the object, he cannot say. But he watches her every movement some nights, unable to breathe, wondering if the fearful something is about to disclose itself. The longer it doesn't, the more desperate he is to return to the scene and begin the drama of anticipation again. Repetition is madness. But stopping just as you are about to get your wish is madness too. So when does sanity say enough is enough? 'Loving Lily does not demand I stay on this whirligig of defeated masculinity,' he tells himself. 'It is a bastard sideshow to my love for her. So why don't I hop off it now?'

Could the answer be that a whirligig of defeated masculinity is exactly where he wants to be? Hence, for all his protestations against the things they are doing, his determinedly going on doing them.

Lily is amazed by his persistence. He now rings her every other day, wondering if she's found a place for them to go at the weekend and what she's thinking of wearing. They book a room at the nearest hotel to the venue, where they change and then wait in silence for half the night to bleed away. There is no talking. Words will break the spell. Then it's off to the latest crypt or catacomb, holding on to each other, gingerly managing the stone descent, smelling the warm bodies packed together as in a nest of rats, beholding the first tableaux of pain and humiliation that minds even more deranged than Quaid's have contrived. All this dispels whatever disappointment lingers from the last time. But his re-arousal rarely survives the night. He catches his reflection in a bar mirror and shakes his head for shame. He looks foolish and out of place in his morose Pierrot mask, no matter that, to his eye, everyone else looks foolish and out of place as well. It could be Disneyland. A toyland of torture in which no one means to hurt or suffer, and children of any age could be admitted without fear of damage to their psyches, unless contempt for their elders can be be accounted damage. Lily is right. Lily is always right. He over-invests and can only ever be deflated. Yet again perdition shows no interest in catching them and leaves them to their fun.

Masquerading has taken over from film-making as a moral justification for their spending every possible minute together. They both know it makes no sense – descending into the city's underbelly hardly constitutes a sacred necessity – but because it entails work: preparation, travel, dressing-up, risk-taking, staying up late, it somehow creates its own category of solemn duty. They are bound to drop everything else, and make every conceivable excuse, in order to spend five or six hours in holy silence in a hotel room, like devils preparing their expressions for Walpurgis night, and then almost as many hours, when it is all over, unpacking the experience, expounding in wordy confessionals on the excitement the event has or has not generated. In the main it's Lily who does the talking and Quaid the listening. Noticing is her business after all. She comes out of herself as Quaid can't, looks around her, absorbs the atmosphere, gets deeper into conversation with fellow deviants, many of whom are only looking for love from a woman who understands their propensities. In other words a woman just like her. But Quaid isn't only wanting her to describe everything he's missed or tell him what sad stories she's been privy to. He's hoping she will have some unholy indiscretion to confess.

Can he be more definite about what he wants from her than

that? Of course he can't. It's what he keeps coming out to discover.

Hell will come at last to those who wait.

For every twenty clubs for weary London taxi drivers to show off their wives' piercings, there's a torture chamber that lives up to its name.

'At least the celebrants are beautiful,' Quaid says one night as they descend unfamiliar steps into an unfamiliar corner of the city's bowels.

'Does their beauty matter?'

'Where there is beauty to mar, there is drama in the infliction of pain. Who wants to pay good money to see the already disfigured and infirm chastised?'

'You sound like a rake from a novel by Samuel Richardson.'

'I am nothing if not literary.'

'You are nothing if not a snob.'

But Lily is pleased to see he is at least taking notice of where she's brought him.

She must have known this club to be a cut above the others. She's had her hair coloured so that it coruscates and she is wearing a black leather corset he has not seen before. It has a diagonal gold zip running across her chest from her right shoulder. Quaid shivers. Would she dare?

In the corner of his eye he sees an angelic young man who is either concealing his genitals, or has none, spinning slowly on a torture wheel. A woman in a monk's habit turns the wheel by hand, chanting in Latin and flicking him with a cane. A ring on her wedding finger catches lights. Is she married to the angel, Quaid wonders, as she flicks her cane again. Or is a husband hidden in the shadows, looking on. Once more the man makes no sound. 'Ouch!' Quaid says for him.

'That's good,' Lily said. 'You're joining in.'

Before his mood changes, she takes him by the wrist and leads him into the darkness. An overweight woman in a fine, flowing African headwrap and wearing a ball-gag face mask is being slowly undressed by two white men in rubber bodysuits who could be father and son. The older man carries a scalpel. Surely not, Quaid thinks, pausing to watch. Lily pulls him away. Best not to look on when what's being performed is ambiguous. Who means what here? 'I'll tell you later,' Lily whispers.

It's a busy night. Nearly all the equipment is in use. Not that Lily needs more than a wall and the Swarovski jewel-handled whip she carries at her hip. She pulls Quaid towards her so that they can feel the warmth of each other's breath, removes his frock coat and folds it neatly over a ducking stool, unbuttons and pulls down his shirt, and pushes his face into the cold Victorian brickwork. To her, he looks like a hero of the revolution about to be led to the scaffold.

'Count to fifty,' Lily says. 'Imagine they are the last fifty seconds you have left to call your own.'

To himself, shirtless in his Pierrot mask, he looks like a character who has wandered into the wrong play. I am an absurdist cliché, he thinks. He is at one and the same time frightened of what Lily intends – for she has never before, at least beyond the confines of the bedroom, taken control of him like this – and apologetic that his twisted desires have brought her to this pantomime of whips and fancy dress. Whips for Christ's sake. And yes, yes, he knows – the whip she wields is a whip he bought for her to wield.

'Lily, I'm sorry,' he says.

'What for?'

'All this.'

'You mean the aesthetics? It's bit late for that. And anyway, I'm fine with it.'

She puts a hand on his neck and squeezes it between her thumb and forefinger. He feels that if she were to squeeze harder he would pass out.

She remembers the girl with the slavering dog in Taos Pueblo. Ancient man made gods of the animals he slaughtered. You must revere those you hurt.

'Just count, my love,' she tells him.

She knows this isn't what he wants; that he doesn't care for the bathos of whips and chains and prison bars; that it's too literal-minded an enactment of what should never be performed beyond the high walls of the imagination. But what are they here for, if not this?

She is not a flagellator by nature, her life until now has not felt the want of a torture chamber, but she hasn't sneaked out of the hotel in full Sloane Street Sadeian regalia in order to stand around and smack an expensive whip against her boots. Are they serious or aren't they? What you start, you go through with, Lily believes, not least to find out where it will end. It's theatre. Grand Guignol – hasn't Sam Quaid, winner of two Laurence Olivier Awards, heard of that?

'Fifty,' he says quietly.

'I can't hear you.'

'Fifty.'

She brings the whip down on his back. Tonight she will not spare the rod and he will consent to her dramaturgy.

Her. *Hers*.

Does Sam think this is all for him? As she brings the whip down on his shrinking body she thinks how fine he looks. The more she hurts him the more she loves him, and the more she loves him the more she wants to hurt him.

Quaid, knowing nothing of what she's thinking, closes his eyes against the unaccustomed pain, picturing what he can't see, the raising and bringing down of her arm, the heaving and freeing of her elegant, slight chest, the diamantes in the handle of her whip going off like artillery, the men, dominants and submissives alike, pausing from the staging of their own mad desires to look at her desirously, wanting her, wishing they were him. He can picture the envy in their eyes. Isn't this what so many of them come out night after night to clubs like these to find – a soulmate in loving cruelty, a woman who understands, who will take advantage of their queer weakness and yet at the same time make herself complicit in it? Such a woman, supposing she exists, is rare, elusive, prized beyond rubies. Night after night the search goes on, and night after night it ends in failure.

But Lily does exist. 'I am the most fortunate of men,' he thinks.

But he still has to bail out before she asks him to count to another fifty.

'Ouch,' he says. 'Ouch, ouch.'

She releases him and laughs. 'My Pollyanna of Perversion,' she sighs, pulling up his shirt and kissing his cheek with care, not wanting to bruise his softness. She isn't worried about his back. She has barely touched him.

Perhaps sensing her annoyance, perhaps feeling the waste of her, as she feels it herself, perhaps seeing a way to the extinction Quaid has feebly declined, a frail, bare-chested, white-skinned onlooker, observing Quaid's retreat, approaches and begs her to do to him what Quaid has shrunk from. Dungeons being places where it is considered bad form to refuse a favour, Lily nods her assent. She sees him eyeing an *estrapada* but is not prepared to go that far. 'I don't use or need equipment,' she says, pleased by her own boldness. 'Other than this.' She orders him to turn his back to her and press his face against a pillar. She raises her coruscating whip and waits. The dungeon falls silent around them. Somewhere in the darkness, Quaid is surely watching what he's missed out on. Then she strikes.

It alarms her to see how quickly the pale man's skin reddens. It seems to her she's barely hit him before a small smear of blood, no bigger than a teardrop, trickles down his side. These men! She knows that an apology will be unwelcome but she does say 'I have Savlon in my bag if you want it.' He shakes his head. 'Put your finger in the blood,' he pleads. 'Now put your finger in my mouth.' Of all the things she's been asked to do in recent months, putting a finger in a stranger's mouth is the most shocking. What would her mother think? 'This is all you're getting,' she says, wiping her finger quickly across his lips. He darts out his tongue like a maddened goat but she is too fast for him. 'Stop!' she hears herself order. 'You haven't earned another drop!' And the moan he makes teaches her that while he wants her to dabble in his blood, he longs for her to chide him more.

EXCESS BAGGAGE: LILY'S LIST

Lily was not a woman to be taken by surprise. Being kerpowed by Quaid the first time she saw him was exceptional. And the effect of that shock had not worn off. But otherwise she made it a point of honour to be prepared. Let Quaid suddenly propose a trip to Prague, Hamburg, Belgrade or Willesden and she'd be ready to depart in an hour. In the matter of luggage, she still followed the advice her mother gave her when she was a little girl and packed her suitcase in strict compliance with a list she'd made earlier. Excluding the small and unremarkable personal items without which no woman of fashion can be expected to travel comfortably, this is Lily's packing list for the period of which we're speaking:

    1 feather boa
    1 pair of thigh-high leather boots
    1 pair of patent leather shoes with spiked
            four-inch heels
    4 pairs of black stockings
    1 rhinestone flogger
    2 sets of wrist shackles fitted with aluminous
            karabiners
    2 sets of ankle shackles, ditto
    Sundry clamps
    2 corsets
    1 pair of long black gloves
    1 studded leather choker
    1 plaited leather belt with a snake's head buckle

1 length of rope
1 pair of scissors
1 bicycle chain
1 pair of pliers
1 Swiss Army knife
1 blindfold
1 ball-gag face mask
1 copy of Jane Austen's *Mansfield Park*
1 box of rubber gloves (small)
1 tub of nitric oxide cream
1 box of Elastoplast (assorted sizes)
Savlon

In the unlikely event of her mother seeing this list she would have been concerned that her daughter hadn't made sufficient provision for cold nights and taken a cashmere cardigan.

As for Hal, it was a rule strictly observed between them in recent years that neither would so much as notice the contents of the other's luggage. They were too wise and too well mannered to spy. Why risk discovering what might upset you or lower the other person in your regard? It was only because they happened to be travelling at the same early hour of the morning that Hal mistook her bag for his and opened it in order to throw in a novel by John le Carré.

He no sooner got the gist of what was in the case than he closed it again. It wasn't for him to ask why, how, or who.

Was he jealous?

A foolish question. Jealousy lies coiled like a sleeping adder round even the most historic lover's heart. Yesterday, today, tomorrow – no one's safe. Lily and Hal did as well as anybody at putting it behind them. Magnanimity – that was the only antidote. Wanting happiness for someone else. The words 'What the fuck?' must have passed through Hal's mind, but after that he wanted only to be sure she knew what she was doing. He held her in high esteem. Nothing that he saw, or imagined he saw, in her suitcase could have changed that. But she was independent and headstrong. She might do anything to show she was afraid of nothing. He wanted to tell her she could call on his support whatever she was up to, should that entail her getting into difficulty. But what she was up to and what trouble that might land her in, he had no idea. And he couldn't ask. If the contents of her suitcase meant no more than that she was off with someone to a tarts and vicars party he'd look silly prying. If they meant a whole lot more than that he guessed how mortified she would be to know he knew. Though he no longer loved her as a lover, he loved her as one who would spare her every pain, and that might just be the best kind of love there is.

He hugged her tightly before they went through different departure gates and told her to take good care of herself.

THEODORA

On an evening which, one way or another, was to have no small bearing on the lives of Sam and Lily, Sam was meant to be dining in Shepherd Market with a precociously brilliant student director desirous of taking a farce of sexual manners he'd all but forgotten he'd written – *Caliban in Cheltenham* – to the Edinburgh Festival. Quaid didn't know Shepherd Market well and had left the choice of restaurant to Gillian, on whom youth sat more like experience than innocence and who had the air of knowing everywhere. The restaurant she chose was Theodora, named after a classical courtesan who rose to be empress of the Byzantine Empire. Restaurants bearing the names of whores and concubines and housed in former bordellos had become fashionable in parts of London that had a lurid past and Theodora was the latest. Because Theodora's mother had been a dancer and her father a bear trainer in Constantinople, the walls were decorated with paintings of bears and belly-dancers. The menu was Armenian with modern vegan interpolations.

Quaid arrived first and was sitting in a cubicle consulting the wine list when Selena and her two daughters turned up in the company of a man who could have been a bear trainer himself. Quaid hoped that if he kept his head down he would not be observed, but his hair was distinctive in its crackling luxuriance and her daughters who were leading the way saw him at once. 'Mummy, let's leave,' Eleanor said in a stage whisper, '*he*'s here.' The word 'he' had a galvanic effect on Selena, almost knocking her off her feet. Though he had been at home hours earlier, the sight of him out made her feel he was no longer ever in. She took two steps back, her feet barely touching the floor, and paused at the entrance to his cubicle. 'Ah – the husband!' she cried. 'On your own? That must be a novel experience for you. So where is she? Left you for someone younger?'

With which she lowered herself as though to make a curtsy, raised the edge of her husband's tablecloth, and peered under the table.

'I am here on business, Selena,' he said. 'Please don't make a fuss.'

'Business! Good choice of venue for your kind of business. A brothel!'

The waiter was leading her daughters and the bear trainer to their table. But Selena did not want to leave before Lily appeared. She wanted to see them meet. Greet each other. Embrace. Exchange saliva.

This is to be the big scene, Quaid feared. This is the one she's been waiting for. But he felt sorry for her at the same time, sorry for all he'd put her through and all she was about to say. And her fantastical pantomime of looking under his table reminded him of the merriment they'd once shared. He almost wished Lily had been there and Selena had found her.

He saw Gillian descending the stairs in time to shout, 'Don't come down. There's unpleasantness here. I'll call you to explain . . .'

'That's it, run, cowardly slut,' Selena shouted after the clatter of the girl's receding heels. 'Unpleasantness? You've seen nothing yet!'

'Not here, Selena,' Quaid begged. He was afraid that she was already drunk. 'We can talk at home.'

'Home! When are you at home?'

'Then let's talk outside.'

Perhaps because she knew her jealousy was feeding on itself and she needed air to cool her down or, conversely, because she hoped she'd get the chance to see and strike her rival, Selena agreed to leave the restaurant with him. Whispering an apology, he slipped the waiter a couple of twenty-pound notes on the way out. And there among the boorish bawls of outdoor drinkers, but louder by far than any of them, Selena gave vent to a rage she had already given vent to over breakfast and would again when he crawled home at whatever time – for it wasn't true that he was never at home, just that he always looked as though he didn't want to be.

He heard only scraps of what she said. He could have delivered every fair but stale complaint for her. At last, she lowered her voice and asked the only question that could deliver her the full draught of anguish she couldn't do without. 'So do you love her?'

'Selena—'

'Do you love her, yes or no? Give me an honest answer for once in your life.'

Quaid didn't say an honest answer would be too cruel, so he gave a dishonest one.

'No . . . I don't love her . . . how many more times must I say it . . . she is not my type.'

Spare one and you wound another.

'Since when did that bother you? Are you sleeping with her still?'

'*Still?*'

'Are you telling me you never did sleep with her?'

'All right, once.'

'Why?'

'Alcohol, I suppose.'

'No – why *only* the once? Didn't you like it?'

'Selena – this is unseemly.'

'Oh, THIS is unseemly! What about when you discussed me?'

'I wouldn't have dreamed of discussing you.'

'No, I bet . . .'

'Selena, we work together – that's it.'

'You're supposed to be a playwright. Who did Shakespeare work with?'

He could have said 'Scholars opine Thomas Middleton and maybe even John Fletcher.' But just because he was a louse of a husband didn't mean he had to be a facetious one too. 'We've been through this,' he said instead. 'Over and over.'

'And is it your intention to go on *working together*?'

'As long as the work is interesting, yes.'

'And aren't you *interested*,' she asks, 'to know who I'm sleeping with?'

'Don't be a child.'

'*I*, a child?'

Why he said what he said next, Quaid had no idea. 'Just so you know, Selena, the person whose receding back you just saw is not who you think.'

'Ah, so you have another one on the go.'

And why he replied as he did, he had no idea either.

'Yes.'

'Does your Mexican trollop know?'

Quaid lowered his head.

Selena's colour rose to meet her elation. 'Serves her fucking right. I can't wait to tell her when she next pants down the phone at me. *May I speak to Sam, please?* No, you may fucking not. Not possible right now. He's got his dick in someone else.'

With which she turned from him and skipped down the stairs to the restaurant, perhaps to take one more look under the table.

How long he continued to stand there, in the self-engrossed, booze-fuelled piazza of Shepherd Market, stock-still like a monument to inadequacy, Quaid could not have said. An hour, was it? A week? Selena had miscalculated if she'd hoped the roaring brokers and estate agents would pause their bottled laughter long enough to jeer at her husband. Why would they, when words identical to hers awaited them when they got home?

As a rule, boozers on expense accounts disgusted the bohemian in Quaid. Tonight he felt a sort of envy for them. They seemed content being the men they were. They drank in unison, laughed in unison, no doubt deceived their wives in unison. He had scorned such men at Oxford. The rugby players. The oarsmen. The company he kept had been poetical and neurasthenic. Joyce and Lawrence would have been his friends had they been there. They hated each other, of course. Or at least, as they never met, hated each other's work. The same with Quaid and the writers he knew. All rage and envy and disparagement and when they drank they drank to kill themselves, not to laugh in tipsy accord. Had I been a man like these, Quaid thought, I'd have been no better a husband than I am, but maybe I'd have been less of a liar.

He couldn't forgive himself. He had betrayed Lily. Yes, in order to spare Selena. But a betrayal is a betrayal whatever the justification for it. He'd denied, again and again, that he loved Lily. Swore he couldn't love her. Insisted she was not his *type*. Never mind that these words bore not a grain of truth and Lily was not here to hear them. Just the fact of their utterance was a betrayal. And then he had betrayed her further by encouraging Selena to believe that just as he'd been unfaithful her, so was he unfaithful to Lily – as though that might somehow make things better. He could tell himself that these were no more than offerings on the altar of a dead marriage, that he owed his wife some piffling consolation. But did he have to steal from Lily to give it? Must a man deny his mistress to placate his wife?

AND DID THE COCK CROW TWICE?

'I want to take you somewhere,' Quaid phoned Lily to say.

'Bed?'

'You are merry, my lady. No, not bed.'

'Where then?'

'Shepherd Market.'

'Do you intend to whore me out?'

'Christ, Lily, have you been drinking?'

'Just a small glass. I've been celebrating with Lucasta. Her husband's just come back. Unless he's gone again. We drank to whichever it was.'

'I have something serious to discuss with you. This is not a line I ever expected to deliver to you, of all people, but maybe we should wait until you're sober.'

'Stick-in-the-mud.'

She was never – all right, rarely – drunk. And looked stone-cold sober, careworn even, apprehensive, when they met in Shepherd Market three days later. It was early evening, warm enough to sit out.

They kissed cautiously, as was their habit in a public place. By way of further precaution she was wearing lowish heels and had brought her blue exercise book out with her.

'So, what's this something serious you need to talk to me about?' she asked.

'A crime.'

'Whose crime?'

'Mine.'

'Am I to hear your confession?'

'In a manner of speaking, yes.'

'Why specifically in this place?'

'Because this is the crime scene.'

'The crime is of a sexual nature then? Are you sure I'd want to hear about it?'

'It's not of a sexual nature. I betrayed you here.'

'Then it is of a sexual nature.'

'Lily, there is more than one kind of betrayal. And the sexual kind is not always the most serious. I denied you.'

'You denied me what?'

'I'm employing the word in the biblical sense. I denied your importance to me.'

'To whom?'

'To me.'

'That's not what I'm asking. To whom did you deny my importance to you?'

'Selena.'

'I'd say that was very sensible of you.'

'No, no. I wasn't just denying that we are lovers. I as good as denied your very existence.'

'Aren't you being a bit dramatic?'

'I'm being a lot dramatic. What I did was terrible. I negated you.'

'I don't feel negated.'

'You weren't there.'

'Then it doesn't matter.'

'I think it matters more. Had you been there my words might have hurt your feelings but at least your presence would have proved you were not to be written out of the scene.'

'This is convoluted morality, Sam.'

'It isn't. I said I didn't love you. I'm sorry. I said you were nothing to me. As Peter denied knowing anything of Jesus – *Jesus? Man I know not what thou sayest* – I denied caring anything for you. It was a disloyalty of the heart compounded by disloyalty of language. It was spoken infidelity.'

'And did the cock crow three times?'

'If it didn't it's because we live in irreligious times.'

She leaned across and kissed him on the cheek. To anyone watching they could have been brother and sister. But in his ear she whispered, 'I wish it had been bed you'd wanted to take me to.'

'So you forgive me?'

'You've done no wrong.'

'I hope you are right. Now teach me to forgive myself.'

QUID PRO QUO

Three days later she rang him. 'I want to take you somewhere,' she said.

'Bed?'

'Yes, but somewhere else first.'

'Not Shepherd Market.'

'No, another market. Camden. I have something serious to discuss with you.'

'Have you denied me?'

'No. Quite the opposite. I have affirmed you.'

'You haven't told Hal?'

'Of course not. I have affirmed you in another way.'

'I am intrigued. Tell me what you have done.'

'You will have to wait,' she says, 'until Camden.'

'It sounds dramatic.'

'It is dramatic.'

'Why Camden?'

'It's a crime scene.'

'Whose crime?'

'Mine.'

'What kind of crime?'

'Just wait.'

'Can't you give me a little clue?'

'All right. Just a little one. I've murdered someone.'

DANCING ME TO THE END OF LOVE

In later years he will remember that he laughed. She too will remember that he laughed. It was the nearest they came, she will tell him, to breaking up.

Quaid believed in laughter. The importance they accorded laughter was the reason he had wanted to interview the sacred clowns of Taos. Like many practitioners of laughter, they didn't laugh much themselves. Like many philosophers of laughter, Quaid didn't laugh much either. 'I am not a great ejaculator of hilarity,' he had warned Lily in the days they were laying their cards on the table. 'Or a great employer of the vernacular,' Lily had replied.

He laughed at that, in moderation. For the Koshare, laughter was a job, strictly limited as to time and place. Away from their work, clowns are not good company. For Quaid, laughter was an idea. The idea was noble. Laughter released humanity from its tyrannies, whether from authority or the self. It welcomed men and women to the great communal dance of life. But the sound, when philosophers of laughter were able to release it, as often as not did the opposite.

What Lily heard after she'd told him she'd murdered someone was mockery.

'What you heard was the shock of disbelief,' Quaid said.

'I know what I heard. Why didn't you believe me?'

'I didn't think you could have murdered anybody.'

'Why not? People are murdered every hour.'

'But not by you.'

'Then why did you tremble to put your life in my hands? Were you only pretending?'

'I was part pretending, yes. Weren't you?'

'Were you pretending to love me?'

'Of course not.'

'Wasn't something dangerous between us at the heart of that love?'

'What does "something dangerous between us" mean?'

'Isn't it a bit late in the day to be asking that? I saw terror in your eyes, Sam. And the more afraid you were, the more you told me you loved me. In those moments you begged me to tell you I didn't reciprocate your love – something it wasn't easy for me to do – your life hung by a hair. You wanted to die rejected by me. You were never sure whether I would take you at your word. Neither was I. How far dared I go? You didn't know. I didn't know either. In the cold light of day of course we had limits. But we weren't living in the cold light of day. In the dark heat of the passion we brewed up together, I was your executioner.'

'I shouldn't have laughed,' Quaid agreed.

LADY MACBETH OF MUSWELL HILL

'You remember the man with the Hermès-scarf fetish?'

'Which man with the Hermès-scarf fetish?'

'Sam, how many men with Hermès-scarf fetishes do we know?'

'I don't know any.'

'We met him in a club.'

'You mean you met him in a club.'

'I told you about him.'

'I don't remember. So what about him?'

'He's the one.'

She had met him originally in one of those deep, dark, iniquitous cellars into which it pleased her to lead Quaid, not on a leash – he knew why men wanted to be treated like dogs, but a leash he found demeaning in the wrong way – but by a light gold chain tied to his wrist. 'Like an item of my jewellery,' Lily said. *That* he found demeaning in the right way. He was wearing his sad blank Pierrot mask that made him at once invisible and conspicuous. He could not speak through the mask but he had increased the size of the eye sockets so that he shouldn't miss anything. The man, taking the blankness of Quaid's mask to be an advertisement of his non-existence, approached Lily with the directness of a suitor, bowing exaggeratedly and introducing himself as Alain. 'And I'm Leonore,' Lily told him. But for a Hermès scarf wrapped around the bottom half of his face like that of a designer bank-robber, Alain was dressed as an Eton sixth-former in pinstriped trousers, a black evening waistcoat, a stiff white shirt with an Arundel collar, and a tailcoat. The room was too dark for her to see that, with an Etonian's disdain for conformity, he wore unmatching socks. 'I would like to make you a present of my scarf,' he said, unwinding himself from it like a dancer.

'He's a yes,' Lily's mother would have pronounced had her daughter brought him home for tea. 'But see if you can get him to lose the scarf.'

'I couldn't possibly take this,' Lily said. But he no sooner handed it to her than he pirouetted away.

A month later, in the same deep dark iniquitous cellar, he asked for it back.

'I thought it was a gift,' Lily said.

'It was. But I hoped that when I saw you again you would be wearing it. As you aren't, I can only assume you don't want it and therefore I would appreciate your returning it.'

'How do you know I still have it?'

'You say you thought it was a gift. I don't see you as a woman who would destroy a gift. Here is my address. I have a shop opposite Camden Lock. I specialise in folk art.'

'You told me you sold rag and bones near Mornington Crescent,' Lily reminded him.

'You see? I was right about you. You remember.' He drew a flyer from his frock coat and presented it to her. 'This is my emporium.'

Lily inspected it. 'Am I to keep this as a gift or return it the next time I see you?' she asked.

Something faintly reminiscent of a smile passed across his gloomy features. I don't like him but I can handle him, Lily thought. As far as she could tell from the flyer, the 'emporium' had no windows. Its frontage was one teeming mural of wild animals and even wilder dancers. The words *Alain's Folkloric Bazaar* were scrawled across it as though in blood. 'As you can see, I am easy to find,' he said. 'I have a beautiful carved Kachina doll above the door. I picked it up on my travels.'

'Ha,' Lily said. 'A Hopi clown.'

He was impressed she knew what it was.

'I too am well travelled,' she said, irritated by his condescension, 'and I have met many clowns.'

He looked at her sadly. 'Are you saying I am another?'

Too intimate. 'Just tell me,' she went on, 'what does a dealer in folk art want with a Hermès scarf?'

'Return it to me and I'll show you,' he said.

'I think not,' Lily thought, even as she was thinking she probably would.

Alain made as though to look into her soul. Lily looked directly back into the slough of misery that was his. These wan, perverted men, she thought. Whatever else, the warps in their personalities did not make them happy. Unless unhappiness was what drove them to perversion. She hoped it wasn't that way for Quaid. She hoped it was love for her that explained his propensities. As it was love for him that drove hers – that and the simple fact that wandering off the straight and narrow energised her.

'Please ring the phone number on the flyer before you come round,' Alain said. 'And make it late. I don't want anybody to be embarrassed.'

Lily blew out her cheeks. 'You can't really think I'm coming,' she said.

But, exactly as he had done the time before, he spun on his heels and left.

Quaid made it a rule not to ask Lily what words passed between her and the men with whom she struck up conversation underground. The point of his mask was to convey the idea that he didn't exist. The room marked Pierrot was empty. To admit curiosity was to admit possessiveness and possessiveness would break the trance. The minute their masquerade began Lily moved in her own sphere, answerable to no one. But on this occasion – so odd a fetish was a Hermès scarf, and so odd a coincidence was the Hopi clown – she took Quaid into her confidence and showed him the brochure.

Quaid nodded silently. It would not have been permissible, by his lights, to evince any more interest than that.

What made her decide to return the scarf? The man who had presented it to her and now wanted it back was not in the least to her liking. He was insistent and humourless. Good reasons, both, to have kept away from him. But the wildness was upon her and a good reason she shouldn't do something was a good reason she should.

She attached no value to the scarf. Why she kept it in that case – or at least why she hadn't thrown it away – she could not have explained. But it took up no room and, as her mother would have said, didn't ask to be fed. Notwithstanding the universal strangeness of the predilections to which she was growing accustomed, she was curious as to the talismanic hold the Hermès scarf enjoyed over its owner. Was that sufficient motivation to do something so reckless as to call on him, alone, in the dead of night? Recklessness was its own sufficiency.

She took a taxi, making deliberate conversation with the driver, so that if he saw a picture of her in the papers describing her as missing, he could give the police the address at which he'd dropped her. She sat huddled in the back of the cab, alarmed at her temerity and folly. Was she excited? Yes, but not in anticipation of meeting Alain. She was excited by the thought of Quaid, by the love she felt for him, by what they had brewed up together, by the loosening of the laws and precautions she had previously – pre-Quaid, pre-She-and-Quaid – lived by. Whatever else – and maybe there was nothing else – this escapade was an expression of infatuated, uncontainable, frenzied love. Was there anything, she had begun to wonder, that she wouldn't do, both *for* him and as a consequence *of* his influence? But she was party to his influence. He didn't simply exert it. She invited and then hosted it. So the question ought to have been: Was there anything she wouldn't do for *them*?

In a stroke of intuitive genius — an act of empathetic prescience attributable to her crazed state — she paused before getting out of the taxi to put the Hermès scarf over her hair and tie it under the neck. To anyone catching a brief glimpse of her in the dark it might have seemed that a senior member of the royal family was going calling. Could she have kept a horse here?

Alain, wearing only an Etonian's gown, opened the door to her and dropped to his knees. He didn't greet her or speak. The headscarf transfixed him. Lily, wearing the impossible spiked shoes Quaid loved, kicked the door closed behind her and, less forcibly, prodded him out of the way. She would discover soon enough if this had been the wrong thing to do but she doubted it. The square of silk that transfixed him empowered her.

'Where?' she asked.

He led her into what she could only think of as a seafarer's cabin, on the walls of which were engravings of harpooned whales and from the ceiling of which hung nets and ropes.

Did he want her to spear him? Or net him like a fish? She'd encountered stranger longings in the club.

'Take off your gown,' she said. 'Now lie on the floor.'

She couldn't have described what he looked like naked. She had no curiosity about his appearance. Afterwards she couldn't even remember if he were fat or thin. Only when she began to tie his hands behind his back, as she had countless times tied Quaid's, did he make a move or utter a sound. 'Uh, uh,' he said, freeing his hands and folding them flat upon his chest, as though in prayerful repose. He could have been laid out in his own coffin, like the poet Donne, posing for a brass rubbing, had he not, a moment later, brought his knees up to his stomach. By means of signs he was able to convey exactly how he wanted to be bound. Not unlike a chicken, Lily thought, without humour or disdain. No aberrance shocked her; no vagary of desire struck her as absurd. She set to work, occasionally allowing him to smell her perfume and feel the corners of her scarf brush his skin. Midway through, it occurred to her that she had never performed a more maternal task. 'For you, Sam,' she thought. 'Come to my woman's breasts . . .'

As she struggled to make the knots tighter, it crossed her mind that women had always to implore a special dispensation of strength and cruelty before they could do what men did naturally. It infuriated her that her trembling fingers were not stronger or more expert. *Come thick night* . . . Did she really need Stygian assistance to truss a naked, unresisting Etonian like a chicken? But it would have to do. He was sufficiently helpless, she thought at last, for her to leave him. They exchanged no words. She unknotted the Hermès scarf, draped it over his face like a shroud, waited to be sure he was breathing beneath it, sucking it in, dimpling it out, then she turned off the light and closed the front door after her. Back out on the street she walked quickly and hailed a taxi. She could hear her heart beating.

The whole thing had taken fifteen minutes.

It was only when she'd found a taxi that fear began to take over from exultation. Should she have left him as she had? She had felt certain at the time that only a seasoned escapologist would have allowed himself to be tied up and abandoned by someone as amateur as she. And if he couldn't escape himself, he would surely have made provision for a friend, a partner, a helper, maybe even a wife, to come around and disembarrass him. But she now knew for herself what desperation human beings were capable of when the lust for abandon was on them. Quite possibly he had not thought beyond the craving to be subjected to a middle-aged woman in spiked heels and a Hermès scarf. Quite possibly, he was happy to die where he was, fulfilled at last. Just as – yes, she had to admit – she was happy, half-happy at any rate, exhilarated certainly, to have been the cause. It wasn't in the slightest bit personal – but if the worst happened, hadn't they both got something they wanted?

She imagined going back and finding a succession of women knocking urgently at his door, each scarfed like the Queen. An intimation of the commonality of her action disappointed her. Halfway home, she had told the driver to go back, but now she told him not to. Alain? Alain who? Who cared!

AND I HAD DONE A HELLISH THING

And, and, and . . . ?

They have not yet arrived at their destination. Quaid listens as though to a death sentence – could it be his own death sentence? – delivered in a language he doesn't recognise.

'You do know,' he says at last, 'that you could have got yourself killed?'

'Yes, I do know that.'

'And you do know that I wouldn't have wanted that?'

'I think I know that too. But getting myself killed isn't any longer the issue.'

The issue . . . The issue being . . . Can they really be having this conversation?

'So what is it,' he asks, 'that has made you change your mind a second time? Why, now, do you think you hurt this freak?'

'Not hurt, Sam. Murdered.'

'Yes, but what makes you think that?'

'He wasn't moving.'

'Isn't that his shtick? You don't ask people to tie you up so you can move.'

'I wasn't sure he could breathe.'

'And you don't ask people to choke you so you can breathe.'

'I met him in a club, Sam, remember. I didn't know anything about him.'

'All the more reason you shouldn't have gone there.'

'I don't need to be told that.'

'But you still haven't explained what's changed. He wasn't moving or breathing when you left him and yet you left him.'

'I wondered about it.'

'But you left him. Why only now do you think you left him for dead?'

'Maybe what's changed my mind was what you said to me in Shepherd Market. If you could fear you'd murdered me with words, shouldn't I fear—'

'—that you'd murdered him with a Hermès scarf? So had I said nothing, you'd have said nothing?'

Lily thinks about it. 'Is that terrible?'

'Not too terrible. You, after all, didn't ask me to deny you. Whereas, as I understand it, the freak did ask you to make a parcel of him. But I see it might be hard for you to argue that distinction in a court of law.'

'Sam, you aren't taking this seriously.'

'I couldn't be taking it more seriously. But at the same time it's all too extreme to believe. I simply cannot connect to the idea of murder. In all the plays I've written no one has been murdered. I do throw a character not far removed from my father into a pyre, but that's different. Otherwise I'm not even able to imagine a murderous impulse. Murder's what other people do. Not us.'

'This isn't about us, Sam.'

'All right – I just can't associate the idea of murder with you.'

'Well maybe you should.'

And it is only when they arrive at Alain's Folkloric Bazaar and find the pavement in front of it cordoned off with blue and white police tape warning the public against crossing, that he does.

'Before jumping to conclusions . . .' Quaid says.

'Jumping to conclusions? A police cordon!'

'Yes, I know, I know. But just stop to think about it. How many days ago was it that you returned the scarf? Seven? Eight? If you did what you think you might have done then, why would the police still be here?'

'Could it be because they have only just found the body?'

The word body affects them badly. Murder itself is an abstract concept until you connect it to a body.

Quaid holds her face in his hands. 'Christ, Lily.'

In a pub across the road she drinks more brandies than have passed her lips in the whole of her life.

She asks him to hold her face again. 'Christ, Sam.'

They are sitting hugger-mugger in a corner, keeping their voices down.

'We must look as guilty as hell,' Quaid says.

'There is no we. I must look as guilty as hell. Sam, I *am* as guilty as hell.'

She goes over, for the hundredth time, all that had happened. Not just the actions but, far more interesting to them both, the wayward impulses that drove her to do so wild a thing.

'There are times,' she says, looking into her glass, 'when I am so overwhelmed by all I feel for you – so excited and disrupted by *us*, by what we've unloosed in one another – that I feel there is nothing, absolutely nothing, I wouldn't do, wouldn't give you . . .'

'I don't ask for anything.'

'I know you don't ask for anything. The thing they call *folie à deux* doesn't have to be the consequence of rational conversation between lovers. You don't need to tell me what you want for me to try to give it you.'

'I don't want anything I don't already have in you.'

'Sam, just listen. It isn't about meeting your requests. If anything it's about exceeding your expectations of me, and my knowledge of myself. It's – I don't know – an audacity, a lunacy even, that can't be reasoned or explained. Imagine all the usual inhibitions and precautions just falling away. Sam, I'm not exaggerating when I say that some nights I feel I could do anything. Love engenders criminal insanity – I shouldn't have to tell you that.'

Quaid tries to take her hand but she pulls it from him. This isn't a holding-hands matter.

'Who is your favourite novelist, Lily?'

'Sam, if this is your way of taking my mind from what's happened, it isn't going to work.'

'I know the answer. Your favourite novelist is Jane Austen. So why are you talking like a character out of Emily Brontë? I feel I've married Heathcliff.'

'We aren't married, Sam.'

'You know what I mean.'

'Love turns the brain, Sam. I don't need any of the Brontës to teach me that.'

Does he understand what she's telling him?

'You aren't saying you were in love with this fruitcake?'

No, he doesn't understand. How disappointing. And he reputedly so clever.

'In love with *him*! What do you think?'

'Lily, all this is shocking to me. I don't know what to think.'

'If you are trying to find out whether I slept with him, no of course I didn't sleep with him. I barely noticed him. This was about you and me, not him. He was merely the occasion. The madness – the liberation, the risk, whatever you want to call it – was generated by us. By what we say. By what we do. You and me. And don't call him a fruitcake. Just remember what you beg me to do to you.'

'Do I beg?'

'Yes. You do. You beg. You'd beg like a dog if I demanded it. And I give you what you beg for. Admit it about yourself. Admit it about me. We're all just a single blow, a single word away from being murderers and victims.'

Quaid stared into her storm-tossed eyes. 'Who the hell are we, Lily?'

Finally, a question to which she knows the answer. 'Lovers.'

THE PHOENIX AND THE TURTLE

After several hours hiding away in the pub, going over and over what she'd done and not done, Lily said she wanted to ask around.

'Ask around for what?'

'Just ask.'

She'd like to find some locals to talk to but almost everyone here was a tourist. Come to Camden to buy pre-shrunk jeans and meet a murderer.

But she did get talking to a weathered, nautical-looking man at the next table who she fancifully thought might know Alain – might *have* known Alain – on account of those nets and pulleys in his dungeon. What was going on across the road? Same old circus was his bet. Drugs, transvestites, prostitutes, weirdos, men in rubber nappies, asphyxiators . . . Asphyxiators? Yep, quite a craze for it in these parts, and that shit-heap of a shop was somewhere asphyxiators were known to hang out if you'll forgive the pun. Why the police presence? Damned if he knew. A couple of chokers were reputed to have been brought out, but whether alive or dead he had no idea. It was immaterial, anyway. They'd be dead next time if they weren't dead this.

Lily turned to Quaid. 'Did you hear that?'

'I heard that.'

'What do you think?'

'I think we need our heads examining. Who have we been hanging out with, Lily? Asphyxiators!'

Now was not the time, in her view, to be judging the company they kept. Feeling that little bit safer, she wanted to return to Alain's Bazaar. Take a second look. 'That a good idea?' Quaid wondered. She sighed. Mr Curious. She was unsteady on her legs. He was unsteady on his. They didn't speak. The silence reminded them both of those hours waiting to go clubbing. When they got to the shop the police were taking the cordon down. 'Crime solved?' Lily asked one of the policemen rolling up the tape. He ignored her. Quaid gripped her hand. What would she ask next? Whether they'd like to take her prints? A second policeman was talking to a man – an Etonian, upright, scarfed and not in a winding sheet. Alain.

'He's here,' she whispered.

'Who's here?'

'Alain, you moron.'

'Alive?'

Now it was her turn to say 'Keep your voice down.'

Quaid gripped her hand still tighter. Don't smile, Lily. Don't fucking smile at him.

He pulled her away into an adjoining shop doorway where they kissed and kissed, as much to hide their faces as in relief. Relief would come later. Relief could not be rushed.

'Jesus, Lily.'

'Jesus, Sam.'

They agreed that Lily should not drive herself home. Quaid flagged down a taxi. He was going to stay in Camden for an hour, shake the day off. They held on to each other before she was driven away. They should have their own home to go to.

Quaid wondered whether, in a tiny, unfamiliar corner of his being, he was disappointed she was not a murderer.

Walking the sulphurous streets of Camden, Quaid rewrote the story as he could best comprehend it. Lily, fizzing with love for one man, had accepted another's dare to visit him and return his scarf. Not much of a challenge on the face of it, but that could only mean it concealed a secondary risk. What wouldn't she do to prove what madness drove her? To prove it not only to the man she loved but to herself. She had described that madness as fomented by her fixated union with Quaid: an induced consanguinity, as deranged as incest, in which, like Shakespeare's Phoenix and the Turtle, two indulged the fantasy that they were one. 'Two distincts, division none'. So she had set out in the darkness, alone, distinct but not divided – so she had set out, poor undivided Lily, alone and in the dead of fearful night, with the intention of returning an unwanted gift to a man she'd met in a rat-hole and, either because he had assaulted her when she arrived, or begged her to assault him (bind him, throttle him, suffocate him, hang him with his scarf), had been unable to prevent play descending into reality and, in the real or pretend struggle, had – almost had, could have – killed him.

Such an eventuality was not unknown where people demanded pain to enhance pleasure. At the furthest extremes, death itself was a small price to pay – and for some the only price to pay – to attain that final, all-consuming throb of ecstasy. Though Quaid was not so far gone in erotic hysteria himself, he could see the road ahead. It was distant yet, but a step, a belt, a buckle, a whip, at a time . . . Clearly, the inexplicable idiot who loved Hermès scarves and Hopi clowns had put in the miles. Good luck to him, then, if he'd got his wish. Maybe he was grateful. Maybe he thanked Lily in the imagined moment of expiry. In which case he was thanking the wrong person. The debt he owed was to Sam Quaid, playwright, pretender by trade, without whose crazed longings to escape the ordinary conditions of love, Lily would not have encountered an answering craziness in herself. He had done this to her. He had put her life in danger, dragged her down, demeaned, degraded, defiled her. He had cared more about the seemliness of a sentence than the dignity and honour of the woman he claimed to love.

And not only her. He thought of poor Selena, reduced to cursing in a public place of horn-mad drunkards – she too was his doing.

Miss Gore had been right all along. A man starts by slavering over a woman's breast, and next . . .

Take murder back out of the equation and thank you, thank you God, all is good. Lily was in the clear. Of course Lily was in the clear. Morally, however, he was not. What she hadn't done she *could have* done. And behind such a *could have* was him, the source of all that was disruptive and rampaging between them. She denied him the credit – how dare he see himself as the author of her desires? – but he denied her denial. He wasn't going to have self-blame snatched from his grasp. Yes, she tied the belt but only after he had offered her his wrists. Lily was sweetness incarnate. He revered everything that was kind and lovely in her. Yes, accommodating, too. The pornographer-in-chief of their wild, weird passion was and always had been Quaid.

Vanity? Without doubt. Lovers' vanity.

And she had her share of it. Who was to say she would not go adventuring in the name of love again? What if this narrow escape were to convince her she could get away with anything? Lily invincible. It was an attractive proposition. Even as he dreaded its consequences he felt himself go weak before the very idea of it. *Lily invincible . . .*

Had he lost his mind?

He stayed in Camden Town long enough to make a number of resolutions. In so far as it was in his hands to lower the temperature, he would do so. They didn't have to burn for each other. Wasn't it enough to glow? No more nights in the stews and sewers of London. Enough with the lewd masquerading. There were other ways of loving. They had loved otherwise at the beginning themselves. They must love otherwise again. They must, like a new Adam and Eve, quit the torture garden they had no business frequenting in the first place, leave deviants to their deviancy and the sordid to their dishonour. They must be all in all to each other, indifferent to the examples of the dissolute and far from the stimulating stares of smutty strangers. If her loose gown should from her shoulders fall, only he must be there to see it.

A FEW THINGS HAVE TO CHANGE
AROUND HERE

How, he wondered, was he going to break the news to Lily that things would have to change?

He took a few days to find the words and summon up the courage, then he said – 'Lily, I think it's time a few things changed.'

Fine, she said.

After all that's happened . . .

Why, what's happened?

OK come on, Lily.

I know. I'm pulling your leg.

Well that's better than choking me.

Can we move on from that?

I can if you can.

Good. Go on.

I think, he said, it's time we stopped.

Stopped seeing each other?

Stopped clubbing.

Stopped doing it or stopped calling it that?

Both.

OK.

I think you should give up wearing leather corsets.

Basques too?

Basques too.

In public or in private?

Let's start with in public.

OK.

Prospero broke his staff. I think you should break your whip.

Not the Swarovski one you bought me?

Yes.

Can't I just hang it on the wall above my bed?

Won't it be seen by the man you live with?

Hal doesn't notice things.

But I do.

You don't have access to my bedroom.

Precisely. I'll be imagining it there, hung on a diagonal like an ancestral sword. Already it upsets me.

OK, but I can't bear to break it. I'll put it on eBay. But don't forget Prospero also drowned his book.

We aren't drowning any books. If anything we should stay in and read more.

OK. Where?

In. Just in.

OK.

And stop dressing up as though we work in a bordello.

Me, you mean?

Well hardly me. I've been dressing for degeneracy like a seminarian.

I thought that was how you saw yourself.

Don't scoff. A little God and a great deal of restraint will do neither of us any harm.

OK.

And maybe we should talk about having children.

OK. I won't be having any but I don't mind talking about them.

And I think I should go back to being a conventional man.

Fine. (Was she suppressing a laugh?) You mean no more belt?

I don't know what you're referring to. But if it unmans me, yes.

Fine.

And in return for that I will show you more respect.

Fine. I think you show me respect enough, but I won't say no to more.

And we must stop talking about how amazing we are.

Why? Aren't we?

We are but I think it's unhealthy to go on about it.

To other people?

To ourselves.

Fine.

They kissed with closed mouths and, though they hadn't discussed enforcing chastity and had, as was usual with them, paid for the grandest bed in the entire hotel – a bed big enough to sleep not only Antony and Cleopatra but Enobarbus, Charmian and Isis too – slept back-to-back for the first time in all their years together.

'How was that for you?' he asked when a grey dawn woke them.

'Fine. How about you?'

'Terrible.'

'Why? What happened?'

'Nothing. That's why I feel terrible.'

For Quaid, lying back-to-back with a woman meant he woke looking out into a terrifying immensity of blank space.

FUTURE PERFECT

Like many lovers, they took pleasure in skipping between tenses, reliving their happiest hours and greatest escapades, then granting themselves sneak previews of felicities to come.

For her sixtieth birthday, he buys her a French diamond and platinum full eternity ring dated *circa* 1935, a vicuña sweater from Peru, crêpe de Chine pyjamas – he had earlier in their relationship bought her silk pyjamas that had wild tigers on them: this latest pair features a woodland scene – and a fish-smoker. Were there such a thing as a cashmere fish-smoker he'd have bought her that.

Ten years earlier than that he'd bought her a black leather catsuit and Batman mask.

Ten years further along he doesn't want to think about, but he knows that whatever he buys her will have to be warm. If shoes, they will be flat. If a handbag, it will be capacious and easy to get into.

She buys him Ferragamo ties, low-alcohol wine and, every year, a new and bigger silver pillbox for his tablets. She has already bought him a dosette box engraved with his name and a Breitling divers' watch, the joke being that he doesn't swim, is frightened of overfilling the bath, and can't understand any of the dials.

There are two ways for couples who stay together to envisage the future. They can see it as an old folks' home or they can see it as living happily ever after.

'We'll be living happily ever after,' Lily says.

Sam drinks to that, but not too much. Too many bottles of wine and you'll be lucky even to make it to an old folks' home.

However determined they are to stay happy, there are pockets of grey reflectiveness in the corners of all lovers' eyes. What will living happily ever after really be like?

It is cruel to concertina a love affair. The time it takes to get to wherever it gets to is the story, not its final resting place.

Sam and Lily don't expect to subside into comfortable amicability all at once, if ever. They are not going to let the fire go out. The tigers might be sleeping but they will not retract their claws. Sam isn't sure what Lily will do or whom she will murder next and still, some nights, wants it to be him.

Time, however, will reveal them to be living together in rare amity, nearly twenty years after the great escape from their previous lives. And they will be talking valiantly – no, not valiantly, that's too ageing a word; more matter-of-factly – of looking forward to twenty more. They have an architect-designed house – designed for a pair of lovers before them – made of glass and stainless steel and overlooking the Thames at Putney. From here they watch the Oxford and Cambridge boat race. Sam supports Cambridge to prove he is still a pervert. They don't go into town much unless one of Quaid's plays is being reprised. They have friends – at least they have Lily's friends – and throw dinner parties, but are largely content with their own company. Each understands everything the other says, even when they aren't speaking. They don't have children, dogs – though Quaid would like a dog – or sex.

They are living happily ever after.

A word about their great escape. Both knew, after they had confessed their crimes to each other, that there could be no going back to their previous lives. Matters had become too weighty. Lovers need a comfy place of their own in which to discuss such matters as betrayal and murder.

The move out of their respective houses, obligations and mindsets had not been easy for either of them. Of the two, Lily managed it the better. When Lily broke up with someone, she didn't leave them devastated. She transformed what might have felt like a rupture into an adjustment. Those she'd loved she went on loving. Sam, who broke promises on a scale commensurate with his making them, had first to negotiate something resembling a nervous collapse, though as was habitual with him when it came to calling a spade a spade, he called it something else.

He called it – amusingly to himself, less so to Lily – an interregnum: a break in continuity, an interval between two authorities.

INTERREGNUM

It is not so much that he has left as that he is leaving home – peeling away his old life a rip of wallpaper at a time, peeling away himself, more like it. He is sleeping in clubs. Smart, high-end members' clubs, not discos or dungeons. And not hotels. This accords with his idea of sophistication and decency. A man spending a few nights in his club has not done a bunk. A man spending a few nights in his club is considering his options and obligations. A man spending a few nights in a club is doing what his father did, but he tries not to think of that.

It's in that same spirit that he changes clubs every few days. It could be said that he is researching a new play, though it would be more accurate to say he is researching himself.

But changing clubs makes no difference to the nightmares he's having – the same nightmare – night after night. The nightmare begins euphorically, Sam happier than he has ever been in his life, packing a bag, expecting no resistance, so light of spirit his feet barely touch the floor, a bird in flight on the loveliest of summer mornings, but ends, somehow, with him staying. It is not a resolution to stay, it is the absence of a resolution – the absence of the capacity even – to do anything else. No part of him can move. Not even his eyelids. Wide open in the grey dawn, his eyes take in a terrain of terrible mistake, a battlefield of remorse, misgiving and dread.

What have I let happen? he asks in the moment before waking. And he is still asking it when he does wake. The weakness of will he dreams about at night cannot be annulled by day. Even before the nightmare begins again he is preparing himself for it, knowing what he will not be able to do. Irresolution leads him into sleep and holds him there.

There is one sliver of solace. Because the nightmare does not allow him to see who it is he cannot leave, it is always possible he has made the right choice and stayed with the woman he wants to stay with. But if that's the case, why the dread that he hasn't?

By nightmare logic there is no right choice. There is only wrong piled on wrong. And that includes wrong to his heart as well as to the heart he will be breaking. Woven into the hair shirt of nightmare is the anguish of craven betrayal. How to tell the other woman, waiting for him in some other dream, that the thing he went out meaning to do he has not done and never will do. But beyond her grief, like a dark, immovable shape in the shadows, is his own. The battlefield strewn with remorse and dread from which he wakes, night after night, in a cold quicksilver sweat, is no less the battlefield of his hopes. His love, too, lies bleeding.

What have I let happen?

Some nights Lily joins him at the Groucho or the Savile or the Shoreditch or the Chelsea Arts Club, and on those nights, God be praised, he is spared the nightmare. He doesn't want her to hear him crying *What have I let happen?* She will wonder if she is the mistake. To be on the safe side, to be sure she hears nothing, should so much as a fragment of nightmare leak out, he imprisons her in his arms. Yes, they have stopped masquerading but they have also stopped sleeping back-to-back. If he could sleep with his hands over her ears he would. His assertiveness surprises her, but she goes along with it. Could it be she understands with her sixth sense that he must assert the primacy of his daytime moral universe over whatever it is that seizes him in the night? Wherever nightmare leads him, Lily close to him when he wakes, Lily not abandoned, is what he wants.

She can feel her importance to him in the tightness of his grip on her.

So why doesn't she stay every night?

He hasn't asked her to. And she will not force herself upon him. His need for her all but devours her, but still she holds a part of herself in reserve. He is still a married man. He still has other obligations whether he acknowledges them or not. And she has obligations to her self-respect. Her honour.

And Hal?

Leaving him, she thinks, will not be the excruciation that leaving Selena is to Sam. Not because he has been less dear to her but because she connects differently. Or at least she connected differently with Hal. There had been no maelstrom of passion. She made fewer promises. She kept one foot outside the magic circle. Though they have only been half together for a long time, she doesn't minimise what she will lose when finally she leaves. It will be like parting from her history – the 'University Years', 'the 'Job Interviews', the 'World of Work', 'Success' – the sequences of their lives ticking over like the calendar marking the passage of time in black and white movies. It's Hal who has charted the course of her life in tandem with his own. These are the things she must have done because he's done them. It would be wrong to call him possessive; he's been protective rather, like a shell. Should a new life sweep him up, what will become of her old one? Will her past cease to exist? Will she have gone straight from childhood to Sam with nothing in between? And what chance of narcissistic Sam – Sam the selfish artist who fabricates what he needs to see and is oblivious to everything else – what chance of him carrying her life in him as carefully as Hal has done?

And vice versa? Will her future life put an end to Hal's past? No. Because she has not been all in all to him she won't leave as cruelly and finally as Sam the flamboyant giver and greedy taker will. She gave less and will take less. And she will not forget Hal as Sam will forget Selena. She will keep him on as part of her life, as he always has been.

Sam is looking tired. He has bags under his eyes and his skin has yellowed. Lily wonders whether he is overwrought because he fears Selena is having him tailed, though if it is true that she knows why he has left her, there would be no reason for her to do that.

'You are being honest with me, Quaid? She does know? I'm not demanding you tell her. I have no right to do that. I just want to know that what you tell me you have told her, you *have* told her.'

'Yes, she knows.'

'You haven't half-told her? You haven't spun one of your impenetrable verbal evasions round her? She doesn't think you've just popped round to the corner shop for a newspaper?'

'She knows I'm leaving her.'

Leaving, not left.

And what he isn't able to say is that Selena knows he is leaving her because he is in love with another woman.

There is something he hasn't thought of until now. 'What if these nightmares are the direct consequence of my obviations? Are they the price I must pay for not being able to look Selena in the face and tell her the truth? Could it be that the powers that control nightmares do not accept that I have left her for another woman until I leave her for another woman in words? Say it, Quaid. Say it!'

What if he meets his nightmare halfway? What if he moves out of the Groucho Club, the Saville Club, the Chelsea Arts Club, rents a flat, asks Lily to leave Hal and move in with him, pops a change of address card in the post to Selena, and resumes a proper life?

Proper! Did he say proper?

Selena deserves to be free of him: of that, in waking hours, he entertains not the slightest doubt. But what of Lily? Oughtn't life to have dealt her a better hand? Given her a better shot at happiness?

False humility. He knows she loves him and believes he can make her happy. His certainty of that is rooted in how much he loves her. How can it not be mutual? But as for proper, he isn't is he? Proper as in owned by himself, appropriate, genuine, decorous, all he should be. He is not a proper man in any of those senses, and therefore not the material of which proper husbands or proper husbands-in-waiting are made.

He has vowed to be a pornographer of the heart no longer, but he is finding that promise to himself hard. Love, for Quaid, just won't stay still or clean.

Nor is he a proper playwright, not having finished a full-length play in years.

He can't write in a club bedroom. He can't read much either. Someone has left a biography of Hemingway on a dresser in the Groucho. 'Now here's an unhappy man,' Quaid thinks, opening the book where the page has been folded down. In love with two women blah, blah. Quaid, who is in love with only one woman and suffers agonising nightmares, wonders how much worse they'd be if he were in love with two. Did Hemingway have bad dreams? Did he dream in short sentences?

Quaid flicks through the book. Surprise, surprise, questions about the great white hunter's maleness. A photograph of him as a little boy in a dress. No doubt someone has a photograph of Hemingway as an old man in a dress. Leave us alone, Quaid thinks. Give men a break. Let us look at whatever we want to look at. Let us look however we want to look. He wishes Lily were here with him this minute. He would like to try on her dress.

Like a proper husband.

LET ROME IN TIBER MELT

Lily can guess that Quaid's bad dreams are made of guilt and indecision, but he won't describe the exact nature of their turmoil to her. It is unspoken but understood between them that the decent interval of time he has given himself is the all-but-certain prelude to their – well what? Coming out? Becoming a couple? Formalising their relationship? Hardly the best time for telling her he leaves her every night in his sleep. That's if it is her he's leaving.

'You are not in two minds?' she asks him after a bad night in Shoreditch.

'About us? Of course I'm not. Why do you ask?'

'You shouted in your sleep.'

'I always shout in my sleep. Sleep is where I go to do penance.'

'What for?'

'Every bad thing I have ever done and every bad play I have ever written. If I shouted revisions to *Shelley* I hope you wrote them down.'

'*Yes/no.*'

'Yes you did or no you didn't?'

'*Yes/no* was what what you shouted.'

'Oh come on. I did not.'

'No, yes, you did not. But I see you fear you might have. I'm getting the distinct impression that you are not as sure as you tell me you are, that one of your minds, at least, is not as made up as the other.'

'Lily, I'm a dramatist. What would I make drama out of if I were not conflicted?'

'You can write a play without being conflicted about me, Sam.'

'I am not conflicted about you. I am conflicted full stop. Isn't that how a lover is supposed to feel, like a firework going off in all directions?'

'That's now how *I* feel.'

'That's because you're in charge of the display. You light the touchpaper and stand back, curious to see what happens.'

'When have I ever stood back?'

'Never. Never. You are and always have been the adventurous one of the two of us. It's just a figure of speech. I only go off in all directions because you load me with explosive material.'

'I'm not sure I like that idea any better,' she says. 'We might both live to regret it.' Her fears already being projected into their uncertain future.

'The only thing I'll regret,' he says, 'is not being with you.'

Yes, yes. But he doesn't know himself.

The picture forms in her mind of God touching fingers with Adam on the Ceiling of the Sistine Chapel, filling him full of the explosive material of life. Men tire of the gods who make them. This is a dangerous period for a married man, when he cuts loose and discovers the woman he has cut loose for might be no more than a strategy for cutting loose altogether. It's preferable that he stays safely stowed in his stale marriage; unanchored, he might do anything, including adding a third or even a fourth woman to his domain.

She suggests a holiday. Maybe Amsterdam. He shakes his head. No going back. Rome then. They can look up at the Ceiling together and she can tell him that she does not want to be thought of as his creator, thank you. Better to be Eve, for all her fatal adventurism, even if that means they have to leave the Garden in shame. At least they'll leave together. She not his creator. He not her creation.

★

So Rome it is.

She packs her most corruscating showgirl corset – no, they haven't all gone to eBay – just to be on the safe side. It's one of those mornings when Hal happens to be home as she is leaving. She catches him eyeing the case. 'Have a good time,' he says, hugging her. 'And be careful.'

She senses something wistful, even final, in the hug. She feels their long-drawn-out parting is finally reaching its conclusion. He intends to leave me, she thinks. He intends to make it easy. That's the highest kind of love – the kind that relinquishes, or accepts being relinquished, in such a way as to make it easy.

I love you so I let you go – that sort of easy.

'You too,' she says. 'You too be extra careful.'

He is in love with someone else, she realises.

Watching her hang the corset in the hotel wardrobe, Sam gives way to remorse. He feels like a child who consented to having his toys taken away from him too early. One more night's masquerading in this city of masquerades? No. What's done is done. As ever, Lily reads his regrets. Sorrowfully, she shares them.

This is the price of our starting late, she wants to tell him. If we'd met at fifteen we'd still be searching out the next low dive.

But to tell him that would just make them both the sadder.

They leave their hotel dressed as tourists not revellers and walk the faded Via Veneto hand in hand, unsure whether they've just won a battle with the past or lost it, fiercely possessive of each other. Everyone else on the Via Veneto looks the same. They have all given up the ghost.

'So much for the Roman demi-monde,' Sam says at last. 'Wouldn't you have expected something more outrageous from Italians?'

'Not any more.'

He wants to cry. *Not any more . . .*

They pause to read a plaque to Federico Fellini *che fece di Via Veneto il teatro della Dolce Vita.*

'Would you like one of these?' Lily asks.

'To take home?'

'No – in your honour.'

'Several.'

'Where would you like them?'

'The hotel in New Mexico where we first kissed. The pueblo in Taos where we made our first film. And our own *teatro della Dolce Vita . . .*'

'Which is where?'

'Wherever we set up home.'

Careful, Lily, careful. She suspects he will have said this to a woman before. That she can't ever believe he means what he says – that he will keep his promises, that he is proof against further temptation – is the price she accepts she must pay for having been temptation herself. This is the tragic fate of mistresses: they know their men's weaknesses and so can never rest assured.

She tries not to look at him. 'A plaque to you shouldn't be about us. It should be about your work. What about where you wrote your first play?'

'My digs on the Cowley Road? Yes, why not. And you?'

'I am not deserving of a plaque but, if I were forced to choose a site, then Lawrence's Wearhouse in Albuquerque where I bought you a belt.'

A belt! She means *the* belt.

Their eyes go off like fireworks in the Rome night.

'Would you call that work?'

'I'd call it a labour of love. But all right, then I'd like my plaque right here, where I met Fellini.'

'You met Fellini?'

'I shook his hand. I'd come to interview him for our sixth-form magazine.'

'How did that go?'

'Badly. He wouldn't talk to me. I had to make do with a handshake. Clammy, I remember.'

'It must have been the sight of you.'

'I doubt that. He'd seen Anita Ekberg walk out of the Trevi Fountain, remember.'

'How old were you?'

'I don't know. Sixteen? Seventeen?'

'And your mother let you go on your own?'

'No. I persuaded her to take me. She sat at an adjoining table to be certain he didn't abduct me.'

'I'd have thought she'd dread him offering you a part in one of his films more.'

'She'd never seen one.'

'And he never spoke to you? Couldn't have been much of an interview.'

'Wrong. I made it all up. I guessed he wouldn't ever read it or sue me or St Paul's School for Girls, Northampton, if he did. I wrote it there and then while the café was trying to find my mother a teabag.'

'Can you remember anything you wrote?'

'Only that I said I found the pose of the self-reflexive wom-anising auteur tedious. My English teacher told me she was proud of me.'

'So am I.'

'It had nothing to do with you. I didn't know you then.'

'Lily, you always knew me.'

They are joined at the plaque by a couple of refulgent, Gatsby-esque Americans in their rampant middle years. 'Ah, Federico *mio*, where are you now?' the woman wonders aloud, throwing her head back in self-delight, the city lights reflected in her lipstick.

'Probably in Hades,' her companion says. 'Where all the best men go.'

He turns to smile at Lily, as though inviting her to join him there. The woman appears to second the invitation. Lily glitters back at them.

The couple move on down the Via Veneto, still loudly delighting in the witticism that is their life together.

'Do you wish we were them?' Lily asks.

'Why should I?'

'They look bold and glamorous, up for anything.'

'We were up for anything once.'

'I can't bear you to be sad,' she says.

He gathers her up in his arms. 'That's such a motherly thing to say,' he says. 'I don't deserve you.'

In years to come they will discuss the motivation for what he did next. Was it to prove that while she would have made a good mother to him, he would decidedly not have made, nor did he have any intention of trying to make himself, a good son to her? Or did her reference to the passage of time make him summon his resolution, quick, quick, before it grew too late for other things as well. Or did he need to show her that he wished for nothing, that he had all he wanted, all he ever would want, right here in his arms? What he did was declaim 'Let Rome in Tiber melt. The nobleness of life is to do thus,' kiss her full on the mouth, fall on one knee and say 'Marry me.'

His gesture did not go unnoticed by a skeletal figure in a black cape drinking alone outside Harry's Bar. The cadaver roared his hoarse approval, clapped his hands and cried, '*Dirgli di si.*'

'I would, were there not a serious impediment to it,' Lily said. '*E cos'è che?*'

'He is already married.'

GHOST

'I think I need to sit down,' Quaid said. 'I feel faint.'

Lily took his arm. 'I hope this isn't my doing.'

'It isn't. It's my father's. I've just seen him.'

'Where?'

He pointed to Harry's Bar. 'There. The man in the cape.'

'The one who wanted me to say yes to you?'

Quaid sank to his knees and blew out air. 'Ah. Then it can't be him. My father's a misogamist. Not just by nature but profession. It's been his life's work to keep people apart, not bring them together.'

'Wouldn't you know whether or not he's your father just by looking at him?'

'I haven't seen him for twenty years. And I tried not to see him before that. He's not a man you see, he's a man whose presence you feel and smell. Like death. My father, methinks I smelled my father. But God be praised I didn't.'

'Is that why you never talk about him? Do you fear him?'

'I fear I might be like him.'

'You're not.'

'How do you know?'

'You're not like anybody.'

'Neither is he. He's made it his business to oppose everything.'

'See?'

'No. I'm just a Sunday curmudgeon. He is the real misanthropic deal. He hated me from the moment of my birth. He hated anything my mother gave him. He only liked what

199

he grabbed for himself. He threw birthday presents in the fire. He wiped his face when anyone not his latest floozy kissed him. He was a philosopher and a fraud, though not in that order. He stole other men's wives and other men's names. He'd been born a Fellowes, but as it was no distance from Fellowes to fraud or from fraud to Freud, Freud he became. Ossian Freud had a better ring than Owen Fellowes.'

'So how come you're a Quaid?'

'I was a Freud until my fifteenth birthday when I decided that with all this name changing going on I'd do some of it myself, if only to dissociate myself from him. I liked Quaid because I was the fourth boy born to my mother and because I fancied shortening it to Q, the Edwardian bookman who edited *The Oxford Book of English Verse*, a work I was seldom without at fifteen.'

'He didn't take satisfaction in your success?'

'He has only ever taken satisfaction in failure. So logically he should have taken satisfaction in my birth, since I was a failure by virtue of coming out a boy.'

'He too wanted a girl?'

'Yes. He wanted to be the only man in a world of women and my mother kept giving him boys. To spite him, he believed. So he tried elsewhere. To the wives of colleagues he did what all philosophers do and freely donated semen. With three of them he had daughters. He was cruel beyond all imagining. Once, he showed my mother a photograph of his illegitimate daughters, saying, as though he were Punch and she Judy, "That's the way to do it." For subsequently trying to brain him with a rolling pin she received a suspended sentence. My father was reputed to be overjoyed when he learnt of the judge's ruling. He thought a suspended sentence meant hanging.'

'This makes no sense. A philosopher would know the meaning of "suspended sentence".'

'He was a bad philosopher.'

'You're making this up.'

She won't forget his smile. 'Why would I make up such a story?'

'Many reasons. Because that's what you do for a living . . . To see how much I will believe . . . To explain why you're so interesting . . .'

'Do you mean peculiar?'

'That too.'

'I have an idea for a play,' Quaid said in bed the next morning. 'A man proposes to a woman in a Roman street. Sitting at a table watching is the Devil. He pretends to rejoice in the proposal though love, of course, is against his nature. When he claps his hands he crumbles to dust.'

'And then?'

'The woman rejects the proposal and the Devil comes back to life.'

'Is there a moral to this tale?'

'Of course there is. You have to marry me.'

'To save you from the Devil or your father?'

'From myself.'

YES

It isn't entirely true that Lily has been keeping the depth of her feelings for Sam Quaid from all her friends. Just most of them. With Amaryllis she's been less circumspect. It's the Hal thing. She is sure Amaryllis has carried a torch for him. This hasn't made her jealous. But that might only be because – to her knowledge at least – nothing has happened. And if it has and they have succeeded in keeping it from her, well, she thanks them for their urbane consideration. Now *she* must show some.

'What's the occasion?' Amaryllis asks as the two women kiss.

'Must there be an occasion?'

'To explain why we're taking tea at Claridge's, yes.'

'I haven't seen you in ages and I love taking tea at Claridge's.'

'I think of you as taking tea here every afternoon. I remember how much you loved afternoon tea at university. The joke was that any man who wanted to get into your bed had first to buy you scones.'

'And none did.'

'None?'

'Few.'

'So?' Amaryllis says when they have ordered.

The question refers to the progress of Lily's affair. It isn't exactly to raise her hopes in relation to Hal that Lily has told her what she's told no one else. It is not her job to match-make. And it would demean Hal to do so. Hal is more than capable of looking after his own love life. But she needed to talk to someone once in a while, and precisely because Amaryllis had an interest in the outcome of her affair but had always been a scrupulously honourable friend, Lily thought of her – perhaps perversely – as the one person she could confide in.

The tea comes before Lily can answer. 'You be mother,' Amaryllis says.

'You want to see if my hand is shaking.'

'Why would your hand be shaking?'

'Because I stand at the crossroads of decision.'

'Let me help. Don't put the milk in first.'

'I'm glad you feel you can make fun of me. But this is serious, Mar. He's asked me to marry him.'

'Well that's wonderful if it's what you want, but I've never thought of you as a woman who waits to be asked. I imagine you asking him. I even imagine you as being the one who buys the ring.'

'To the degree that I could never trust Sam to buy a ring, you're right. Left to his own devices he has the aesthetic of a savage.'

'The last time we talked you said he was the only man you'd ever met who loved shopping. I didn't suppose you meant for groceries.'

'Loves shopping with *me*. I take him to Bond Street. I try on the clothes. I tell him what I like. He agrees. I see him eyeing off miniskirts and I daren't let him near shoes, but yes, if I come out of a changing room enthusiastic about a winceyette nightie and a pair of bed socks he'll feign delight and buy them for me . . .'

'A winceyette nightie, you?'

'Well, not quite yet. But you take my point. When he's with me he isn't visiting Soho sex shops.'

'What does a Soho sex shop have to do with an engagement ring?'

'That's where he'd go to buy it.'

'Oh, Lily. I don't believe you. Where's that refined mind you used to rave about?'

'He's refined only when it comes to words. Anything else and

203

he might as well be a footballer. Had Hal and I married he'd have bought me an exquisite ring.'

Silence between them, as the sandwiches arrive.

'But none of this is the point,' Lily continues. 'I don't know that I want to be married. Don't forget, I've always subscribed to the "marriage-as-prostitution" theory. Sam tells me his father is a Professor of Misogamy. It's a position I wouldn't mind holding. Marriage! You exchange independence, sexual favours and the right to your career, for a house you don't like, a two-car garage, masses of jewellery and the fact that your husband will never be at home because he's working all hours to "accumulate" more of the above. That's partly why Hal and I never did . . .'

'I always thought that was your excuse for not quite loving him enough.'

'Oh, I think I cared for him well enough. Though it wasn't love in the way I wanted to love or to call love. Sam I love in all the wrong ways, which *is* how I want to love. Maybe I can only think of love in all the wrong ways. He's brilliant and fluent and charismatic and egomaniacal and every other seductive thing I like, but . . . till death do us part, in sickness and in health? I know how it will be. If he's sick I'll look after him. If I'm sick he'll disappear. I don't think he even knows how to call an ambulance. Wouldn't I be crazy to swap a man who probably loves me and certainly respects me and definitely knows how to fix the boiler, for one who can make grandiloquent speeches about love but who swoons every time a glamorous woman – or man not too much more famous than he is – throws him a compliment, and doesn't have a clue what a boiler does let alone where it lives.'

'Listen, Lily, if you want my opinion, this is a pretty speech to reassure yourself of your feminist credentials.'

'You might be right. But I can't part with them just like that, on the say-so of an arrogant man with a voice like hot macadam.

Yes, his world fascinates me. He's always complaining he isn't writing enough, but he never stops writing. I am engrossed by his imaginative energy, even if it makes him a bad listener. And it will be great travelling with him to see productions opening abroad and that sort of thing, but what about *my* world, what about *my* work? I love it, you know I do. I love the access it gives me to the unfamiliar – to people for whom Sam has only contempt – and the compliment of being respected and trusted enough for interviewees to let me into their stories and their secrets and their psyches even – and I'm not going to give it up for anyone.'

'I think you'll just have to deal with that as and when. Lily, my beloved and best of friends, you *know* you're going to marry him. Just get on with it.'

Without doubt, Lily thinks, she is pleased for me. And for herself?

As much out of habit as precaution the lovers took separate taxis from the airport, Lily going home, Quaid to the Savile Club. They had only been away four days but that was long enough for him to have forgotten where he'd been staying. He'd moved out of the Savile Club ten days before, and out of the Groucho Club a week before that. Unable to remember where his clothes were he hailed another cab to take him to his house. He was surprised to find his keys still worked, and more surprised to find the house empty. On his pillow was a letter and on the letter a PS. 'Gone. Don't come looking for me.'

The letter was dated two months before and the house had the air of not having been lived in for even longer. He found it oddly vexatious to think that while he'd been carting his belongings around from club to club, and having nightmares about leaving and not leaving, there had all along been no one here to leave.

The letter went straight to the point. The chap she told him she'd been seeing – and in whose existence he had steadfastly refused to believe – had asked her to marry him. She had said yes. So had the chap's wife. So had her daughters. That left only Quaid. She hardly needed his blessing but hoped he could find it in himself to let her go without unpleasantness and would be amenable to facilitating a quick and cordial divorce. In the meantime, she was gone and had no intention of telling him where. Giving him time to remove all trace of himself from what had once been a home but he had turned into a hell.

He thought of writing back, 'Do you love him?' but didn't have an address for her and on reflection decided it wasn't worth pretending, even for a joke, that he was anything but delighted. When someone hands you a full tray you don't make any sudden movement that might spill it.

He couldn't believe his luck. He had taken the coward's wager and won. The marriage he hadn't had the courage to end had come apart without his having to tell his wife he loved another.

Couldn't believe his luck, but couldn't meet his reflection in the mirror. This was what pusillanimity looked like. Too grand a word. This was what a wretch looked like.

Wretched or not, his first instinct was to ring Lily and tell her the good news. But wouldn't such haste be indecent? Didn't he owe Selena a day's respect? Didn't he owe it to Lily not to suppose she'd been hanging on for dear life to hear him say he was now all hers? If he'd learnt anything from adultery it was how difficult it was not to insult all parties to it.

And there was something else: would he dare tell Lily that it was Serena who'd delivered the *coup de grâce* because he lacked the nerve and probity to do any such thing himself? How would the conversation go? 'Hey, Lily, guess what? Thanks to Serena . . .'

But wouldn't a new life erase the old him? Wasn't it to wipe the slate of their dishonour clean that adulterers laid waste to all around them? Sometimes again and again. Well, Quaid was only going to do it once. After weighing all the compunctions, he couldn't wait to be the new him.

Lily had only recently taught him how to text so he texted her.
Where are you?
Claridge's
Shame I have news
What news?
I'm available
What for?
Matrimony
You've always been available for matrimony
He took a taxi to Claridge's and waited outside for her. He had already bought the ring.

He helped her into the taxi with exaggerated courtliness and sat beside her as immovable as a pharaoh. The minute the taxi stopped at lights he turned towards her – after Rome he was not going to drop to his knees – and in silence handed her the box.

The ring resembled a tortured oyster and comprised two bands cradling a large round cut diamond that bloomed like a carnation and hurt her eyes.

'I'm told it's called a Capri,' he said. 'I thought—'

She kissed him before the lights could turn to green. 'It's beautiful,' she said.

PART 5

AND IN ONE
BOUND . . .

NEXT

Cut loose, they smell the air and survey their options. The world is all before them. Hand in hand, with wandering steps and slow, they take their solitary way. Only, unlike Milton's first pair, they don't leave the garden, they enter it. But of course, if they are to live happily ever after, there's horticultural work to be done.

Happiness fares poorly in the literature of love. Call no man happy, the wisdom has it, no, nor woman neither, until they renounce the flesh. Sam and Lily don't mean to wait that long.

They house-hunt, hovering outside the windows of estate agents in alien suburbs, amazed by unfamilarity, transfigured by hope. They could be Bunyan's tremulous elect – Christian and Hopeful – clothed in new raiments, each carrying a golden harp, hearkening to the bells of the Celestial City. They are at first, on undeclared principle – each wanting nothing to inhibit choice – unable to agree what sort of habitation would, in the spiritual as well as the physical sense, accommodate the people they are, the people they have been and the people they see themselves becoming in the future. A loft in Dalston, should it be? A penthouse in Docklands? A mansion with river frontage in Oxfordshire? Quaid would like a sloping garden down which he could roll with his dog. Lily reminds him he has no dog. No, but what's to stop them getting one? – ideally something big and brown like a bear, with melancholy eyes and not too wet a mouth. 'Fine,' Lily agrees, 'so long as you don't expect me to—' Which puts paid to the dog idea. Lily is relieved. She was jealous of the dog. If Quaid sees the future as roly-polies down a lush lawn to the very fringes of the Thames it should be her he's roly-polying with.

As for what *she* wants – a ballroom, an editing suite and studio, a walk-in dressing room – no, two walk-in dressing rooms – and four guest bathrooms. Quaid reminds her that she's said she doesn't intend to have guests. 'That's four guest bathrooms for me,' she tells him.

He doesn't ask about where his friends will stay. He doesn't have any friends. That's why he wants a dog.

'Otherwise,' Lily tells the young estate agent, 'we have no stipulations. Oh, except that my partner here rather fancies the idea of a dungeon.'

'That could limit your choice somewhat,' the estate agent tells her without changing her expression.

'As to size of property or as to neighbourhood?' Lily asks.

'Both the above,' the estate agent answers imperturbably, not looking up from the questionnaire she's filling in. Clearly she has dealt with the dungeon prerequisite before.

'Noted,' Lily says.

So. For Quaid at least, that's no friend, no dog and no dungeon.

'Was that entirely necessary?' he asks when they are back out on St John's Wood High Street.

'Are you telling me you've changed your thinking about having a dungeon?'

'I've never thought about having a dungeon.'

'You used to say that once we were masters of our fates we would maintain a lifestyle consistent with the unconventionality we'd espoused when we were young, hopeful and in hiding. I was to be your jailkeeper forever, remember. You would wake to the sound of clinking manacles. I recall your exact words. I didn't suppose you meant them.'

'Then you supposed wrong. I meant them metaphorically.'

'So was your dread of declining into a featherbed of domestic mediocrity also metaphorical?'

He recalls the circumstance of his voicing that fear only too well, his hands bound, his breath constrained, his burning eyes imploring Lily for more. It was this, this theatrical abnegation of his will to hers, that he wanted never to forgo – the psychic condition, not the props. 'I remember that conversation vividly,' he says. 'But if I mentioned a dungeon I can only imagine I was hyperbolising to conceal my embarrassment.'

'I didn't know you were embarrassed.'

'I'm using the word in the embarrassment of riches sense.'

'I was using the word dungeon in the same sense. Out of an abundance of high spirits. I'm happy. That's all right, isn't it?'

The change in circumstance has made them nervous of each other. They have to keep checking a) that they are still happy, and b) that they are still in accord. Now the gates are open will they run off in different directions?

'Yes, it's all right. More than all right.'

She has just bought a new summery dress and gives him a twirl. 'Sure?'

Her skittishness delights him. So many expressions of love between them have been tinged with the terror of transience or discovery. Suddenly, with nothing to hide and no eventuality to fear, they are as children. 'Sure. I, too, am happiness itself.'

He hears himself. The pedantic word-orderer. Why can't he just say 'I'm happy, too'? Happiness is not a word he's used often. It takes some getting used to, that's all.

His pomposity is yet another cover for his embarrassment, Lily realises.

They kiss on the High Street. Don't ask them which High Street. This must be the hundredth estate agent's they've kissed outside.

Anyone would think they are both setting up house for the first time.

There's unenthusiastic talk of a wedding. There's been talk of a wedding for some time. She's never done it before and doesn't know what it entails. He has and does. So no rush. Something for the future, no more.

They worry a wedding would mark the end of their lawlessness.

'We aren't *that* lawless,' Lily reminds him.

'Maybe not. But we were gifted amateurs. We pushed a few boundaries. We did things that would have made our mothers gasp.'

In private he wondered whether he'd been a good boy all along and feared marriage would make him even better. Even Lily wondered that.

The other thing she wondered was whether marriage would make her too good a girl.

That this was what marriage does his father had maintained for over half a century. In gathering his things from his old house Quaid found a review of the play in which he'd imagined killing his father.

Not such a good boy, after all.

DO YOU TAKE THIS MAN?

One minute marriage is on the back burner, the next it's in the microwave.

Quaid puts it in. Lily takes it out.

Lily is, of course, flattered by Quaid's urgency, but she's managed fine without for so many years and can't imagine why she ever accepted Quaid's second proposal with such alacrity. Was it just because it came without the baggage of his being indefinitely married to someone else? Did she just want to hear herself say yes for a change? Wasn't that what women did? Yes, darling, yes.

It isn't quite true that she couldn't imagine why, other than for sweetness's sake, she'd acceded to Quaid's proposal. She saw it as a promissory note, from one to the other, that they'd stay together, not for a while but forever. Of course such an assurance didn't need marriage: there were other forms that keeping a promise could take. But a contract concentrates the mind, reminds you in later years that when you swore in front of witnesses you meant the words you spoke.

Quaid was a hard man to read generally, but on the subject of marriage he was a sphinx. For all his ardour now, there's no knowing how he'll feel in a fortnight. By his own account he had been married all his life – actually married to Selena, but imaginatively married to almost every women he met, a mental husband, partly because he thought every woman he met wanted to be married to him and he couldn't bear to disappoint them; partly to spite a father who held a personal chair in marriage-loathing in an East Midlands polytechnic and whose books were too explosive to be on sale in the usual places and could only be found in the Marriage-as-Tyranny section of anarchist bookshops in Bloomsbury, alongside Plato, de Sade and Kierkegaard. Lily hadn't met the infamous father but she felt his malign influence. Who was to say his genes wouldn't make a late appearance in his son?

'We don't have to do this, you know,' she said. 'You don't have to put a ring on my finger to make me feel secure. Just swear a blood oath that you won't go off with other women and tell me you understand I will take a knife to you if you betray me. That will suffice.'

'Is that a threat or a promise?' Quaid asked.

'You are all talk.'

'We are both all talk that's why I want to marry you.'

'How will marriage further talk?'

'Well in the first place by our having a talky ceremony. Speeches, blessings, liturgy, the pomp of promises that take aeons to express. Not simply "I do" and "So do I" but here are the reasons, pro and con, like one of your lists, why after full consideration we think we probably should. Let the humdrum plight their troth humdrumly. We must have an exceptional occasion. I'm only sorry it can't be a coronation.'

'Didn't you go to Oxford with the Archbishop of Canterbury's son?'

'Did I say that? Don't believe a word anyone who's been to Oxford or Cambridge tells you. They say they were happy when they weren't. They say they met people they didn't. I even lie about which of the two I went to. As it happens, though – and this too might be a lie – I did row in the same boat as the Archbishop of Canterbury's cousin, but I hate asking for a favour.'

'I'll settle for a golden coach.'

'Two. One for you, one for your mother.'

But there was another, less fanciful argument for them marrying. It would prove they were, and always had been, serious.

Theirs was not just another affair between a director and the talent. They hadn't fallen into each other's arms because they were far from home and had nothing else to do. Something out of the ordinary, something exorbitant, had happened. *Kerpow*. And its longevity – no, its sempiternity – would be the proof of that. Odd as it was to say, they felt they owed it as much to Hal and Selena as to themselves to make a go of what had started, looked at coarsely, as something on the side.

Once, under a fearsomely large orange moon, joined at last as though dreading ever to be unjoined again, they admitted as much to each other. 'This is our time and our opportunity,' Quaid began. 'If we should fail.'

Lily didn't know whom he was addressing. The moon? Heaven's cherubim? The witches?

But she knew how to answer. 'We fail?' she said, tightening her grip on him.

Under a moon like that it was impossible to feel they existed only accidentally. Out there on the night the sightless ones were listening keenly, the unseen judges, the divine arbiters of desire against whose holy expectations all lovers who are vain and crazed enough to believe themselves ordained measure their actions.

Neither of them needed telling that it was no longer any skin off Hal's and Selena's noses what they did. It was for themselves they made this promise not to fail.

'We are not flibbertigibbets or serial betrayers who absconded on an idle impulse,' Quaid asserts.

'What are we then?' Lily asks. She has her own answer to that but she wants to hear Quaid declare his.

'In deadly earnest.'

Easy to make fun of them. All lovers are preposterous if you don't look away when they're talking about themselves.

They fail? Not if there's a god of love.

★

Meanwhile, at a less hallowed, more domicillary level, there were obligations to themselves to consider. All very well being celebrants of love, but where, in that case, was their church? Shouldn't candles burn around their bed at all hours of the day and night? Shouldn't the air be perfumed with holy incense?

Released now from the urgency that living in hiding conferred, weren't they in danger of sliding from the high-wrought poetry of their first amazed encounters into the prose of mere familiar cohabitation?

A dungeon was never a serious suggestion, but oughtn't they to have done more in the way of stocks, cages, pillories, smother boxes, spiked Spanish Inquisition iron maidens for renouncing your religion in, *fin de siècle* dominatrix chairs for renouncing your masculinity under? Feeling bad about it, they went to a restraints-equipment fair in Earls Court where they bought a raffle ticket for a weekend for two in the Marquis de Sade's old asylum in Charenton, but – citing Lily's unwillingness to commit to cleaning anything bigger than a handcuff and Quaid's not wanting anyone to know that he and Lily had recourse to anything other than the lips they'd been born with – they excused themselves on the grounds of preferring minimalist design and left Earls Court empty-handed.

'Your documentary-maker's love of low-life doesn't appear to extend to your taste in furnishings,' Quaid twitted her.

'You should talk,' Lily said. 'It was you who used to rub down my whip with antiseptic wipes when we got back to the hotel.'

'And it was you who used to rub down the hotel.'

'I was brought up by a mother who kept plastic on the sofa. One can enjoy slumming without wanting to live in a slum.'

'So you were only ever playing?' He was mocking her old complaint against him. That he was never fully committed to the oaths they made. That he didn't really want to end his life – that minute – in her arms.

'No. Not *only*.'

'When then weren't you?'

They had not so far put their old life behind them that she could throw up the opportunity to torment him. 'Wonder and suffer,' she said.

Whereupon they kissed voraciously, as they'd been kissing outside the window of the Conran Shop on Fulham Road, Harrods in Knightsbridge and of course Heal's.

'Never fear. Our bed will be our dungeon and our bridal chamber our garden of exquisite torture,' Lily said.

'Promise?'

'Promise.'

'And in the meantime?'

'We need to confirm the new roster with the cleaner.'

Hush. Listen carefully and in the jesting can be discerned stirrings of inevitable change. They won't be the first outré couple to find degeneracy too demanding to keep up. Once you have someone in to change the sheets and sweep the floors, you are limited as to what you can use your living quarters for. Besides which, they are getting older. 'We are getting older only if we let ourselves get older,' Lily says sternly. Now that she has twenty-four-hours' oversight of Quaid's domestic routines, she is shocked by how careless he is of himself physically. She knew he ate big hotel breakfasts and liked wine in the evening, but didn't realise he ate no smaller a breakfast at home and could be drinking his first glass of Shiraz by lunchtime. She hadn't been aware how little he walked. 'Do you know I've never seen you run,' she says two weeks into their new life together. 'And you never will,' he promises her. He is a tall man. He can get away with indulgences a smaller, rounder man cannot. But now that he is Lily's forever, she has the right to demand he stay well forever. If they are going to install any equipment in their bedroom it will be a rowing machine not a gibbet.

He is drinking freely, he tells himself, to make up for everything else he isn't doing freely. Since Shepherd Market and Camden, those sites of shamefulness and sin, he has been under self-imposed house arrest. Drink's the only tawdry adventurism he has left. As for Lily — though it isn't she who is throwing in the towel — she has less zest than of old for the whole caboodle of preparation and pageant, the long wait for the evening to start, and then, in harlot's heels, the long walk down the cold steps to the catacombs, followed by the long looks of Quaid's lugubriousness should the night not pan out as he wants it to. They are not quite living out of a suitcase. They take short-term leases on mansion-block apartments in Marylebone and Regent's Park while looking for the house that will simultaneously enable and thwart the louche amenities they once imagined indispensable to the expression of their love. But in the meantime they are too comfortable plumping cushions for each other to want to venture out to the cold cellars of Vauxhall.

And now, as if they aren't making concessions to normalcy enough, they are talking about a wedding again. Are they losing their minds? Getting married is so against the spirit of the never-ending bacchanal they swore their life together would be, should they ever break the shackles of the life before, the thought of it positively takes their breath away.

'Are we mad or what?'

'You say.'

'No, you.'

GOODBYE TO ALL THAT

The trouble is, their happiness, contentment, tranquillity – call it what you will – is not leaving them with enough to do. Not in the work sense: professionally they are both busy enough, Quaid with two plays simultaneously on the go (one a tragedy, one a comedy), and Lily lecturing to the old and making programmes she cannot pretend she is proud of for the young. But what will fill the hours they used to put into dodging and lying, the time spent wondering if and how they'd next meet, what hitherto unimagined desires they'd stimulate in each other, what declarations they'd make, what hellholes in the sewers of London they'd dare penetrate, who'd see them, whether they cared, whether they *wanted* to be seen, how they'd bear the subsequent hours apart?

That the happiness of unhampered mutual access would come at a cost they hadn't realised, neither having been happy in this way before. What they are face to face with now is the tricky material afterlife to the great spiritual adventure that has brought them to this point. Guardians of public morality, among whom are to be numbered the spouses of adulterers, will, in all likelihood, have trouble with the word 'spiritual' to describe what Quaid and Lily said and did and thought in each other's company; but both experienced ecstasies not a million miles from those recorded by saints and mystics. Lily had been the controlling moon of Quaid's transports and that, on occasions, without having to touch him at all. And Quaid could create turmoil in Lily's soul simply by staring deep into her eyes until she thought she would faint. As a teenage girl she had told her mother she had no desire to be penetrated, and meant it. Yet Sam Quaid she allowed to make invasive psychic inroads into her against which she put up no defences. Leonard Cohen made a song of touching Suzanne's perfect body with his mind. Lily permitted Quaid to go a lot further with his mind than that.

But that was then. The situation had since changed. There could be no duplicating any of the old ineffabilities once they had bills to pay. The material world is everybody's enemy but it has it in for lovers most of all. Pay, pay, pay for your daring to think you can escape what no one else can. The body ages, ardour cools, expenses mount, and all the while the Lords of Comeuppance grin from the sidelines.

So what are those who have thrown in their lot with love supposed to do? Admit their mistake, try not to meet one another's eyes, and turn their thoughts to pension pots? Or take the other route and whip their bodies into ersatz ecstasy one last time? Lily's friend Amaryllis, whose heart broke a little when Hal sadly admitted himself unable to return her patient devotion, has found a new profession as relationship coach and instructor in intimate massage.

'If it works why is she so unhappy?' Quaid asks.

'Because she meets so much resistance from cantankerous old bastards like you.'

'Old! You're forever telling me off for saying I'm old.'

'You're old when I say you're old, otherwise you're not.'

'Got it. Now can I interest you in an intimate massage?'

They were as one on this: it was sacrilege to simulate what was no longer real. Nothing was over forever in their view, but they had to honour the moment. That which – for the moment, *for the moment* – they no longer had ravening appetite for, should be left alone as fields are left fallow. Who could say what would grow again in the germinating darkness? And if nothing did?

Then nothing did. Love showed more than one face. Knowing when to fall quiet was no less an expression of love than commotion had been.

Nevertheless, from time to time they felt the need to check that everything was all right between them.

'You OK?' Lily periodically enquired.

'Aha, you?'

'You still in love?'

'For all time. You?'

'We aren't getting smug about ourselves?'

'We are a bit.'

'Does it matter?'

'Only if we don't remember to be sad about ourselves too.'

'What do we have to be sad about?'

'That, my dear, is a smug question.'

Materiality might have been their enemy but they made a sort of peace with it, seeing it as a backdrop to the enactment of those sentiments and desires that weren't material at all. Just as at first they had kissed outside shops selling a chair that was an earnest of everything they were looking forward to doing together, so now they embarrassed gallery owners by their fervid displays of mutuality when they bought a painting or a pot which pleased them identically, and embarrassed shop assistants who caught them in a tight embrace in changing rooms, no matter that Lily had just tried on a winter coat and sensible shoes, not a leather corset Quaid would have to lace her into before they plunged into the night.

They were hardly to be distinguished from other couples – devotees of Eros or not – in the pleasure they took in extravagantly designed restaurants with outlandish menus. Food was making fools of rich and poor, friends and enemies, alike. Whatever of meaning or unmeaning happened, now had to happen over food. But Sam and Lily, cheek by jowl at one or other of their favourite tables, made every meal seem as though prepared especially for them. Over food, they were celebrants of themselves again. Serve them snow crab and they fell upon it as they'd once fallen on each other, only this time they didn't have to hurry home to someone else, spraying their throats with breath fresheners in the taxi.

The sacramental wine, too, was as good as they could afford it to be.

'To you, Sam.'

'To you, Lily.'

'Are we being smug?'

'Yes.'

'Yes. But we're allowed,' Quaid said. 'We're old.'

'We aren't old.'

'We are experienced, then. And entitled. We have suffered—'

'How have we suffered?'

'Let me finish. We have looked into the jaws—'

'Of joy.'

'That too. But into sorrow more. We have eschewed triviality. We don't watch reality television. We give to charity. We support good causes—'

'*I* support good causes.'

'Yes, *you* support good causes. But with my blessing. *And* we've dedicated our lives to the making of art.'

'Plus we've worked hard,' Lily agreed.

'More than that,' Quaid said. 'We've loved hard.'

Lily corrected him. 'We're loving hard.'

Amaryllis accompanied them one night to their currently favourite restaurant in Barnes.

'You eat like you're in bed together,' she said.

Quaid laughed. 'We are,' he answered.

Under the table she took notes. For those to whom she taught

224

the arts of intimacy Quaid guessed. *Try to eat like you're in bed together . . .*

The following day she rang. She was worried she'd spoken out of turn. Lily assured her she had not. 'Then tell me,' Amaryllis said, 'you both looked so happy. What's your secret?'

'Eating,' Lily laughed.

'I mean the secret of your looking so euphorically post-coital.'

'We're euphorically post-coital.'

'Are you telling me you had sex just before going to the restaurant?'

'I don't know about "just". Post-coital doesn't have a use-by date. We had a lot of sex for nearly twenty years.'

'It's not the experience of most women that post-coital euphoria can last that long.'

'Then they've been doing it wrong.'

She wished she'd had the nerve to add, 'And they haven't been doing it with a pervert.'

'I DO'

Where they wanted to live turned out, to their surprise, to be Kew. Lily loved the idea of being close to the Gardens. Quaid loved what she loved. They weren't exactly on the river but they could smell it. The house was painted white, enjoyed good views of the sky from the extensions, and breathed an air of wholesomeness.

'Do you think this might be the only suburb of London without a bondage club?' Quaid wondered.

'Why? Are you starting to miss them?'

'On the contrary. I like the idea that we might be free at last of the taint.'

'Oh, taint. There is no taint. We didn't murder anyone, remember. We didn't catch a disease. No one did us harm. I danced a bit, that was all. You hid in a mask. Haven't you always been hiding in a mask? Taint! You know you worry me. Can we ban that word from our vocabulary?'

'Willingly. How about blessed?'

'That's just as crackers, Sam.'

'I'm a hyperbolist.'

'That's also what worries me. What you overvalue one day you'll undervalue the next.'

'I promise I will never undervalue you.'

'We'll see.'

'When will we see? In some unimaginable future? We're in it, Lily. This is what's to come. This is how we turn out. Do you remember fearing we wouldn't be be able to adjust to each other? Well we adjusted, didn't we? This is what adjustment looks like. We've made it through.'

But sometimes they both worry. Quaid recently bought a 5,000-piece jigsaw puzzle and then a games table to put it on. Why? A question that never fully answered itself to Lily's satisfaction was this: would they survive the everyday?

Thanks to Quaid's father, they finally get round to discussing wedding dates. Quaid receives a phone call from the mother he has never forgiven for having married his father, for having wanted him to be a girl, and for those reasons rarely thinks about. 'Your father is dying,' she tells him.

Quaid is flabbergasted. 'You're in touch with my father? Promise me you haven't let him back into the house.'

'Only for a cup of tea. He begged.'

'Oh, Mother. I suppose he told you he'd changed.'

'Far from it. He's still fathering children on impressionable students. He shows me the photographs. This time he's fathered twin girls. Be happy for me, he says.'

'And are you?'

'I'm happy he's dying of testicular cancer.'

'I'm surprised he has testicles left. I'm surprised he has anything left. I thought he died years ago.'

'You probably thought I died years ago.'

'No. I saw you recently.'

'Six months ago isn't recently. Such loving children I have.'

'You have my brothers. I'm sure they love you. How are they, by the way? You have loving grandchildren. You have loving great-grandchildren. How much more love do you want?'

'I could ask you the same question.'

'Don't.'

'Are you still with what's-she-called?'

'Lily. Yes.'

'What happened to the other one?'

'Selena? She married someone else.'

'Without telling you?'

'She mentioned it.'

'So what about you? Have you remarried yet? I don't like to think of you unmarried.'

'I know. I'd make a beautiful bride.'

'Bride, groom – what difference? Just get married. You'll go to the bad if you don't.'

'I want to go to the bad.'

'No you don't. You only think you do. You don't have your father's flair for it. Just get married.'

'It's under discussion. If you promise not to cry I will invite you to the ceremony.'

'You can say that because you know I don't leave the house any more. I have two new hips and am waiting for a third. Invite your brothers.'

'I don't really know my brothers.'

'Whose fault's that?'

'Yours. But I don't harbour grudges.'

'Good. Then invite your father too.'

'Invite him to my wedding? Of course not.'

'I think you should. He's too ill to accept but he might appreciate the gesture.'

'Mother, it would kill him. Or is that your intention? Are you hoping I'll finish him off?'

'It would be nice if you were reconciled at the end. It would make me feel we'd turned into one big happy family after all. Think about it at least.'

'I've thought about it.'

But after thinking about it some more he was ready to reverse his decision. I fancy asking him to be best man, he told Lily.

'Your father!'

'Yes. Can you imagine his face when he opens the invitation?'

'Sam, why would I want the country's leading advocate for free love at my wedding? Why would you?'

'Because he's my father.'

'That's a reason for keeping him away.'

'All right. To show him his teaching has made no earthly difference to his son. I see it as my final act of defiance. Look, Dad, I've won. Not that he'll come. He must be at least ninety. My mother assures me he's too ill to leave his bed, let alone come to the Ritz.'

'The Ritz!'

'Or wherever we have the party.'

'If he's ninety, why don't we wait until he's a hundred to be sure?'

Quaid thought otherwise. If they waited for his father to die he'd lose the unutterable satisfaction of infuriating him to death.

'And for that unutterable satisfaction you're prepared to risk infuriating me?'

'Lily, do you want to marry me or not?'

'I have already said I do.'

'How many years ago was that?'

'If you can assure me that your father will be too ill—'

'—or too dead—'

'—then all right. But not the Ritz.'

'Why not the Ritz?'

'Too showy for my mother.'

'I have always thought of your mother as a very smart woman.'

'The essence of my mother's smart is knowing when not to go too far.'

'Like mother like daughter.'

'If only.'

In the event, Ossian Freud wrote his son a charming letter, calling him 'my verdant boy' and thanking him 'from the bottom of my rancid heart' for reposing such unexpected filial trust, but regretting the indisposition that prevented his accepting. He would, though, like to take the opportunity to congratulate Quaid for marrying a second time and hoped he would marry many times more in the future. He hoped thereby to correct the imputation that he was a marriage hater. It was only *staying* married he objected to.

Quaid did not show Lily the letter. He would sooner have made her a gift of a poison spider. Instead he washed his hands a dozen times and told her that the old bastard had said no. So they could go ahead and book the ballroom at Claridge's.

But Lily still hesitated until the news came that her father-in-law-to-be had fallen into a fire at the old people's home.

'You do think he's flammable, don't you?' she asked.

'Better to burn than to marry was his motto,' Quaid said, 'but I wouldn't bet on his burning if he could stop a marriage some other way.'

Before they could agree a date, Lily's mother was rushed to hospital. Lily had been wondering if the wedding would be painful to her mother. Would she owe it to her not to look too radiant? Was this another parent they needed to die for decency's sake?

Well, soon she would. But there could be no wedding until she had.

Quaid was fond of his mother-in-law-to-be and thought the idea of her daughter's nuptials might cheer her up, even if she couldn't come to them. They could video-link it to her bed. Lily could visit her in her wedding dress.

'What wedding dress?'

'The white one I'm going to buy you.'

She snorted. 'The leather one?'

But no. There could be no wedding yet. It would be cruel to her.

'Not marrying,' Quaid said, 'would be cruel to me.'

'You're not dying.'

'That's what you think.'

He was one of those men whom love made morbid. Her kissed Lily and thought about the grave. He took her in his arms and heard the melancholy, long withdrawing roar of the sea as it retreated from the naked shingles of the world. The eternal note of sadness. And it wasn't just his own extinction he listened out for. What if Lily died before him? Many a night he would lie on his back to stop himself snuffling into his pillow like an adolescent, imagining the cold wind blowing across a Lilyless universe.

He reminded her they would soon have been together nearly twenty years, counting from – well, whenever it was seemly to start counting from. Marriage would make it a double celebration. It always amazed Lily how conscientious a keeper of their personal almanac he was. Like Hal, he never forgot her birthday. This didn't mean he would get round to organising a special event to mark it as Hal would – a house party for her and all her friends in the Seychelles, a helicopter ride around the Shetlands, a box at a Rugby League Cup Final. Sam remembered the day, sent a card, gave her a bunch of flowers, and then forgot about it. But at least that way she was spared having to say thank you but she didn't want to go cliff-jumping in Negril. Sam knew to the month how long they'd been together and could tell her what, in any of those months, they'd done and, no, not only which of his plays they'd seen premiered together at what theatre. Lily lived more in the moment and often, unless she was on a shoot, couldn't have said what day it was. It worried her that Sam was an almost frantic time-watcher. Shouldn't he have lost himself in work? What did he always have an eye on? Why the wall *and* the desk calendars? Why the three diaries? What was he desperate not to miss? What event was he steeling himself against?

★

Lily's mother agreed with Quaid. The idea that her daughter was marrying cheered her up. 'Do it quick, before I die,' she said. 'I'll go happily knowing I've finally got you off my hands.'

Which left no time for a coronation. So they married one sunny morning at Chelsea Register Office and then walked to the reception at the Chelsea Arts Club. This was Lily's idea. Invite the membership, she said, since you have no friends. It would be good for you to be surrounded by fellow artists. He reminded her that he had never sought the company of 'fellow artists' before.

'You weren't married before.'

'Yes I was.'

'Not to me.'

Midway through the wedding breakfast a ghostly waiter came looking for Quaid. 'There's a guy in the garden who wants a brief confidential word with you,' he whispered in Quaid's ear. Quaid shuddered. This was the very sentence the Devil's emissary had whispered into Don Juan's ear in Quaid's early play about the Don in Oxford.

Who would remember that? Christ no, Quaid thought. Fortunately Lily was working the room, accepting kisses and compliments. She looked marvellous, to Quaid's eye, in streetwise Yamamoto pleats and a pencil in her hair. He rose from the table and followed the waiter to the French doors.

'This guy,' he asked, hesitating. 'He's not on fire is he?'

'On fire?'

'He doesn't have burn marks?'

'I didn't really notice.'

'About ninety?'

He shrugged. 'No idea,' he said. Who that is twenty knows what ninety looks like?

Doing his best to be surreptitious, though he was drunk and

halfway to being disorderly, Quaid slipped into the garden. A tall gaunt man with wrinkly expat's skin and a glittering eye was curled like the snake around a tree.

'Here,' he rasped.

'I can see that,' Quaid said.

The man unwound himself and extended a skinny hand. 'There was a ship,' quoth he, thought Quaid. 'If you have a terrible tale to tell I've already heard it,' he said skittishly. It was his wedding day. He was happy.

'I do actually,' the man said, 'but that's not why I'm here.'

Quaid was not prepared for these words to issue like the final cough from a hole in the man's throat. He stepped back, as though frightened of what deadly cocktail the man might cough at him.

Should he apologise for his reaction or would that only make the situation worse? 'So who are you and why are you here?' he asked. Rude, he knew, but what else was he to do – invite him in to drink champagne, that's if he could drink champagne without spraying it about, and terrifying the guests? He could hear what Lily would say. 'Are you mad?'

'I'm here to give you this.' The stranger held out a brown envelope. 'It's a wedding gift. But you might not want to give it to her right away. You might not want her to know I've been here.'

Though every instinct in his body told him to back away, Quaid knew he had to extend his trembling hand and accept the envelope. 'If it's for Lily, why didn't you give it to her directly?' Quaid asked.

'To answer that I'd have to embark upon my terrible tale after all. And believe me, you wouldn't want to hear it.'

'I'll settle for knowing why you were hiding behind a tree.'

'I shouldn't have to tell you of all people that that's what characters in Shakespeare do when they want to see but not be seen.'

'Ah. By your daughter, presumably.'

Not much of a guess, even by a drunk, Quaid thinks.

'Yes. Forgive the cloak-and-dagger, but I know she wouldn't want to see me. I respect her feelings. I came only in the hope of catching sight of her. And I have. You are a lucky man. She is very beautiful, like her mother. But don't tell her I said that. In fact, better you don't mention I came at all.'

The voice reminded Quaid of the fetishists in rubber suits and snorkels who'd asked Lily for a dance in Amsterdam and Slough. Face to face with Lily's father, Quaid felt a rush of shame that they'd been to such places. *You allowed my daughter to do that!*

Well, Quaid was not her – or anyone's – father.

Maybe I should have tried harder to be one.

'And this?' he asked, tapping the envelope.

'It's a forget-me-not brooch. Don't throw it away when I leave. It's set with sapphires. I don't know what she likes. But her mother would have worn it. Sell it if you think she won't and buy her something exquisite with the money. It'll be enough for me to think she has something from me, even indirectly. Take care of each other. God bless you both.'

And with a wave of the hand, he disappeared, coughing first behind one tree, then another, before quitting the garden altogether. So did the Devil take his leave of Don Juan in Magdalen Garden.

Quaid watched him go, uncertain whether to call him back and embrace him – no, he didn't have the courage for that – uncertain whether to run inside and tell Lily what had just happened. Would she want to meet him? Would he have to prepare her for what she'd see? Or would knowing he'd been there spoil the day for her?

He was not a man who took decisions. The point of Lily was that she did the deciding. But he couldn't ask her to decide this.

He stayed a little longer in the garden, sure that if he returned immediately to the reception his face would give the game away.

Her fucking father, for God's sake. Ill. Quite possibly dying. Quite possibly dead. Spirits visit weddings. The dying were everywhere. It could have been any of them. Even his own father – as he'd first expected the unholy ghost to be – looking for a bit of pity.

He took the liberty of opening the envelope. The delicate sapphire brooch was bound with a ribbon of fine gold to which was attached a label engraved with the words 'Ne M'Oubliez Pas'.

Funny. He had once bought Lily that very perfume.

It touched him beyond measure to think that someone else loved Lily as much as he did, craved her love as much as he did, and that she did not know and, even sadder, did not care to know it. In asking her not to forget him, her father showed he would not forget her. Would Quaid tell her eventually? He didn't know. Should I tell you eventually, he needed to ask her.

Paradoxically, what had happened made her, in his eyes, the more in need of protection. No love lasts long in which one of the participants isn't part-parent to the other. He first asked Lily to marry him in Rome when, like the best of mothers, she had told him she could not bear to see him disappointed. Had he knelt down on one knee to his mother?

Lily had not looked to him to be her father. She knew him too well. He was not father material. But did he owe her what she hadn't asked for?

Here, anyway, was his first fatherly test . . .

No – he would not mention a word to her of her real father's appearance.

Not yet. Perhaps not ever.

We have been married barely an hour, he thinks, and already I'm keeping secrets from her.

Lily's mother didn't need to be told either. She died the next night.

FATHERS AND SONS

They agreed to postpone the honeymoon. 'I owe her that,' Lily
said. She was not overwhelmed by grief. Her mother had lived
a long life. But she fell into a state of melancholy, almost surly,
reserve. Was it her fault her mother had closed her heart against
men who traipsed filth into the house? Was it Lily she'd been
protecting? She sobbed quietly for a week believing she was the
cause of her mother's loneliness. She had OK'd Quaid and
seemed to like him. 'You'll have your work cut out with him,'
she said, 'but he has a faithful look.' Lily hadn't told her mother
he was married. But she'd already guessed. 'Of course he is,' she
said. 'He has a married look too. But that needn't matter if he
loves you. You can be faithful to one woman while you're married to another. And you can be faithful to your wife while
carrying on with someone else. I think I judged your father too
harshly. But it's too late to be doing anything about that now.'

Lily's mouth fell open. A lifetime of example extinguished just
like that. But if it was too late for her mother to change the way
she lived, it was too late for Lily to change the way she felt. Let
Quaid traipse filth into their Kew cottage and he'd be out of it.

'I think,' Quaid said, about two months into Lily's mourn-
ing, 'that I'll visit my father.'

'I thought he'd fallen into a fire.'

'He had. It turns out that you were right. He wouldn't burn.'

'Why do you want to see him suddenly after going fifty years
without wanting to hear his name?'

He couldn't tell her that it was obscurely connected with his
having seen her father in the gardens of Chelsea Arts Club. And

now with her mother's death. It seemed wrong that he should be so implicated in her family history and so without any of his own.

'Time to clear the decks,' he said.

'Why? Won't they clear themselves?'

'Not in the spirit I want to clear them.'

'What do you intend to do?'

'It's more what I intend to say.'

'*I love you Dad*?'

'How did you know?'

His father had a slightly different expectation. 'If you've come to tell me to fuck off, don't waste your breath. You're the last in a long line of visitors. They've all told me to fuck off. I hope you'll be more original.'

He was propped up on half a dozen pillows, his pointed beard full of breakfast, his matted eyebrows falling like spiders into his eyes, black spiky hairs growing in clusters on the bridge of his nose. Quaid wondered if he ought to complain to the matron or whoever was in charge of the care home. Shouldn't someone be looking after the old man? But that would have been hypocritical. He didn't want anyone looking after his father. He wanted him to perish, uncared for and alone. (As I will be, he added as an afterhought, if anything happens to Lily.)

A torn piece of paper, sellotaped to his father's door, read

OSSIAN FREUD
PROFESSOR OF MISOGAMY

Who could want anything good for such a man?

'Ah yes, now I have you, you're the one who refused my name,' he said. His voice was fainter than Quaid remembered but he still sounded as though he were forcing words through a steel trap.

'You know very well who I am. You wrote to congratulate me on my wedding only a few weeks ago.'

'Did I? That was uncharacteristically charitable of me. I hope it went well. Are you still fucking her?'

'I won't answer that question.'

'That must mean you aren't.'

'Not your business.'

'That you are or you aren't? Do you know, eighty-seven per cent of men who have been married more than five years no longer fuck their wives. And the other thirteen per cent do it thinking of someone else. But that's after five years. If you've stopped fucking yours after only five weeks something's seriously wrong. Have you tried looking at porn while you're doing it? I've got some stashed under my mattress you can borrow. Nurse!'

Quaid waved away the offer. 'Can I get you a tea or anything?'

'I never got round to asking you when you were a kid – that was very remiss of me – I'm sorry – how old were you when you started fucking?'

Don't answer, Quaid told himself. Don't give the old swine the satisfaction. But he feels there's so much unfinished business between them, he has to make a start on it at least.

'I wasn't a fucker. Fucking wasn't what I called it. You must have taught me badly.'

'So what did you call it? Coitus non startus?'

'You can fuck without fucking,' Quaid said.

The old man all but choked on the mirth of it. '*You can fuck without fucking*! Which bitch sold you that story? Ah, yes. Now I remember – you were the mollycoddled one. I suppose your mother told you fucking *with* fucking was a sin. She sinned quite a bit, in that case. I'm surprised you didn't turn out to be a nancy boy, unless you did. Are you?'

'I suspect nancy boys do their share of fucking.'

Why did he say that, he wondered. What was the magnetic quality of his father's odious vocabulary that he had to answer it in kind? Was it some infection in language or his genes?

'Well, you'd know I suppose. Yes, I'll have tea. See if you can get Nurse Iglesias. She's an occupational therapist. Her occupation's looking after me.'

'Then why doesn't she wash your fucking beard?' Quaid wanted to ask. 'And while she's at it why doesn't she pluck those fucking hairs off your fucking nose? And disinfect your brain?'

'Do they ever take you for a walk?' he asked. 'You look a bit yellow.'

'A walk? I've never walked in my life. Why should I start now? So that I'll live longer? Who wants me to live longer? Do you want me to live longer? Be honest. You want me dead.'

'I don't want you dead.'

'Then I've failed as a father.'

For one mad moment Quaid thought he ought to try exonerating him. You? Fail? Perish the thought, Pa.

'So how would you have succeeded as a parent?' he asked instead.

'Not parent, father. There's a difference. Your mother felt she succeeded as a parent by apparently teaching her boys how to fuck without fucking. Had I succeeded as a father with you, you'd have come in here brandishing your cock like a battering ram, shouting *my turn, my turn*, and smiting me with it. I'd be cowering from you, not laughing at you.'

To his surprise, Quaid rather liked the picture that evoked. 'I could come back and try again,' he said.

'You? Not a chance. A man who can't fuck his wife five minutes after he's married her is no threat to his father.'

'You should have more sympathy for me. I'm told your fucking days are over.'

'Who told you that? Call Nurse Iglesias. Nurse, Nurse! This

little shit who is no son of mine thinks my fucking days are over. Tell him.'

Quaid rose. 'I won't kiss you,' he said.

As he closed the door he heard his father shouting after him. 'If I'd fucked your mother without fucking her you'd never have been fucking born. How would that have been, eh? Eh?'

'Fucking wonderful,' Quaid shouted back.

'So how was that?' Lily asked when he returned.

'Fucking awful.'

LOVE ISLAND

What with one thing and another, it took them a year to arrange their honeymoon

They were scrupulous about not going anywhere they had been before, whether for business or for pleasure, whether separately or together. The wisdom about honeymoons was that nine out of ten were cruel disappointments. The fewer comparisions a honeymoon invited, therefore, the better. How it was that neither of them had been to Bali, either to shoot a documentary or lecture to visiting Australians at an arts festival or research the series it now seemed they were never going to make, they couldn't explain, but Bali got their vote. Maybe it was an omen. The Island of Love had been under wraps, waiting for the hour of their arrival.

They needed a fillip. It had not been the best of years. Lily could not quite climb out of the depression into which her mother's death had thrown her. She woke to an unlocated sadness that wasn't wholly attributable to her mother's wasted life. She suffered one health scare after another. And Sam's low spirits bothered her. He had suffered a bad fall himself, put his shoulder out and lost two teeth, and was struggling to breathe life into a new play about a foul-mouthed old roué who addressed the audience from a hospital bed in four-letter words he coughed out from a hole in his throat. 'It's hard to imagine anyone liking this,' the director of the theatre who'd commissioned it said.

'Is liking a *sine qua non* suddenly?'

'Let's say it helps.'

'Would you have said that to Shakespeare had he walked in here with *Timon of Athens?*'

'Had Shakespeare walked in here with *Timon of Athens* I'd have fainted. But as per your point about liking, perhaps audiences were different in those days.'

'Hamlet mentions seeing a play that pleased not the millions. But it was still staged.'

'We could workshop it.'

Which sounded to Quaid too much like submitting it to an intimate massage.

'You could do with a break,' Lily said. 'We both could.'

'A break! It's meant to be a fucking honeymoon.'

'And what you most need a break from is your father's influence. We owe ourselves a honeymoon. Let's take it.'

Separately, they wondered if a glamorous location might just rekindle some of their old verve. She wanted not to go on thinking about her mother. He wanted not to go on thinking about fathers. Rekindling their old verve didn't have to mean finding a way back to Taos or Capri. There was no way back. What they needed was a way forward.

'Frangipani,' Lily declares, as they enter their hotel.

Quaid tosses his head back like a wild animal, testing the air for danger. It's an act. His sense of smell is poor. But he wants to show Lily that he smells what she smells and is equally overcome by it.

The feature of which the butler who shows them to their room is most proud is the outside shower, a simple bamboo spout protruding from the side of a rock on which orange and purple hibiscus grows and kaleidoscopic lizards take fright. Lemon-grass candles burn around the heart-shaped pool. 'Totally private,' the butler tells them with a smile, meaning they can swim here naked. Quaid kneels to feel the water. Warm, warm. Lily has a flower in her hair

'God Almighty,' Quaid thinks. 'Do I have the capacity for satisfaction equal to this?'

Dinner is a beaten copper platter of aromas. The bay sighs, throwing back reflections of the stars. They kiss each other with mouths tasting of champagne. How many days is it since they first kissed? They agree there has not been a single one of those days they have regretted. But what if this is the hour of hours, the peak from which no more can be expected and all there is left to look forward to is decline? Each feels the other's nervousness. They get up from the table to dance slowly, no matter that it isn't dance music that the gamelan band is playing. Tightly, tightly, they cling to each other as on a boat that's slowly sinking.

The bedroom door recognises their breath and opens automatically. There are rose petals on their pillows. Christ, Quaid thinks, has Amaryllis been here? No sooner do they lie down than they fall asleep. It's been a long flight.

Over fourteen days they shower in the open, swim without clothes, inhale rare odours, dine on rare fragrances, sip sweet coconut milk, dance to music that isn't designed to dance to, repeat the rhyme of their extreme good fortune at having met, retire to beds of the crispest linens, and fall asleep. For his part, Quaid marvels at the faerie spirits of his new wife: her floating golden on the perfumed pool like a princess from the *Arabian Nights*; her padding noiselessly through their marbled rooms like a faun; her sitting under the shower on the artfully arranged rocks, combing out her dripping mermaid's hair – but the sight of her so engrosses his senses that he wants nothing more, seeks neither to possess her nor be possessed by her. And Lily, too, takes pleasure watching her new – all right, new*ish* – husband crouching beneath the bamboo spout every hour that

God sends, letting the water spill like stardust down his chest, then striding dripping into the bedroom like the dog he is never going to have – without asking for anything further. She has, of course, brought their accoutrements of desire, the corsets for him to lace her into and out of, the bordello spikes, the belt whose magic properties she must have discerned in New Mexico before being able to give them a name or understand their function, and whatever else might just, from one passing hour of experimentation and fantasy to the next, make both of them gasp anew. But she will not bring them out of her case; it would be a profanation to use them as the bellows to inflame a lust which, for whatever reason, and for however long, has cooled.

Has it?

Cooled, no. Wrong word. It matters what words you use. Words are like those ignes fatui that lure travellers into bogs and marshes. You have to interrogate every one. Check their papers. Make sure they have a right to be here. *Cooled*, never.

Ask another question then – Have the winds of your desire for Lily died down or just taken a different direction?

And the winds of hers for him?

Ask another question.

No, ask nothing.

Quaid is not sure, as their old patterns stubbornly refuse to return, how much trouble he's in. Has the man in him finally given up the ghost as he has so often feared it would, or has it mutated into a new aesthetics of appreciation, loving Lily for herself, for the shape she makes in the world rather than for the dents, or whatever one wants to call them, she puts in him. He sees her at the end of a passage unaware of him, engrossed in some thought he cannot guess at, or descending a staircase with childlike concentration, or sitting at the dinner table, awaiting his return, looking out for him, ever so slightly anxious, as though afraid he never will return – and he is overwhelmed by his sensory dependence on her, not her company or even her presence but the never-ending astronomic fact of her, the starlit heavens he cannot now imagine ever looking up and not seeing her presiding over. Well, he is a strange man and these are strange times. Excesses in a man his age are to be forgiven.

'You are no age,' Lily is forever telling him.

Sometimes she's right, sometimes she isn't. But consciousness of ageing is a poison there's no getting rid of once it's entered the bloodstream. There are remissions but there's no cure.

Their room is like a temple with a golden cupola for a ceiling. As he lies on his back, looking up into it, reliving every sight of her he's enjoyed today, a new thought forms – *Am I loving her for the first time?*

He's been alive too long to suppose that desire must always take the same form. He has waxed and waned a sufficient number of times never to be sure what manner of man he's going to be when he rises from his pillows next, but this migration of ardour from his selfish generative parts to his self-renouncing, all-receptive senses is not like anything he has experienced before. At any moment, as he lies there, he imagines Lily rolling into his arms, and asking, 'What is the matter? Have you stopped loving me?' and he answering, 'Stopped loving you? God, no. If anything, at this moment I love you more than I have ever loved you. More variously. More surprisingly. Less urgently perhaps, because I don't hear the chariot of lawlessness at my back, but with a grander apprehension of all the world and time we have, all the changing relations to each other we can map.'

The coalescence of honeymoon and anniversary would always have worked some sea change in them both, and even more dramatically in Quaid for whom dates are a potent influence, but there is also the meeting with Lily's wounded, wheezing father to take into account. Has Lily been handed over to him, as from one parent to another? It has detracted nothing from the sensual attention Lily has always lavished on him, that she is able, at any moment, to worry about him as a mother might. The mistress in her has never been at war with the mother. If anything, the more of every other role being a mistress has encompassed, the more being a mistress has become her. Is Quaid the lover now to encompass Quaid the father? Will he know where the father in him is to be found? Will he even know where to start to look?

Well, there's one clue. He won't be looking to the example of his own dear dad. But what if he has no choice? What if his father is a warning? Don't even try it, Quaid. You won't ever know how.

They have not stopped touching but they touch with an unaccustomed diffidence. Suddenly a touch is not a signal for something else to happen. Nor is it in all circumstances as appropriate as it was before. Should he be asking permission?

Quaid watches and waits.

Lily waits and watches.

He spends time under the outdoor shower because he can think there. He is not quite a stranger to himself but his body is behaving differently. Normally, water running down him is arousing. But he is not aroused. Does he have a different body now he has a wife?

Wife.

And here's another thought – *could he grow to like having a different body now he is a husband?*

Husband. It's as though the force of that has only just struck him. It has taken a honeymoon to bring home to him the fact of marriage.

Yesterday, or however long ago it was before things changed,

Quaid moved within Lily's electric field like so many charged particles, any one of which might, without warning and without any say in the matter, hiss, sizzle or even explode. I might as well be Frankenstein's monster in its earliest stages of development, he told Lily, and while that wasn't exactly a plea for her to turn off the power, he did on occasions wish he could escape from her electromagnetic influence just long enough to think about something else. I do have plays to write, he'd tell her. I know, and wonderful plays they are, she'd say, laying her cheek on his shoulder, whereupon his torso would light up like a pinball machine.

Queerly, his seeming impotence feels like a promise, though he doesn't know of what. Independence, is it? Not from her but from the world and its expectations. This is who he is, this is what he does, this is what he doesn't do. Anyone got an argument with that? It is not an independence that is in any way disparaging of his wife. He is, if anything, more aware of her than ever. He absorbs her with his eyes. He approves her with his heart. But if there is no further call on his manliness, does it matter?

Well to Lily it does, yes. She doesn't need a warrior for a husband. She has never much cared for being an invaded country, anyway. So she can live with him sitting brooding in his tent; but she cannot live with not knowing how long he's going to be in there or if he's planning to make a dash for it under cover of darkness.

Honeymoons do strange things, she has no doubt. She came with no naive anticipations of rapture. And anniversaries do stranger things still. Twenty years, Sam says. Could he be right? He tells her he sees in her the girl he saw in Alburquerque. Age cannot you-know-what, he says, nor custom stale your whatsit. You continue to astound me. Though I sleep the sleep of an innocent child every night of our honeymoon, the fires still rage within me.

Lovely of him to say it. But it is one thing for a husband to feel this way about his wife, quite another for her to believe it. She looks after herself. Is careful what she eats. Dances for exercise. Creams her limbs each night from expensive pots and tubes – a ritual he loves to watch. Edgar Degas – *Woman Bathing in a Shallow Tub*. But she wasn't a girl when she met him and is many years further on from being a girl now. Infinitely flattering to be told she is a faun, a Nereid, a faerie princess, but how long will it be before he sees, or admits he sees, the ugly truth beneath this allegory of eternal beauty?

Floating on her back in the perfumed pool she wonders if her question is already out of date. What if, here in Bali, the man she loves in full knowledge of his faults, now sees only faults in her?

This much difference is there between a woman's love and man's – a man lacks the emotional intelligence to live with disenchantment.

Since Quaid does not know that this is what Lily is thinking, he cannot answer on his own behalf. But if he could, he would say that, yes, he was light in the emotional-intelligence department; yes, he lacked what people were starting to refer to as empathy, and lacked even more what people had always called curiosity; and that while this could be accounted a drawback in a playwright, it was not when he was writing plays that he was most himself. Who it was that took him over he couldn't say. A better self? Someone else entirely? But as Lily's lover – both as writer and as man – no, no, *he was not disenchanted*. He had crossed that river which all lovers must cross if they were not to fall out of love: Lily's every fault now became her and in his eyes her every vice had become a virtue.

She will do nothing to break the becalmed mood. It's part of Quaid's idealisation of her to believe she holds the happiness of both of them in her hands, runs the carnival that has been their romance, and can effect any change simply by wishing it. But however much of that is true, it has been achieved by an attentiveness to Quaid's wants and whims, his scares and susceptibilities – many unknown even to himself – that has been little short of superhuman. Right now – though this is not what holidays are supposed to do to you – she feels wrong-footed. She senses him eyeing her from his lounger as she climbs out of the pool. She would like to shake her hair in imitation of the sea nymph he has told her he sees, showering him with jewelled droplets like shooting stars, but wonders if the comedy of extravagant sensuality is the right note to strike today. She blows him an operatic kiss. The air is suddenly perfumed with sadness. What if she has not proved desirable enough for the island?

THE CICADA AND THE SEA SQUIRT

'Sex is not a memory pillow. Once it loses its shape it can never return to what it was.'

Lily started when she heard those words. They were spoken by a character in the first of Quaid's plays she went to see in his company. Shifting in her seat, she had fanned herself comically with her programme. 'Jesus!' she whispered just loud enough for him to hear. She returned to it in the interval. 'That's a bleak view,' she said.

'Well as long as you remember it's not mine,' he said. 'The character speaking is hardly one whose opinions I share.'

'I understand that,' Lily said. 'But some statements have the power to stay with you, whoever makes them.'

Years later, floating in the pool of petals, she has not forgotten it. Nor has she forgotten what she thought at the time but didn't dare say – that whoever spoke the words, Quaid wrote them. They had passed through him. For a fleeting moment, the words and Quaid shared the same space and breathed the same air.

Would they share the same space now, she wonders. Does Sam, showering continuously under the bamboo spout as though to shower his old self away, think their relations will never return to the shape they were?

She feels as though bereaved.

Ought they to put a black sheet on their bed?

How has it come to this? And what will be the consequence? Because she is a catastrophist she must first fix the origins of it and then confront the worst eventuality. By sex she doesn't mean what other women mean by sex; by sex she doesn't mean the ingress and egress of a man of steel. As if! when that man is Quaid who likes – who *liked* – her to tie to him to the bed. No, by sex she means the entire drama not the act – the orchestra, the overture, the prologue, the libretto (especially the libretto), the applause. Not *Rheingold* but the Ring entire. Back she goes over what she has done, what they have done together, to cause their drama to lose its form. Is it because they married, because they set up home together, because they left their spouses, because she danced like a showgirl in disreputable cellars, because they slept together the first night away from home, because they met? *Kerpow*! Was that the sin for which it was decided there and then that they would one day have to pay? *Kerpow*! And now *kerpow* again – from the beginning to the end in a single word.

For the moment at least, Quaid is not taking whatever it is that's happening to them as badly as she is. Not having much liked the man he was, he's well positioned to embrace a new version. He hopes he is not going to become one of those ingrate geriatrics who welcome the waning of desire as relief from an oppressive burden. It is not desire that's oppressed him all his life, only himself, and of course the teaching of Edina Gore. Nor does he believe that desire has waned in him now. There's been a subtle shift – in direction, in intensity, in concentration – that's all. And even that might be no more than temporary. Love, he is beginning to realise, is like authorship. You don't know where it's going to take you. And you mustn't hold out for your original plan. To be creative, in love as on the page, is to let yourself be buffeted by the gales of surprise and change. But Lily needs to know where she's been and where she's going. The more intense the looks of protective love he throws her, the more she thinks he is working out a way to divorce her.

She has – she must never allow herself to forget – been witness to his doing this before.

All she knows of him as a married man – again she must remember – is that he once found the condition irksome. Why did she agree to his embracing it a second time?

There is an argument that some people are too in love to marry. Too engrossed in the minutiae of each other, too fascinated by the chemical phenomenon of themselves – the correspondences and correlations, the freak affinities and benign incompatibilities – too indifferent to the side benefits which some look to marriage to provide: law, legitimacy, security, progeny, position in society.

This is not to embrace Ossian Freud's view of monogamy as contrary to natural law. From an earlyish age – let's say seventeen – Sam Quaid, already a playwright and a sentimentalist, believed he was the author of his own laws. So long as he was in love with one woman, he could never imagine being in love with another. But until Lily he had never been in love with one woman long enough to put monogamy to a rigorous test. Post-Lily, he was a one-woman man again. Fidelity, he was now prepared to tell the world, wasn't just honourable, it was as exciting as hell. Fidelity, where its object was self-willed, more than a little reckless, not false but capricious, was the high-wire act of love.

Why Sam Quaid welcomed wedlock, when it was really a circus he wanted to join, was a question Lily, in her distress, pressed upon him.

'I love you and am proud to be your wife,' she told him on their return, 'but did we really need to do this? Weren't things going well enough before?'

Before! Before when? So long and sorrowfully did she look at him, she could have meant that things were going well enough before they met.

After Bali, she settles on marriage as their big mistake. Everything fine until then. It was their own fault. They had grown used to listening only to each other. Eyebeams plaited, fingers intergrafted, ankles locked, they had become an entire universe unto themselves, beyond counsel or example. Marriage, once they embarked on it, would be its own New Creation. Where they went from there they didn't know but the illusion of marriage was that you must be going somewhere. That was what ruined Bali for them. They forgot to live in their own present. You don't go to paradise-promising places when you carry paradise around with you. If they were ever to renew their vows they'd honeymoon in Harlesden.

They'd been relieved to get back home. A commission to write a new play for the Chichester Festival Theatre boosted Quaid's spirits. Then Lily was headhunted by an important museum to design a programme for interviewing women film-makers. Both were flattered and excited until they remembered that Lily hated gender-specific work and Quaid hated commissions. They were both occupied enough already. They didn't need a leg-up. So why did the idea that fortune was giving them one please them, even if only for five minutes? It must have been because they were still under matrimony's charm, still expecting more to happen.

On the morning they decided to say no to the museum, no to Chichester and no to anything else that came in the post, Quaid laughed, opened his empty hands and said, 'Welcome to a blank slate.'

Lily shuddered.

'Be not afeared my pretty one,' he went on. 'At least we have each other.'

Though meant to be jocular, the remark touched a raw nerve. What few high spirits were left in the bed fled as though from a punctured balloon.

'Isn't the trouble,' Lily replied, 'that we *only* have each other?'

'Who else would you like us to have?'

'Children.'

'Children! Lily, I've rarely seen you look at a child and when you do it's as though you've seen a cockroach. You've told me every day I've known you that you never wanted children.'

'And I still don't. But we have to face the consequence of not having any.'

'Yes – a quiet life. Allelujah!'

'Since when did you want a quiet life?'

'Since you started wanting children.'

'You don't get it, do you. I don't *want* children. But they're the natural consequence. Love, marriage, children. Without them we cut ourselves off mid-performance. As though the end of all our exploring is to arrive where we started – with ourselves. Children lead you out into the world. They connect you, Sam. Don't you ever ask yourself where all this is going? What are we for?'

He rose on one elbow to kiss her. 'Let Rome in Tiber melt—'

She turned her cheek. 'This isn't Rome, Sam.'

'You've never turned your cheek from me before.'

'We've never been here before.'

'Where's here?'

'Without a future.'

He tried to kiss her cheek again. 'We *are* the future,' he said. The new Sam Quaid. Impotent and all-powerful. Flaccid and imperturbable.

But there was no new Lily. 'No we are not. We are just ourselves and when we're done we're done. My mother often said her main motive for staying alive was wanting to see what happens to me. It gave her something to live for.'

'Isn't that because she kicked your father out?'

'That's a cruel thing to say, Sam. But all right, if either of us kicks the other out, what then? What would have been the point of it all? It would mean we'd led to nothing.'

'No, it would mean it had led to us.'

'Us, us, us! Is that it?'

'I think it's quite a lot.'

She thought about it. 'I too. That's the trouble. We're self-consumed, like those fabulous creatures that eat themselves, starting with their own tails? What are they called?'

'Sea squirts.'

'You're making that up.

'No I'm not. Sea squirts. I'm a world expert. I did a dissertation on them at school. But I could have said artists.'

'Don't be smart with me. I'm being serious. How will our story end, Sam?'

'It won't. You know the Thomas Hardy poem: "Yonder a maid and her wight / Come whispering by: / War's annals will cloud into night / Ere their story die." Well, you're the maid and I'm your wight. Our story has no end. We aren't an event. We just go on and on. Like nature itself.'

'Not a very satisfactory story in that case. Who'd want to read us?'

'Other lovers.'

'What if I'd like to be read by someone else?'

'You mean readers of whodunnits and fantasy fiction? Forget it. We aren't that kind of story. We don't begin and end. We are not linear. There is no end to us.'

'What kind of story are we, Sam?'

'We aren't a story at all. We're a poem.'

She took consolation in that. But which poem?

HOTCONSTANCY

The character in Quaid's play whose opinions he didn't share turned out to be on the money. Sex isn't like a memory pillow. It doesn't spring back into its accustomed shape.

Lily didn't spread a black sheet on their bed, nor did she deck herself in widow's weeds. But she and Sam, like all one-time adulterers who'd scaled the wall, had yet another bout of serious readjusting to do. Instead of understanding the rest of their lives as the freedom to explore an intimacy which hitherto they had only enjoyed piecemeal, they had now to face the fact that intimacy was not an end in itself but the means to enjoy the rest of their lives. The aftermath of adultery is a sort of purgatory in which lovers must face the unconditional nature of their passion. It was as it was because it couldn't be anything else. The only way they will enjoy anything comparable at such a frenzied pitch again is by replicating it with other people. And if Lily and Sam agreed on anything it was this – only by remaining everything to each other today did being together yesterday retain its legitimacy and being together tomorrow its promise of felicity.

'So we find another word for frenzy? Is that what we're saying?'

It doesn't matter which of them asked that question. They each thought it.

'Yes, that is what we're saying.'

'And that word would be?'

'Hotconstancy.'

'That's two words.'

'Not if you say them quickly.'

'And how are we to attain hotconstancy?'

'That's what we are charged with finding out.'

'You mean charged as batteries are charged?'

'No, charged as emissaries from God are charged.'

'So we're introducing the idea of religion now.'

'Not introducing. We were always doing God's bidding.'

'Isn't that all a bit self-importantly Lawrentian, even for us?'

'Yes, which is why we need to import something self-amusedly Joycean.'

'You mean sex in the head.'

'Wise lovers take it wherever they can find it.'

'So who's to be Molly Bloom?'

'Whichever of us isn't Leopold.'

They didn't follow up too literally on that apportioning of roles. Making adjustments needn't entail immediate action. It was enough they were talking. Talking was something they had always done well, even when it hadn't been strictly necessary to the business in hand. And something of the heat of those earlier times could still be generated by words alone. This was hotconstancy in action – that friendship which intense passion can bequeath, friendship that's not residual or consolatory but the very fruition of what was there before, as though the whole purpose of sex – if you discount children – had been to make intimates in language of those who'd been intimates in body.

They entered, anyway, into what could seem to them like a higher state, a rich period of wordy companionship, pleasing each other with vivid reports, not from the small self-referring world of themselves, but of the great life beyond. Not long after giving a class for the University of the Third Age, Lily was asked to present a lecture series on documentary-making. 'Would it be all right if I show them out-takes from our Taos film?' she asked him.

'Do I get a royalty?'

'It's a charity,' she reminded him. He didn't think people should be allowed to laugh at him gratis. 'They're getting on in years,' she said, 'they need a laugh.'

'I'm getting on in years.'

'No, you're not.'

References to senescence were not exactly proliferating, but they were never far away.

'When they say University of the Third Age . . .' he jested roughly the day she began teaching there, but she wouldn't rise to his bait.

'Enrol if you want to find out,' she said.

They had given up hope of making more television programmes together – 'He's not relatable enough,' commissioning editors told her, 'in fact he's entirely unrelatable' – but Lily didn't allow commisioners to turn her against him on that account, nor Quaid to sour her against making programmes with others more relatable.

'Just don't relate too closely,' he told her. Well, let him wonder. It did him good to be without her for a couple of weeks, she thought. And it did her good to have stories to tell him when she returned. Absence made him a good listener.

Especially he liked hearing about the silent short she'd shot in Rothko's chapel in Houston, a site so holy that not a word dared be spoken there. 'I'd like to have presented that,' Quaid said.

'I'm glad you didn't,' Lily told him.

No less intriguing to him was her film about a twin who couldn't cook until her other half enrolled in the Paris Cordon Bleu whereupon she was immediately able to cook any dish provided it was French. 'How much of that was true?' Sam asked.

'As much of it as you'd like to be true.'

'I'd like to know if it's science or telepathy.'

'I knew you were going to say that,' Lily said.

Unaccustomed to spending a single evening alone, let alone

weeks, Quaid started into space, ate pizzas, watched television, read books he didn't like, flirted with being jealous, then flirted with not being jealous, counted the hours before Lily returned and finally got back into the rhythm of writing again. A college production of *The Man Who Wasn't Jealous* enjoyed good sales at the Edinburgh Festival. 'So is the main protagonist you?' an interviewer asked him.

'Main protagonist is a tautology,' he told her. 'A protagonist can't be anything but main.'

Just as Sam Quaid couldn't be anything but unrelatable.

But he was learning to relate to himself at least. In the past, the sight of an empty bed had make his heart sink: going back to his student years, an empty bed denoted failure. An empty bed meant Edina Gore had wrested the initiative. Now, he counted it a moral triumph that he did not look on Lily's absence as an opportunity to wrest it back. So this is what maturity looks like, he told Lily beside him on the bed, no matter that she wasn't beside him on the bed. Maturity was talking to yourself.

So time passed in that slow, hypnotic way it does for lovers, the hours eating themselves like sea squirts, a happy expenditure of months and years beneath which a dangerous sense of nothing really happening, nothing tangible having been achieved – just a continuous present of contentment promising more of the same – lay in wait to stab and stab again the heart should they wake one day and discover they no longer loved.

GIVE A THING A NAME

To our bodies turn we then . . .

Shakespeare was characteristically precise about the number of natural shocks that flesh is heir to. A thousand.

Quaid and Lily had not yet – jointly at least – suffered quite that many when, some five years – was it? – into their happily rekindled marriage, Lily returned from the Women's Hospital in Hampstead and told Quaid to pour himself a drink and sit down.

Yes, bad news. No, not that bad, but bad enough. She breathed deeply and took a long time to begin. Had she not feared Quaid was going to faint she'd have taken even longer.

'Look,' she said at last, 'we're going to have to be very grown-up about this.'

Cold with fear, Quaid nodded. Not just grown-up, *very* grown-up. Did he have that much grown-up in him?

For the last few weeks – he must have been aware of her anxiety – she'd been taking the sorts of tests no woman wants to talk about and no man wants to hear, and now . . . She paused again. Sparing him. Always sparing him.

'Just tell me, Lily.'

Ha – just tell him. *Just.*

'So – the upshot is that there are things we will no longer be able to do . . .'

'You aren't dying?'

'I'm not, but our marriage might be.'

'If you aren't dying, we aren't dying.'

'You haven't heard the worst.'

If she wasn't dying there was no worst.

So she gave it to him, sparing his absurd squeamishness where she could. What would no longer be the same. What would have to be worked around. What would be the severest test on them both. Not being medically able to do was not the same as not doing. Not doing was a choice. Not being medically able was a sentence. Did she know how long she might be like this? She shook her head. Did people get better? She shook her head again. He opened his arms to her and she cried. He did the same.

She shook herself free, as though the last place she'd find resolution was in his arms. 'We mustn't give in to this. I have another appointment with Dr Umlaut in a fortnight.'

He guffawed. He needed a guffaw. 'Doctor who?'

'Don't, Sam. Just don't bother. She's a leading consultant in her field. I don't care what her fucking name is. We're going to have to be very grown-up about this if we're going to survive it.'

'You keep introducing the phrase "grown-up" as though it's a new idea.'

'It is.'

'So if we haven't been grown-up, what have we been?'

'Playing.'

'My love, I am a playwright. Play is what I do.'

'That's why I am concerned. I've been happy to play along with you.'

'That's what love is.'

'That's what love *was*.'

She calls him to her and throws her arms around his neck. They fall silent, as in prayer, to say goodbye to play.

With too much decisiveness for his liking, she breaks free of him as though to begin their new life. 'There must be no denials or recriminations,' she says. 'I don't accuse you, you don't accuse me. When Dr Umlaut asked me if I'd been under any stress of a sort that might, you know, I said no. Ours is a strong marriage based on a strong adultery, I told her. She raised an eyebrow. What did I mean by "a strong adultery"? We were sincere, I told her. We'd loved being together. She wondered how long our strong adultery had gone on for. She was surprised when I told her. And you were very active? Very. You could have worn yourselves out, she said. Was that a joke or did she mean literally worn ourselves out? You mean wear and tear? Like tyres? Not the image she'd have chosen but yes, like tyres. There must have been stress in all those years, she said. I told her the only stress was when we couldn't be together. Not being together didn't cause vaginal atrophy, she said.'

'Vaginal *what*?'

There. She'd told him.

The blood drained from his face. Atrophy. Us! No, Sam. *Me*.

He stood up and at once needed to sit down again. 'Put your head between your knees,' Lily told him. Some help he'd be.

Atrophy!

He shook his head as though to empty it of the word.

She tried to make a joke of it. 'Think of me,' she said, 'as what every husband wants – an Atrophy Wife.'

A joke? Quaid believed he would never laugh again. 'What else did the doctor say?' he asked. He would rather not hear but he had to ask something.

'She asked how I thought you'd take it. I said I couldn't say. What I didn't tell her was that for all I knew you'd be relieved. I was giving you the best of all reasons for leaving me. If I could no longer be your wife, why stay?'

'Why stay! Don't be ridiculous.'

'I am being realistic, Sam. Ever since you turned away from me in Bali I've been half expecting you to leave. If you want to go, I will not stand in your way.'

'I did not turn away from you in Bali. I turned away from myself.'

'I don't know what that means, Sam, and I doubt you do. I beg you to think before you speak. Don't smother me in words. There are a thousand reasons we should call it a day.'

'I can't think of any.'

'Haven't you been listening to me?'

'There's more than one way of living, Lily.'

'That's exactly what Dr Umlaut said. "There are remedies". I didn't ask her to enumerate.'

'She called them "remedies"?'

'She's German.'

'Are you sure she didn't call them "solutions"?'

'I'm glad you can find a joke in this.'

'Who's joking? We aren't Germans. We don't need remedies. We aren't ill.'

'What are we?'

'Older, wise, subtler . . . We don't have to give it a name.'

'Better to give it a name than to pretend it isn't there.'

'Give a thing a name and it becomes your master.'

'That sounds like something the person who said sex was not a memory pillow might have gone on to say.'

'I've no idea who you're talking about.'

'It doesn't matter.'

She kissed him. She wanted to say nothing mattered as long as they loved each other but she knew everything did.

They wept softly and silently in each other's arms. How many weeps had that been?

They had been toying with amateur dysfunction and its impish cousins, lassitude, overfamiliarity, distraction, moodiness, marriage, now they were up against the real disabling thing – the ageing body, the troubled mind, the heavy heart.

It was as though they'd been told their adult lives would begin that minute.

Or end that minute.

Lily and Quaid, lovers for the ages, the pattern for all lovers to come, how like you this?

She put that very question to him that night, before sleep.
'Will you be all right with this, my love?'
'There is no "this". Yes.'
'Don't just say it.'
'I'm not just saying it. I'll be all right. Will you?'
She took so long to answer he wondered if she'd fallen asleep.
Finally, she said, 'I don't know.'

And the evening and the morning were the Last Day.

PART 6

NON FINITO

SHAME WASTING

One day, it doesn't matter when exactly – nowish – she asks, 'Do you love me?'

He replies, 'More than that, I like you. Liking is rarer than love. Liking has its reasons. Liking *is* reason.'

'But do you love me?'

'I more than love you. I admire your character, I revere your intelligence, I venerate your being. I tremble in your presence.'

'But do you love me?'

'I find you endlessly, limitlessly, absorbingly interesting.'

'I ask if you love me.'

'You engross all my waking thoughts and nine-tenths of my sleeping ones. I am overburdened by what I feel for you, in the sense that you outweigh and occlude all else.'

'So you don't love me?'

'I'm searching for a bigger word.'

'The smaller one would have done just fine,' Lily says.

One day he asks 'Do you love me?'

'I love you,' she says. Her eyes say it too. Her skin says it. 'I love you.'

He wonders if that means she doesn't like or find him interesting.

Sam Quaid, a rationalist much given to superstition, feared that the concurrence of marital mishaps – his mysteriously keeping his distance from her in Bali, her tactfully keeping her distance from him now – was no coincidence. How to explain what had gone wrong other than as a punishment for their selfishness? So far, things had worked out altogether too well for them. This was the backlash. In a moral universe, you can't just leave your spouse and seamlessly take up with your lover and expect to get away with it. Their success to date bred smugness, and in love the smug will always pay.

Lily, too, thought the fault was hers. She had let her guard down and thought she could be happy. She had taken another woman's husband. Now, another woman could reach out and take him from her. He was a sitting target. If it came to a battle, Lily was bound to lose; she no longer had the weapons with which to fight back. *I am an old lady.*

At a further extreme of superstition, Quaid wondered if what had happened on his honeymoon was simply the love gods softening him up for a different life with Lily. In the not too far distant future he would need to be a lot less demanding and lo! – less demanding he was.

And Lily? Had she too been readied for the coming change by the slackening of her husband's avidity, or weren't the Balinese gods of love interested in women? In such matters, Lily had always been hard to read. For her, the company of a man surpassed all other considerations. No disrespect to Quaid, but he was a better talker than he was an anything else. There were worse things Umlaut could have told her. She might have lost her hearing. Her husband might have lost the power of speech.

The idea that Dr Umlaut's diagnosis served to balance the books was not one Quaid was willing to entertain. No, these things happen – wasn't that all there was to say? Something arbitrary happened to him; something arbitrary happened to her. Looked at one way, it was as it should be. To all things there is a season: as adulterers they had been as amorous birds of prey, who loved with their teeth; now that they were husband and wife they pecked each other's cheeks like suburban garden birds. Except – well, let them find their own way to describe wherein they were different from the commonality.

In the meantime Quaid grew – even by his own lachrymose standards – ever more tearful. Retiring to his study where Lily couldn't see him weeping for her, he reproached himself unremittingly. It was his fault. Don't ask what. All of it. Could he have 'worn her out' in Dr Umlaut's unlovely phrase? Had he been alpha male enough for that? He doubted it. But how else to explain what had happened? Besides, there was more than one way that a man could wear out a woman and, in the end, himself. He had loved her too demandingly. Wanted too much from her. Wanted her to take too much. Overburdened her with his lovingness. With his wanting to be loved.

He retired contrite, woke in contrition – but didn't dare allow Lily to see it. 'What is it, my love?' she would ask and the concern in her voice would be too much for him.

Was such a condition as his consistent with happiness?

Yes. The mistake is to think that to be happy in love is to be forever smiling. Contrition too can minister to a soul's contentment.

Quaid had increasingly come to rebuff the charge that he had no friends with the assertion that Lily was his friend. Had anyone said friends and lovers enjoyed a different order of intimacy – higher or lower according to your point of view – he'd have answered that that depended on the versatility of the lover. Lily moved effortlessly between both orders. The one disadvantage of Lily being his only friend was that he couldn't discuss with her, as he could have discussed with male friends, the commonality of what ailed them. So he missed out on learning that everyone his age was as troubled as he was.

Lily was more fortunate in that she did have friends most of whom were unhappy and envied her for what they took to be the perfect union she enjoyed with her husband. She had no intention of disabusing them. Her married life was as private as her single life had been. And what would she have told her envious friends anyway – that while on honeymoon in Bali Sam had gone on a queer, somewhat mystical journey from which he had not yet returned, that he had begun to stare adoringly at her more than he used to, that he had taken to falling asleep touching her fingertips with his, and liked to wake to find the contact still intact, that (waking or sleeping) he seemed to be (and indeed described himself as) distraughtly happy, that one of the country's most eminent gynaecologists had just advised her that her body was worn out by sexual overuse, but that otherwise, yes, yes, a thousand times yes, she did indeed have a perfect union? Truth to say, little of this would have changed her friends' minds even had she confided in them. Compared to the hazards of the ageing marriage-bed they had to endure – depression, diabetes, low testosterone, high testosterone, nerve damage, hyperthyroidism, late-onset gender dysphoria, serial infidelity, not to mention such attendant marital malfunctions as shoplifting, making inappropriate remarks to other women, dressing like a child, getting tattooed and driving under the influence of drink – Lily's life with Quaid was a stroll in the park.

'Given how much remedial work my friends are having to do on their love lives,' Lily told Quaid, 'you'd think that half of London over the age of sixty was under the care of Dr Umlaut.'

'Maybe if they stopped thinking of themselves as having love lives . . .'

'Oh, Sam. Let people think of themselves as they choose.'

To the list of her own undeclared marital malfunctions Lily might have added the ponderosity of her husband which had been getting worse since he'd rearranged the vocabulary of their relations. If she missed anything about their old lovemaking – and don't let Sam catch her using that phrase – it was the unpoliced directness of their desires. *Now let us sport us while we may* left no time for nice verbal discrimination. *Come back to me, Sam. I don't say take me. I will just as happily take you. But come back to me full of the old hunger. And joy. To devour or be devoured, I don't care which. Your sadness is growing palpable. Am I the cause or the occasion of it? I know I am in no position to demand anything. But surely I too am allowed to look back in sorrow.*

The remedies at which Dr Umlaut had hinted figured at some point or other in Lily's conversations with her friends but the details were of a grossness that made her think twice before passing them on to Quaid, who found the most harmless of them insulting.

'Has she been talking to Amaryllis? "Touch each other with tenderness." What the hell do they think we did before?'

As for 'touching *oneself*', whether in private to obtain surreptitious relief or openly to excite a neglected partner, Quaid had little to add to the words the Lord spoke unto Moses and Aaron, to wit, 'When any man hath a running issue out of his flesh, *because* of his issue he is unclean.'

Lily thought *running issue* sounded a mite torrential, to which Quaid retorted that to some ears an *expense of spirit in a waste of shame* sounded a mite cataclysmic, but you don't get to be a moralist by judging an event by the quantity of fluid it spills or the chagrin it misspends.

Lily didn't think Shakespeare meant expense of spirit to describe the act she dared not name. Quaid said he read it as he read it. Waste of shame? Come on!

'Do you think you might be exceptionally odd about this?' Lily wondered.

'Well there's God, Moses, Aaron, Shakespeare if you read between the lines, D. H. Lawrence, Jean Esquirol who diagnosed it as a cause of insanity, and me for starters. I would expect there to be millions more.'

'Every one of you insane.'

'Every one of us driven to insanity by the practice in question. Madness is bound to be the consequence of turning an outward act inwards. One might as well be ingesting one's own being. The very language of it replicates the brutality – jerking, beating, whacking, spanking . . . As do the visuals. All acts of love find their celebration in art, except this one, which has nothing of love or beauty in it. Man crouched in an act of supplication to himself, like an ape at the water's edge, worshipping his own reflection. It is the last resort of sex.'

Lily stared long at him. 'So when did you finally abjure it?' she finally asked.

'Who said I've abjured it? But I long to every time. I've been trying to find the strength of character to abjure it and then cursing myself when I can't for half a century.'

'I hope you aren't saying that to placate me. I am not made jealous by your doing it. Especially now.'

'Nor should you be. You play a starring role every time.'

'Who enjoyed that privilege before you met me?'

'It was always you. You before I knew thy face or name. As an angel is worshipped in a shapeless flame.'

'You make it sound so beautiful I can't believe you hate doing it.'

'Please don't speak of me *doing* it. It does me. Now can we change the subject.'

The worst, unless it was the best, that could be said of these conversations was that they were good-humoured when something closer to desolation might have been expected. Was this because Lily and Quaid had not yet taken full significance of what they'd lost? Did they think that there was a chance they would somehow win it back? Or were they able to convince each other that they had resources enough to compensate?

Hubris?

Wisdom warns that mortals who think they can escape the routine fate of mankind are riding for a fall. Lovers, in particular, must expect to take a tumble. Among the great heroes of art and literature lovers hold the most estimable place because they are not individually ambitious. To love is to approach the self-abnegation of religion. But because lovers are not in fact divine, they need to burn. They cannot be allowed either to surpass the common or defy the gods. They must not have a happy ending.

Not everyone shares this vengeful predilection for censure. Some who study love think that, in a world of rage, lovers deserve all the encouragement they can get.

Happy endings should neither be begrudgd nor scattered like confetti. To the deserving, the laurels. What made Sam and Lily deserving?

Their gravity.

NOW YOU SEE HIM, NOW YOU DON'T

Lily wishes she still had her mother to talk to. All very well having Sam, but some conversations about women you can only have with another woman.

Remember Lucasta, Mother, whose husband left her for another, older woman and then came back? Yes, you know what's coming . . . he is in the process of leaving her for another woman again. Also older? No, he's done that. This time younger. Maybe next time he'll find one exactly Lucasta's age.

She can't be quite so dry with Lucasta. She was younger herself when she arched an eyebrow at her friend's decision to forgive and forget. There were more men in the world then. And poor Lucasta was more capable of landing some. Age is cruel. 'I told him that if he was going to leave me again he shouldn't wait until I was an old lady,' she said to Lily, showing her the flaps of loose skin under her arms.

'We all have those,' Lily said.

'But some of us have husbands.'

Lily sighed. 'Is there any reason to think that if he goes he won't come back again?'

'There's always a reason to think he won't come back again, but even if he does – and his record suggests he will – it will be the same old complaint: that we got together when we were too young, that we never experienced life, that he's missed out—'

'Whatever you do, you miss out on whatever you didn't do.'

'I know that. Though I don't feel I've missed out on all the things he thinks he's missed out on—'

'Those things being?'

'Oh, you know. Playing the field. Wife-swapping. Hand-cuffs. Troilism. Visiting prostitutes. Being gay. Bestiality, for all I know. Topless bathing—'

'Who stopped him topless bathing?'

'Ho, ho. He says we've been too straight. Oral sex . . .'

'What about oral sex?'

'The usual. Missing out on it.'

'Which version?'

'How many are there? I've never liked the two I know.'

'Oh, Lucasta. *Liked*.'

'Well what's your secret been?'

'Secret of what?'

'Being happy with a man.'

'That's a very dangerous condition to admit to. But the truth is—'

She hesitated. How would the truth – the truth about the reckless woman she'd been, the wild acts she still couldn't believe she'd initiated – help the not-at-all-reckless Lucasta? If you want to help a friend you don't boast about yourself. You stay within the range of that friend's capabilities. Or is that to be condescending? Lily shrugged inwardly. 'In my experience, at least,' she went on, 'it helps to go along with what you might not like especially if the man you love does.'

'Lily! That's so Victorian.'

Ha! She couldn't wait to tell Sam that.

'Just good manners,' she said. 'That's all. No one likes doing everything.'

'You once told me you'd been to a sex club.'

'I told you that?'

'Only in answer to the question have you ever been to a sex club.'

'Ask me again.'

'Lily, have you ever been to a sex club?'

'Lucasta, my whole life has been a sex club. But why did you ask the first time?'

'Jules wanted us to go. You were the only person I knew who might have been to one.'

'I shouldn't have answered you. It wasn't really a sex club anyway.'

'What was it?'

'A dressing-up and smacking-people club.'

'You let strangers smack you?'

'No, they let me smack them.'

Lucasta screwed up her face. 'How could you enjoy that?'

'Who said I enjoyed it?'

'You did. You said you had a good time. You said it was fun. You said everybody should try it.'

'Everybody should. Better to try than to wonder. But I hope you didn't tell Jules that.'

'I did. Only I made up that Sam didn't like it quite so much and that you didn't think you'd ever go again. Did you?'

'I'm not telling you. But what did Jules say?'

'That just the once would have sufficed him. That he'd thrown his life away doing nothing and going nowhere and then wondering what doing something and going somewhere would have been like. He said he was afraid of dying unused.'

'We will all do that, Lucasta.'

'Will we? You won't. You've been to a sex club.'

Lily laughed. 'There's more to a fulfilled life than visiting a sex club.'

Lucasta didn't laugh. 'Is there? I'm beginning seriously to doubt that.'

'Remember Lucasta?'

Quaid nodded. 'I remember you talking about her.'

'Her husband Jules was leaving her as I was meeting you.'

'I hope his leaving turned out as well as our meeting.'

'It did for Lucasta. He came back.'

'Good.'

'But now he is leaving her again.'

'Why the present-continuous tense?'

'Because that's the continuous state he's in.'

'For another woman, another man, more space, the chance to find himself . . . ?'

'On the surface for another woman, but from the way she tells it, I'd say a combination of all those things.'

'Presumably she wouldn't let him have a dog either.'

'Are you warning me?'

'Of course not. I don't think a dog is a leaving-home issue. In the end I doubt any one thing is—'

Lily put up a hand. 'Can I stop you there?'

'My love, you can stop me anywhere.'

'Would you speak to Jules?'

'Me?'

'You.'

'Jules?'

'Jules.'

'About?'

'What constitutes a leaving-home issue.'

'A man I've never met wants to talk to me about his marriage? Come on. Why?'

'He admires your work.'

'I admire a lot of people's work. That doesn't mean I want to discuss matrimony with them.'

'Sam, you admire no one's work.'

'That's not an answer to my question. What possible reason can he have to discuss love and marriage with me?'

'It's more what Lucasta thinks. She exerts a strong influence over him.'

'But not strong enough to stop him leaving.'

'He always comes back.'

'Then why doesn't she just wait for the cycle to complete itself?'

'For fear that one day it won't.'

'So where do I come in?'

'He needs a man to talk to.'

'I bet he didn't say that.'

'No, Lucasta did.'

'And what does Lucasta hope I might say to him?'

'*Stay with your wife.*'

'Ha! Does she know I didn't stay with mine?'

'I'm your wife.'

'But does she know that I had to leave an earlier one to be with you?'

'Details, details. It's more that she hopes the secret of *our* marital happiness will rub off on him.'

'Christ! Does your friend Lucasta think happiness is infectious?'

'Is that idea so implausible? Would you write plays if you didn't think words have the power to affect?'

'Can't I just send him a play in that case?'

'No, darling. He needs to feel the happiness coming off your person.'

'Ooof. Do I deserve that?'

'You are always saying how happy you are. I know that's to make me feel better—'

'It's to make me feel better.'

'I didn't know you had been feeling bad.'

'A little depleted, that's all. It happens to men my age.'

'Then drink less.'

'I know. And walk more. And stop complaining.'

'I would never accuse you of complaining. I appreciate it that you don't. Many a man would complain more.'

'So I'm to urge Jules to complain less? What if when I meet him I take his side? What if I think he should leave Lucasta and this time never go back?'

'You won't tell him.'

'I'm to lie for your friend Lucasta?'

'No, you're to lie for me. You're a persuasive person. Persuade Jules!'

Persuade Jules! Kill Claudio! They both heard it and laughed. Like Prospero's Island, a good, properly self-satisfied marriage is full of sweet airs and detected echoes that give delight and hurt not.

'The way I see it,' Quaid began, but it was plain Jules wasn't listening. Quaid realised he had made a big mistake arranging to meet him at an outdoor table in a café in Soho. There was too much that looked like the life Jules had never lived walking past on the pavement. Thoughtlessness was it, or sadism? Quaid didn't know Jules and had nothing against him so it must have been the former.

In fact he did know Jules but didn't know he knew him. 'You won't remember but we were in the same English class at school,' Jules said during a lull in the parade.

Quaid turned his own gaze from the street to scrutinise Lucasta's husband. As a rule he didn't look much at men. Some were interesting, some were not. It wasn't as though he were looking for a friend. This man had a big, tired, granite face that appeared too heavy for the shoulders that supported it. His eyes, though, were soft and imploring.

Something came back to Quaid. 'My God, it was you Miss Gore chose to read Othello in place of me. You took the sex out of it, I remember.'

'I took the sex out of everything.'

Well that wasn't long coming, Quaid thought. A beggar holding out a black top hat interrupted their conversation. Jules gave him a pound coin. Quaid gave him nothing.

They drank coffee, moved on to wine, and talked about things that were supposed to interest men. There was a European football match being played somewhere and the sounds of excited supporters watching it on television rang out from Bar Italia. They both smiled parentally. A special tolerance is granted to fans of football when they happen to be Italian.

'I can't imagine,' Jules said suddenly, 'that it bothered you much.'

'Losing to you? It bothered me greatly. I was a sensitive boy when it came to sex.'

'I'm surprised. You seemed so worldly, with all those erotic poems you knew. And it was rumoured you visited prostitutes.'

'*Visited* sounds a bit decadent. And there was only one. I picked her up on a street corner in Streatham.'

'You see.'

'Anyone can pick up a prostitute.'

'No they can't. I couldn't have.'

'Maybe you didn't know where to look.'

'I wouldn't have dared try. I had Miss Gore dinning the importance of respecting women in my ear.'

'Picking up a prostitute wasn't a mark of disrespect to women. It was a mark of respect to prostitutes. And it was desperation not worldliness. I had to kiss a woman before I went up to university.'

'And?'

'*And* what? How was it? She took the pocket money I'd saved for months and offered me sex in a car park but wouldn't kiss me. I told her I loved her but she still wouldn't kiss me.'

'Did you have sex?'

'That's between me and the prostitute.'

'Amazing. I envy you.'

'I don't visit prostitutes any more.'

'But at least you've done it. I've done nothing. Someone in one of your plays quotes a Chinese proverb. *The twisted tree lives out its life, the straight tree ends up as a board*. I've never forgotten that. It could have been a description of me. I'm the straight tree.'

Quaid was becoming embarrassed. So this was what being friends with a man was like. 'We are who we are,' he said.

'But not always who we want to be.'

Because it would have been impolite not to ask, Quaid asked. 'So who do you want to be?'

'Someone shocking. The first time I left poor Lucasta I thought I'd achieved it. I imagined that running off with a woman my mother's age would show I was a sicko.'

'It's not a bad start.'

'It was, actually. Everyone, including Lucasta, thought I'd done a grand thing for post-menopausal women. SAGA invited me to give a course of lectures on the subject on one of their cruises. That's a joke, by the way. But what's not a joke is ending up a board no matter how twisted I've struggled to be.'

Quaid tried a laugh and ordered another bottle of wine. Italy scored a goal and Bar Italia exploded. He felt a pang of sympathy for Jules. He knew himself how easily debauchery could slip from one's grasp.

'It strikes me,' he said, 'that you're going about it the wrong way. I take it, since you keep coming back to Lucasta, that you love her.'

'Unconscionably. She's an angel of forbearance.'

'Then instead of finding danger in leaving her, what about finding it in staying? Fidelity's an underrated perversion. You say you love Lucasta, well love her obsessively, love her against reason, make yourself think of no one and nothing but her.

Make her your religion. Make yourself sick with her. Has she ever been unfaithful to you?'

'Not that I know of.'

'Pity. An unrequited fidelity is the most giddying of them all. But don't despair – she will surely be unworthy of your love in some other way.'

Jules stared wild-eyed. He needed to support his heavy head with both hands. 'I'm listening,' he said, 'but the situation is complex. I have a girlfriend.'

'You mean a mistress?'

'No, I'd say she's more a girlfriend.'

'Then she's halfway to being a wife, which means your wife's halfway to being your mistress. That's ideal. What can be more crooked than having a torrid affair with your wife?'

'Secretly, you mean?'

'That's up to you.'

'But then I'd be deceiving two women.'

'Morally that's no worse than deceiving one.'

'I can't just up and leave Sara.'

'Spoken like a husband.'

'So?'

'You want to be a twisted tree? Do your duty. Up and leave neither.'

A straggle of cheering Italians stopped at their table. One of them recognised Quaid, introduced himself as Sandro who'd been the cameraman in Taos, and opened his arms. 'We won,' he said. Though he'd never much liked Sandro whom he'd suspected of colluding in some indefinable way with Lily, and didn't care whether Italy had won or not, Quaid had no choice but to return the embrace. Having embraced one, and being almost as drunk as they were, he thought it behoved him to embrace them all. Anyone watching would have thought he'd spent the afternoon cheering himself hoarse in Bar Italia. Jules looked on with the rapt attention of a child in the world's biggest toyshop.

They sat a little longer. It seemed to Quaid that Jules had fallen just a little bit in love with him. Not impossibly, he'd leave both the women for me, he thought. All he really wants is to be somewhere else.

They shook hands. 'Keep writing plays,' Jules said inanely.

'And you,' Quaid said, 'keep – but I don't know what line of work you're in. Do you still review plays?

'No, that's long gone. I run a travel agency.'

'So how did that go?' Lily asked when Quaid got home.

'As badly as could have been expected.'

'Did he ask your advice?'

'No.'

'But you gave it anyway?'

'Yes. At length. You know my only mode of conversation with men is sententious hectoring.'

'No, that's your only mode of conversation when you're drunk. But what's the upshot? Will he be leaving or staying?'

'My guess is staying.'

Lily kissed him warmly. 'Thank you.'

He didn't mention that he'd also be leaving.

THE LILIAD

If beauty is truth and truth is beauty how much more beautiful is truth when it is deftly woven out of sinuous half-lies?

Some time into their tenth year of marriage, after another annually disappointing consultation with Dr Umlaut's successor, Lily fell into a mode of historical and yet at the same time fantastical reminiscence for which the model could best be described as Epic.

Fell into?

Is that a euphemism for *was pushed*?

To trace the subtle tracery of responsibility for such a stratagem would test the patience of even the keenest student of Sam and Lily's marriage. The lovers themselves couldn't have said how it started, though it clearly had its origins in the debriefings that followed those long-gone nights of masquerading in Slough and Vauxhall. Locked away behind his Pierrot mask, Quaid missed much that happened in the dark cellars they frequented and looked forward to Lily describing it all when they got back to their hotel. It didn't matter if she lied. Indeed the more he could believe she invented, the more Quaid liked it. This was not just professional admiration for her narrative skills; what took his breath away was the degree to which she was willing to connive, if that was the word, in all that had gone on in those salacious crypts. What she spoke of, he had not seen. If anything, listening to her describe or, better still, invent what had gone on beat seeing it. In her elaborations she became more than just a player, she became the night's convenor and historian. 'Has anyone ever told you,' her asked her once, 'that you are a pornographer of genius?'

'Often,' she replied, 'but I prefer to hear it from you.'

Whereupon he offered her his wrists to bind.

The idea that Lily's genius might be needed more than ever, as circumstances of age and health forced them to cede to words those acts to which words had originally been a shocking augmentation, struck both of them, let us guess, simultaneously.

Despite their refusal to accept that they'd been invalided and that adjustments needed to be made to the way they lived, they held their heads a little lower than they once had. Bali had not left the pair unbruised and not all the mutual reassurances in the world could mitigate Dr Umlaut's diagnosis. Quaid, as we know, would not hear of alternative forms of intimacy. As far as he was concerned, nothing new needed to be introduced. Their past had been immense enough to feed on for all time. All that was necessary to prevent their repining was to hand – language, besotted fondness, exclusive kindness, mirth, the selfish pleasure they took in each other's company, her pride to be with him on a first night, whatever the critics said, and his to be with her at awards ceremonies, whether she won the Bafta she deserved or not, the words they exchanged in their hundreds upon hundreds of thousands, no matter if the subject was Dostoevsky or a Danish pastry, but above all, far, far above all, the constant visual delight that each was to the other. 'I look at you with no less desire than I ever did,' he told her, remembering to add, 'which isn't to say that I look at you *only* with desire.'

'Nor I you,' she said.

'Looking is a species of love,' he said.

'I agree,' she said.

'Listening too,' he went on, 'especially when you are speaking.'

'As is speaking,' she returned, 'when you are listening.'

All a bit saccharine maybe, but they had obstacles to surmount and never intended their words to be for public consumption.

Though Quaid was the more natural reminiscer of the two – the Instant Nostalgist, Lily called him, a man who prepared nostalgia before her eyes, reminiscing fondly about that morning's breakfast before it was even finished – it fell to Lily to be the Homer of their little family, at once its chronicler and its minstrel, whispering her Liliad – the things she did before they met, the things she did or didn't do while he wasn't looking, the things she would have done had the chance arisen, and therefore the things it is always possible she will do again – into Quaid's never less than receptive ear.

Ask why Quaid never picked up the baton of ambiguous Epic narration to give his wife a breather and the answer can only be that Lily's ear would have been nothing like so receptive. Quaid had a tolerance, not to say a predilection, for the anguish of half-knowing, Lily did not.

'So when was that exactly?' Lily would have asked, and down would come the insubstantial pageant.

Whereas Quaid would sit or lie or listen at the end of a phone if they were briefly apart, and barely stir for fear of causing it all to melt into thin air.

'I was the more deceived,' the much-wronged Ophelia cried when Hamlet told her he'd never loved her. By preference Hamlet, in this encounter Quaid took the part of Ophelia.

'Deceive me more,' he begged Lily. 'Or truthfully tell me today how cruelly you deceived me yesterday.'

Did deception have to assume this importance? Hadn't enough truly happened to them since they met – wasn't that first *kerpow* itself sufficiently extraordinary – for actual events alone to keep them going without having to cook up fantasies?

Quaid explained it this way: poor Lily's powers had been curtailed. No, their revels were not ended, but it would be no surprise if she no longer felt herself to be the magician of desire she'd been. Reminding her of her one-time powers, augmenting them with fantasias of fact, as though to double them in the remembering, was restorative.

For her part, Lily understood what Quaid was about. Yes, sexual jealousy played its part and, as an experienced producer, she knew to a nicety how and when to regulate its flow, but she understood it above all as an expression of appreciation for what he saw as her boldness, a courage not to say magnanimity he didn't have, a largesse of spirit that comprehended him but wasn't comprehended by him. And she could hardly be anything but grateful, post-Umlaut, for that.

Steeped in *Hamlet*, Quaid played all the parts, including the old king who so exorbitantly loved his wife, the faithless Gertrude, that he *might not beteem the winds of heaven / Visit her face too roughly*. Even as he encouraged her to speak disreputably of herself, Quaid stood between Lily and the elements. In him, idealisation worked both ways at once. No, Lily was neither Madonna nor whore to him, but to have imagined her as the one would have been no impediment to his imagining her as the other.

Hard as it was for her, sometimes, to go on rehashing her *Thousand and One Nights* with any zest, she didn't dare release Quaid from their spell and, if anything, grew bolder in the tales she told. Yes, she was playing a dangerous game, but what choice did she have? 'You didn't!' Quaid would exclaim as the latest preposterous story – preposterous but always just the right side of conceivable – neared its climax. He could hear his heart beating.

And where at first she would have teased him – 'Ah, wouldn't you like to know?' – she now laughed, 'Of course I did. You know me well enough. You know that wasn't something I could ever have given a definitive no to.' Not giving a definitive no being ever so subtly different from giving a definitive yes.

And all along, the more invention swelled and made a slave of Quaid, the more her body remained closed against him.

How long they would be able to sustain their complementary roles in this recitation of the Liliad there was no knowing; but for the time being, at least – that is to say as time passed and they grew no younger – Lily sailed the wine-dark sea of fact and fabulation with a strong wind at her back.

He liked it best in the late afternoon, with the curtains closed, when she half-cradled him, his cheek on her breast – pillowed but not at rest – her breath like a desert wind in his ear, her words flitting about him, like small crazed jungle birds that nipped him with their beaks before flying away to show off their beauty and dexterity. Sometimes he didn't hear what they whispered and had to entreat them to return. Sometimes he dozed off for a fraction of a listening second. The attention he paid to her was so intense it knocked him out, Lily didn't mind. If she could bring rest to him, that too was what a wife was for. All he missed, he castigated himself for missing, as in the clubs when his attention wavered and he lost her. What if the word he didn't catch, like the blurred sight of Lily dancing with her breast just visible (was it?) above her corset, was the most revelatory of all?

'I'm sorry, can you say that again?'

And now the word would fly back past his ear, and now it wouldn't.

'Hush, my love,' she wanted to say. But the hunger was on him again.

One episode of her *Thousand and One Nights*, perhaps it was the Thousandth and First itself, stirred him more than all the others, for which reason she was careful to change and ration it. More than some, it was a duet of sorts, and she would gauge his appetite for it by the greed and candour of his catechism.

'Did you shock yourself?' he would ask, which was code for 'Will you now shock me?'

Well, she owed him.

'Shock myself? I have rarely done that. But this time, I always suspected I might.'

'Might what?'

'Go further?'

(How much further?)

'Weren't you frightened?'

'Of being there on my own at night? Yes, a little. But the risk was part of the excitement.'

'No, I meant weren't you frightened of yourself? Of what you might do.'

'Yes. But isn't that the reason we do these things – to find out?'

He shifted his position in the bed. 'And what did you find out?'

'Do you really want to know?'

'Yes.'

'Be sure of that before you ask . . .'

'Yes, I want to know.'

'I found out—' Now it was her turn to change her position in the bed.

'What did you find out?'

'That I am capable of anything.'

'What sort of anything?'

'What sort of anything do you imagine? Do you want to know if I kissed him?'

'Yes.'

'I kissed him.'

'And?'

'He kissed me back.'

'And did you enjoy it?'

'What do you think?'

'I think yes.'

'You think right. I enjoyed it very much. So did he.'

'How do you know he enjoyed it?'

'He told me.'

'And did you tell him?'

'That I was enjoying kissing him? Yes.'

'What did you say?'

'I told him he kissed well.'

'Did you kiss for long?'

'Long enough.'

'Long enough for what?'

'Long enough for my teeth to ache, and to want to go on to the next stage. But you might not be ready for the next stage.'

'I won't know until you tell me what the next stage entailed.'

'I think you can guess?'

'Did you let him touch you?'

'Of course.'

'Did you touch him?'

'Eagerly.'

'Where were you when this was happening?'

'Well we began standing up in the stockroom to his shop. But by the next stage we were on the floor.'

'You hate floors.'

'Normally yes. But this was an exceptional circumstance. A dirty floor seemed the least of my sins.'

'Did you undress?'

'No, he undressed me. Slowly and selectively.'

'What does selectively mean?'

'He wanted me to keep on my shoes.'

'Anything else?'

'Yes. My stockings.'

'So far so conventional.'

'Like you, you mean? Yes. Like all men. Only with you I have never done yoga.'

'You did yoga with him naked?'

'But for the shoes and the stockings, yes.'

'Wouldn't that have been—'

'Unusually exposing? Yes. And what made it the more so was that he remained fully clothed. As though he were my teacher.'

'Would there be any point in asking you to describe some of the positions he taught you?'

'None. You wouldn't recognise them. And he didn't so much teach them to me, as manoeuvre me into them. A hand on me here, a hand on me there.'

'You let him put his hands on you?'

'How else was I going to learn? Of course I let him put his hands on me.'

'Which you enjoyed?'

'Doesn't it sound as though I did?'

He fell silent.

'Is that enough?' she asked.

'No, it's never enough.'

'What if it's all there is?'

'I won't believe you.'

'In the end you have to be content with what I tell you.'

'Even if that means never knowing?'

'Even then.'

So he never would find out if her yoga teacher existed, and whether or not, out of love or hate or simple good manners, she'd choked him or anyone else with a Hermès scarf.

But how was he to know that the next time she told it she wouldn't reveal more?

'Again,' he would say.

'You are like a child,' Lily laughed.

'Well I am at your breast.'

And then, one afternoon, he wasn't.

AN ENDING

'I've something to tell you,'she had told him, coming in to his study and taking him by the hand. She had worn one of the vintage Japanese dragon housecoats he loved. It opened and closed, belching fire, at the behest of his breath. He had followed where she led him, to the bed of course, but whether to hear familiar verses from her epic or new lines altogether he didn't know.

He could hear his heart beat in his chest.

She'd been at her best, improbable yet convincing, funny and fearsome, touching him so lightly, as with feather fingers, he couldn't be sure she was touching him at all. Long ago he'd conceded to her the power to reach him remotely, as though by witchcraft. Enough just to raise her eyes to him or speak his name. *Sam.* And he would cry out as he cried out now. 'My love,' she'd said, at a point in the epic when it wasn't clear whom she was addressing. Did he shake? She remembered Dante's description of Paolo kissing Francesca – a point of frequent reference between them – *tutto tremante.* 'All palpitating, he kissed her on the mouth.' How often had they played at being Dante's lovers. She lowered her mouth to his – but his face had fallen to one side and there seemed not to be a tremble left in him.

Full of a lover's self-remonstrances and forebodings – resigned to letting go of what would never let go of him – Quaid gave in to the sort of weariness a drowning man must feel as his clothes begin to pull him under the waves. He left mementos for Lily to find wherever she might go looking for traces of him after he'd gone: in his drawers and wardrobes, between the pages of his favourite books, in his filing cabinet, behind cushions, in his files marked 'Private' and 'Work in Progress', and even in food cupboards. He scattered letters he had started to her but not finished, short stories about her, portraits of her he had tried to draw but failed, fragments of thoughts about love, a one-act play entitled *Lily in Lilliput* (the Lilliputians, of course, were all facsimiles of him), and far back in one of the drawers of her jewellery cupboard he placed a sapphire forget-me-not brooch with the label 'Ne M'Oubliez Pas', a new bottle of the perfume with the same name, and an accompanying card saying 'Remember to love those who loved you.'

Of these mementos the most agonising to Lily was George Eliot's rumination on her relationship with George Henry Lewes, some of which Sam had had finely engraved for her on the back of the divers' watch she'd bought him for his last birthday. They had spoken the great heartbreak sentence so often – he to her, she to him – they knew it by heart. *Our unspeakable joy in each other has no other alloy than the sense that it must one day end in parting.* Memorialised on Sam's watch were the words he wanted to last forever: *unspeakable joy.*

He had known he would never survive a parting from her. Though they were twinned in anticipation of a finality they could not bear to name except in borrowed language, he was confident she would initially do better but at the last would not survive a parting either. This was not arrogance. It is not arrogant to know you're loved. Leaving reminders of himself around for her to go on discovering was his way of making his absence progressively easier for her. Maybe in the end, as she went on looking for him, he would just peter out.

Sam's death certificate said he died of an embolism, aged seventy-four.

Lily disputed that. He hadn't looked seventy-four. He

couldn't have been seventy-four. And he didn't die of an embolism. He was in her arms – she knew what he died of.

She had much to blame herself for. She had known he was mournful and unfit. The life he lived was morbid, sedentary and unhealthy. And he drank. Yes, she did what she could to get him to give up drinking and to take exercise. But she had promised to love him – *him*, not some other person. Whoever would change a man might just as well *ex*change him for someone else. He had loved her for who she was – sometimes wanting her to be more so, but not complaining when she wasn't. She was still herself when her body wanted her not to be. He loved her not a whit the less for that. This was the great example they set each other – love who you love, and no Sam, not this time, not *whom*. To the degree that she had disappointed him in any regard, she felt disappointed in herself. But she took great draughts of comfort from wearing her husband's watch and turning it over three times every hour to read of their unspeakable joy. But at the same time as they gave her comfort they took it away. Was there some fatal constituent in unspeakable joy that made the grief of losing it beyond bearing?

But for Lucasta coming round and trying to rouse her she would not have left her bed.

She didn't want to talk to Lucasta, yet she did. So how was Jules?

Jules was strange. Sometimes there, sometimes not. And when he was there he followed her around the house in the most peculiar manner, staring at her, telling her he loved her and wondering if she'd consider having an extramarital affair.

Who cared?

That will do now, Lily said. I once experienced unspeakable joy, that's more than enough.

Lucasta reminded her of the advice she'd once given her. 'You mustn't give up. There's always another story.'

I don't want another story, Lily said. And anyway, I'm a poem.

She did not believe her husband's death certificate. He was a young man and love had killed him. He had agreed with her – they led to nowhere but themselves. There was a perfection in it.

Exactly one year after he expired she did the same. She did not care what it said on her death certificate either. She knew what she had died of. She was holding Sam's watch.

She had never been good with time and couldn't have said how old she was. She knew only that her consummated heart had stopped but she had not, that her story had no end because she was not a story, she was a poem. Stories came to a conclusion; poems turned this way and that, backwards as well as forwards, gathering memories and echoes about them like skirts. Lily swirled away in hers.

In so many silent looks and embraces, and later in so many protestations and assurances, they had promised each other a future-perfect life. And they had been as good as their word. They had achieved their happy ending. But they were not gods or magicians: what they couldn't promise was that they'd stay alive to enjoy it.

Howard Jacobson has written seventeen novels and six works of non-fiction. He won the Bollinger Everyman Wodehouse Award in 2000 for *The Mighty Walzer* and then again in 2013 for *Zoo Time*. In 2010 he won the Man Booker Prize for *The Finkler Question*; he was also shortlisted in 2014 for *J*.